THE APP

Paul Ruthven

Balance Press
www.paulruthven.com

For Lady Justice

ACKNOWLEDGEMENTS

It's never too late to follow your dreams, and I'd like to thank some of the wonderful people who've helped me chase mine. My immediate family, for your support, proofreading, and keeping me fed during the lean times. Tania Jacob, for your constant encouragement and regular deliveries of red wine. Alicia Perera, for all those coffees at university and happily proofreading anything I gave you. Alana Parera, for fanning the flame of creativity. Jeremy Jacob, for showing me that the road to happiness and success isn't always the one you expect. My 16-year old nephew, Campbell Ruthven, for designing the cover of *The App* when he probably should have been studying. The regular BBQ and games-night crowd who kept me sane during a difficult period; Soph Blount, Adam Blount, Ian Jones, Madlen Jannaschk, Matt Pollard, and Gizmo. My tutors at Curtin University, including Brett D'Arcy, Sam Carmody, Bonita Mason, Andrew Cameron, and Rebecca Higgie. The regulars in the Curtin Writing Group; Jonathon "JD" Denholm, Holly Stubbs and Erin Scott. Chris Hunter, for introducing me to South Park in Vancouver, and letting me use your name. Doug Harris, for your friendship, advice, and cool head on the hockey field.

Special mention goes to the planners at the City of South Perth, who recommended the approval of the 20-storey monstrosity next door to me. The two year construction period coincided nicely with my career change, and the vibrating desk, pneumatic drills and piercing reversing beepers made it so much easier to write. I dedicate *The App* to you.

THE APP

CHAPTER ONE

Decisions

He decided to have a beer.

And to kill them.

In that order.

Simon smiled as he opened a Corona. He drank the beer and made a list. At the top he wrote a word.

Revenge.

CHAPTER TWO

Rhyme and Reason

In Simon's mind, they only had themselves to blame. The Global Financial Crisis had hit the world hard, and the IT sector was no exception. Many people had lost their jobs.

Simon had lost *his* job six months earlier.

He'd arrived at work one morning to discover his swipe card wouldn't open the door. A security guard had escorted him to Human Resources.

The Employee Experience Manager, Donald Cowper, had lumbered into the room and squeezed into his padded chair. His forehead was clammy from the effort of walking. He acknowledged Simon after he'd regained his breath.

"We've had to tighten our belts," said Cowper.

Simon's eyes shifted involuntarily to Cowper's waist and he scratched his head. "What does that mean?"

Cowper frowned. "We have to let you go."

Simon's stomach clenched and he tasted bile. He clung to Cowper's desk for support. "What? Why?"

Cowper looked at his watch. "Because of the GFC."

The security guard had handed Simon a cardboard box then led him away to collect his things. Simon wasn't given a chance to say goodbye.

On the bus ride home, he'd clutched his possessions and replayed those words.

Because of the GFC.

Several weeks later, Simon had listened to an interview on CBC radio. It was with a homeless man, who'd been living on food scraps plucked from dumpsters.

The man said that he used to be a computer programmer, earning a decent wage. Then he'd lost it all; his job, his girlfriend, his apartment.

The man's new home was a pile of blankets over a subway grate.

When the reporter asked *why* he was living on the street, the man had replied:

"Because of the GFC."

The story resonated with Simon and he began searching for the true meaning of those words.

The answers made him angry.

Greedy financiers and bankers had created investments that were impossible to understand. They'd repackaged sub-prime mortgages to hide the risks and then sold them on to unsuspecting buyers. The regulators — thwarted by lobbyists and politicians — had failed to act in time.

The result was carnage.

People homeless. Starving. Dead.

But not those responsible. They were unaffected.

A few weeks after the *Homeless Man* story, Simon was woken by his cell phone as it shivered against his leg.

It was a message from his best friend, Alan.

As Simon read Alan's text message, the hairs on his arms rose to their full height.

"I need a huge favour Si. Please … tell Mom and Dad I'm sorry. For letting them down. I can't face them after what's happened. I've left my will in the glove compartment. Thanks

for always being there. Al."

Simon swore as he leapt out of bed and dialled Alan's number. He prayed for his friend to pick up the phone.

But there was no answer.

Simon called the Vancouver Police Department and convinced them to trace Alan's cell phone. They eventually found it near the town of Squamish, at the bottom of a cliff face named *The Chief.* It was next to Alan's body.

In the days that followed, Simon learned that Alan had convinced his parents to invest heavily in mortgage-backed securities. Alan told them they were "safe as houses". But he hadn't known their investment was backed by sub-prime mortgages.

When the housing market collapsed, Alan's parents lost everything. Their money. Their house. Their son.

"Why?" cried Alan's mother at the funeral.

Simon held her tightly as she wept.

Because of the GFC.

The final straw arrived for Simon when Dick Gelderman escaped fraud charges on a legal technicality. Dick was one of the greedy high fliers of the financial world who had landed with a multi-million dollar parachute. In Dick's case, the parachute was worth 80 million — more than enough to hire a good lawyer.

As Simon sat at his computer, filling out another doomed job application for a software developer role, the news bulletin on CNN caught his eye.

Dick Gelderman. Free.

"What?" said Simon. "That's bullshit."

He shook his head. There's *got* to be a way to make him pay.

And there was.

Like most ingenious ideas, the one that formed in Simon's mind was surprisingly simple. He would build an app for a cell phone.

But unlike ordinary apps, this one would allow people to bet on the time and manner of someone's death.

Anyone's death. Anyone they didn't like.

The more people who placed a bet, the bigger the prize pool. And the more likely someone would die.

Simon was convinced his idea would work. It was innovative. It filled a need.

It brought contract killing to the masses.

The legality of "The App" was a somewhat grey area.

It was legal to bet on all sorts of things — including the year a celebrity might die.

The App just extended this practice and made it accessible.

At least that's what Simon believed.

If enough people bought tickets in a lottery, someone eventually wins. It doesn't mean they rigged the draw.

Simon concluded the same logic applied to The App. If a person correctly predicted the circumstances of someone's death, it doesn't mean they killed them.

And even if they were responsible, proving a connection would be difficult. Especially with the protective features Simon had in mind.

Having made his decision, Simon phoned Pete Madden, a former colleague who was sympathetic to his plight of long term unemployment.

"I'm thinking of starting a business," said Simon.

"Doing app development."

"Cool," said Pete. "Let me know if I can help."

"Actually … that was kind of why I called."

"Hey, no probs. What do you need, man?"

"It's a bit daunting starting from scratch. I was hoping I could get a jump start with some of the framework code … for the different cell phone platforms."

Pete laughed. "By jump start, I assume you mean raid the software repository of your former employer?"

"That would be correct," said Simon.

"Happy to help. Those cock suckers deserve it for getting rid of you, man."

"Thanks. I'll let you decide what to copy … just use your judgement."

"Leave it with Uncle Pete."

"Oh … make sure you include that high end encryption code they have as well."

"No problem. Consider it done."

Simon's next step was to design The App. He kept things simple, since he was the only developer. The result was a user interface that was easy to operate.

The App's main features allowed a user to display the current prize pool for a betting subject, make a bet, and claim a prize. The minimum bet was set at a dollar, to encourage participation.

All user interactions would be encrypted using the technology 'borrowed' from Simon's former employer. The time and manner of the betting subject's death would be stored on a central server, and would remain encrypted until a prize claimant submitted a decrypt key. This ensured that Simon had no potential foreknowledge of how or when someone might die. An important legal point.

All bets would be made using anonymous digital cash.

The App initially targeted the two major cell phone platforms. Together, these accounted for about 94% of the market.

Simon started coding as soon as he received the library of source code from Pete Madden. He worked tirelessly for three months, relieved to finally have a purpose after six months of depressed inactivity.

To fund the necessary server infrastructure, Simon dug into his savings. He settled on a Cloud Service Provider that offered scalability and a location in Eastern Europe.

Once the coding was complete, he tested The App on the most popular mobile devices.

Finally, Simon submitted The App to the two major platform vendors for approval. The App would be made available for free to ensure the widest possible uptake. The revenue would come from skimming a percentage of the bets. After a nervous wait and a couple of email exchanges, he was given the green light.

The last thing Simon did before The App's release was to pre-populate the back-end database with some bets of his own. He'd identified the major players responsible for the financial crisis. Dick Gelderman was at the top of his list.

Simon sat in front of his computer. The persistent rain that had drenched Vancouver for the past three days, eased to a trickle.

He wiped his sweaty hands on his T-shirt and typed some commands. The App went live.

On the first day there were less than one hundred downloads. But things changed dramatically when one of the major tech blogs mentioned it. A cascading waterfall of blog posts and social media shares flooded the Internet in a matter of days.

"Check this out. Radical app serves up a cold dish of revenge," said one blogger.

"Hate your mother-in-law? This could be the app for you," said another.

By the end of the first week, the number of downloads had reached fifty thousand. Growth became exponential as people shared it with friends, who in turn shared it with more friends. The number of downloads exploded.

At the end of the second week more than 1.5 million copies had been downloaded.

Simon was pleased when he saw the large number of bets being placed against those responsible for the financial crisis. Millions of ordinary workers had suffered from its effects. And they wanted retribution.

It was only a matter of time before one of them took the next step.

CHAPTER THREE

Ignition

Tom Roberts adjusted his goggles at the top of the ski run and turned to the man he'd been guiding for the last five hours. Fortunately for Tom, the mirrored surface of his goggles hid his real feelings from the man who'd hired him.

Dick Gelderman had decided to celebrate his victory over the legal system with a skiing holiday in Canada.

Tom couldn't believe his eyes when he saw the man who'd hired his services for the next three days. He recognised him immediately from the news coverage. Like many others, Tom had been stunned by Gelderman's acquittal on a legal technicality. Tom's brother Mike had been a hardworking executive before the financial crisis, who'd invested his life savings in a 'low risk' fund. Unfortunately the investment turned out to be in sub-prime mortgages, and his life savings were snuffed out in an instant. Mike took his own life two weeks later.

"I hope you're going to find something more challenging for me tomorrow," said Gelderman. "I'm paying you good money to find me fresh back-country powder, and all I've seen is a lot of tracked snow today."

Tom bit his tongue.

"Yes, Mr Gelderman," he said. He'd been subjected to comments like this all day, which were quite unreasonable. Most of their runs had been completely empty, and only a few of them had shown the tell-tale signs of other skiers.

"You'd better," said Gelderman. "I'll expect you in the lobby of my hotel at seven o'clock tomorrow morning." With that, he pointed his skis straight down the home trail and took off, weaving in and out of the less experienced skiers at high speed. He cut across the back of one beginner's skis, causing her to lose her balance and fall. Gelderman didn't stop.

"Wanker," said Tom. He skied down to help the woman, then headed off to his favourite pub, the Dubh Linn Gate. He'd earned a beer.

Two hours and four pints of Guinness later, Tom was bitching to his mate, Norman, about his client.

"Dick Geldermann?" said Norman. "I've heard of him."

"I'm sure you have," said Tom. "He's been all over the news."

"No, not in the news. I just downloaded this app that someone told me about. He's at the top of the betting list."

"What betting list?"

Norman pulled out his phone and called up the list of betting subjects in The App. Dick Gelderman's name was at the top with a dollar figure next to it.

"$63,876?" said Tom. "What's that for?"

"It's the betting pool for how and when he'll die," said Norman.

"What?"

Norman spent the next five minutes explaining how it worked. Tom listened intently before downloading The App to his phone.

Then he quickly finished his pint and made his

excuses.

Tom had a back-country skiing trip to plan. One that Dick Gelderman wouldn't be able to complain about.

The next morning, Tom was waiting for Gelderman in the lobby of his hotel. He was early and fidgeted with his hands.

At ten past seven, Gelderman exited the lift and strode towards him. Gelderman ignored Tom's outstretched hand.

"You'd better have some decent skiing for me today, Roberts, or you can kiss your tip goodbye. I'm not paying you good money to take me places that *anyone* can afford to go to."

Gelderman's attitude had a galvanizing effect on Tom. It reassured him that he'd made the right decision.

"I've spent several hours planning your route today, Mr Gelderman. I think you'll find it very exciting."

"I'll be the judge of that," said Gelderman.

Tom smiled at him. "Sir, I'm so confident, that I'll offer you a money back guarantee."

"Really?"

"Yes. A full refund."

"Okay, but be prepared to lose your money."

Gelderman decided to complain regardless of what he thought of the skiing.

An hour later, they were dropped off by Skidoo at the boundary gate on Blackcomb Glacier. The sign said "Ski Area Boundary, Not Patrolled". It also warned of avalanche dangers and numerous other hazards.

In the distance was a vast expanse of white, where the fir trees drooped under a fresh layer of snow.

Tom unloaded their skis and backpacks from the

snowmobiles. "From here we hike," he said.

He unpacked his climbing skins and put them on, handing another set to Gelderman.

As a member of the local ski patrol, Tom had a good knowledge of snow conditions in the many back country areas, including those with a high avalanche risk.

He also had access to the equipment that the ski patrol used each day.

"What's that?" said Gelderman.

Tom was repacking an orange bag into his backpack. He'd removed it while retrieving the skins.

Tom hesitated before lifting his eyes. "Explosives."

"Explosives?" said Gelderman. "Are we planning on doing something dangerous?"

"You wanted some decent skiing didn't you?"

"Um, yes," said Gelderman.

"Don't worry, it's nothing that I can't handle. These are just a precaution to eliminate any avalanche risk."

"Oh. Okay." Gelderman fitted the skins to his skis. The moisture from his breath froze in the air, causing it to shimmer.

Tom looked at the man who'd contributed to his brother's death, and searched himself for forgiveness. He found none.

He turned away, and they set off into the mist.

For the next hour, Tom travelled a circuitous route that took them far into the back country. In the last half hour, the only signs of life they'd seen were a few tracks made by deer. The remoteness was exactly what Gelderman wanted.

It suited Tom as well.

The recent weather conditions had created layers that increased the risk of an avalanche. In some cases, the weight of a skier was all it took to trigger a deadly slide. In other cases, more direct assistance was required.

As they reached the crest of their latest climb, a steep run of untracked snow appeared before them. They were standing to the right of a dangerous looking overhang. Below them was a steep slope that ran for about six hundred metres before converging into a narrow chute. The chute was several hundred metres long. It eventually opened out into a wider clearing.

"That's more like it," said Gelderman before remembering the money back guarantee. "Still, not quite what I was expecting," he added.

They took off their packs and removed the skins from their skis. Gelderman drank greedily from his water bottle.

Tom pulled the orange bag from his backpack and placed it on the ground. Next he retrieved a small video camera.

"You get to make the first tracks on the run, Mr Gelderman. I'll start filming you from here and then meet you at the bottom."

"I should think so," said Gelderman.

While Gelderman adjusted his skis and tightened the straps on his backpack, Tom removed his gloves and picked up the camera. The orange bag rested against his feet. Tom aimed the camera at his client and started filming.

Gelderman grinned. He pointed a finger at the lens. "Enjoy the show, boys. Watch and learn."

He shuffled on his skis to the edge of the slope and planted his poles. "See you at the bottom, Mr Ski-Guide. And make sure you bring that refund." Before Tom could respond, Gelderman pushed off and dropped into the run.

Tom waited a few seconds then he fell to his knees and opened the orange bag. Inside was an object the size of a large can of soup. A fuse protruded from one end. Tom had reduced the length of the fuse so the burn time was twenty-five seconds instead of the standard ninety.

Below him, Gelderman's shrinking figure carved its way through the knee-deep snow. There was no time for second thoughts.

Tom ignited the fuse and hurled the charge into the middle of the overhang, then he crouched behind a rock. From his position he could just see Gelderman in the distance.

Gelderman was three hundred metres away when the blast went off. The sound took a second to reach him. The crump of the explosion was followed by a crack as the overhang collapsed, and a thick slab of snow broke away.

Gelderman turned when he heard the noise and skidded to a halt. He swiftly confirmed its source.

"Fuck."

High above Gelderman, Tom stood to get a better view. He gripped the icy rockface with his exposed fingers.

Surely the bastard couldn't outrun an avalanche?

Tom held his breath as Gelderman jump turned and launched into a downhiller's tuck.

Gelderman accelerated quickly.

Behind Gelderman, the river of snow flowed rapidly down the mountain, its rumbling passage shaking the trees. A white cloud billowed in the air.

In front of the plume, Gelderman shifted his weight as he tried desperately to find the perfect line. But there was nothing he could do.

A few seconds later, the cold wave crashed over Gelderman and dumped him into the chute like a broken toy. He didn't come out the other end.

Tom exhaled slowly and nodded towards the entrance of the chute.

"Let me know if you want that refund, Dick."

CHAPTER FOUR

Burning

Simon was asleep in bed when his phone started beeping. He was dreaming about the blonde from the weather channel. The noise forced him to open his eyes.

"Why now?" he groaned.

Simon reached over to the bedside-table and felt around with his hand until he found his phone. He squinted as he read the message.

Someone had claimed a prize.

"Jesus," he said.

All thoughts of the weather girl vanished as he jumped out of bed to turn on his computer. He paced the room while it booted up.

The blue Windows screen appeared and he logged on to The App's admin screen. A little red symbol appeared above the claims inbox. An unprocessed claim.

Simon clicked the icon and selected the only row in the displayed list. Dick Gelderman.

"Fuck, yeah," said Simon, thumping his hand on the desk. He fist pumped a few times.

His dog, Gizmo, a Basenji cross, started barking and running in circles. The bark turned into a howl.

"It's okay, Gizmo," said Simon. "Calm down."

Gizmo stopped next to Simon's chair. He stood on his hind legs and rested his chin on Simon's lap.

Simon rubbed him behind the ears.

"First things first, eh, Giz? Let's make sure the

bastard's dead."

He opened a web browser to his local newspaper, *The Vancouver Sun*. He didn't have to look very far.

The second item in the *Latest News* section gave the story.

"Avalanche claims wealthy banker at Whistler," said the headline.

Whistler? That's just up the road. Simon wished he'd been there to see it.

The report gave the essential details.

"New York banker, Dick Gelderman, has died in an avalanche while skiing off-piste near the Whistler ski resort. He was skiing with experienced local guide, Tom Roberts, when the accident occurred at approximately 10:00 am PST. Unconfirmed reports say that he died of a broken neck. Gelderman was recently acquitted of charges stemming from his role in the Global Financial Crisis. His ski guide, Roberts, survived unharmed."

Simon smiled. "Not guilty my ass. You were found guilty in the court of public opinion, Dick."

Simon returned to his administration screen and examined the claim. The claimant's decrypt key was valid. He pressed a button to decode the bet and the deciphered text appeared on the screen.

"Dick Gelderman. Thursday, 27th February, 10:00 am PST. Avalanche."

"We have a winner," said Simon. "Tom Roberts, I presume."

He pressed another button which closed off any further betting on Dick Gelderman. He also broadcast a notification to anyone who'd bet on Gelderman. Under the Terms and Conditions for The App, claimants had twenty four hours to stake their claim once death had been established. Given that The App didn't allow retrospective betting, it was unlikely there would be multiple winners. Unlikely, but not impossible.

Another important legal point.

After twenty four hours, there were no additional winning claims. Simon confirmed the payout via the administration screen, which sent digital currency worth $65,628 to the winner.

Another payment was sent to Simon's account. Ten percent of the total prize pool.

Simon closed the pop-up window and his computer's background image filled the screen. It was a photo of his friend, Alan.

After using his avalanche transceiver to locate Gelderman's body, Tom Roberts had used his two-way radio to call for help.

Twenty minutes later a rescue helicopter had arrived from Whistler. The medic, who was a friend of Roberts, confirmed what he already knew.

Gelderman was dead.

His explanation of events had been accepted by everyone, including the police. Off-piste skiing was a risky sport, and avalanche deaths occurred every year in Canada.

They agreed that it was a tragic accident.

Tom had gone home after making a statement, and following a shower and a stiff drink he turned on his phone. He launched The App and selected his bet on Dick Gelderman. His finger paused over the 'Claim' button as he thought about his brother Mike.

"For you, bro."

He pressed the button.

A popup window appeared. "Thank you for submitting your claim. Your share of the prize money will be transmitted to your specified account as soon as the claim has been validated. We hope you've enjoyed your betting experience as we work together to create a better world."

Two days later he confirmed the transaction and booked a skiing holiday in Switzerland.

Simon was elated with the news about Gelderman. He wanted to celebrate and tell people what he'd done.

But who could he trust? His only close friend was dead, and his mother wouldn't approve.

He opened a beer while he considered his options. When nothing came to mind he logged back in to The App.

"Who's next, Giz?" he said to his dog. Gizmo opened his eyes and raised his head briefly. Then he went back to sleep.

Simon sorted the targets by the value of their bets and limited the results to the top five candidates.

The first was Stephen Hinkley. Simon recognised the name from the media. He was a priest. A paedophile priest.

Hinkley had been publically accused when several of his victims objected to him being made a Bishop. Although his appointment as Bishop was rescinded, he was never prosecuted because of the Statute of Limitations.

"A worthy candidate," said Simon.

The second was someone that Simon knew well. He'd placed the first bet on Jerry Upton himself, on the day he launched The App.

Upton was another banker who had made a lot of money from sub-prime mortgages.

Simon wasn't satisfied with Upton's position on the list. He bet another two thousand. Hinkley and Upton switched places.

Simon smiled and drained the rest of his beer.

He walked into the kitchen and grabbed another from the fridge. The television was on and his favourite weather girl was doing her thing.

She gave him an idea about how to celebrate.

He walked back to his computer and searched for erotic massages in Vancouver.

The *Erotic Playmates* website provided 'models' who came to your house. It also allowed Simon to book online.

He made his booking and went to get ready. For Sienna.

Stephen Hinkley was sitting in his car. He wore a hat and sunglasses as he watched the children playing in the school yard across the road.

Ever since his former altar boy had gone to the media, Hinkley had found it hard to go anywhere without being recognised. He was forced to wear a disguise when he went out. Hinkley hated the little shit for what he'd done.

A young boy was sitting on the swing across the road with his legs apart. He had wispy blonde hair. As he swung towards Hinkley, his slender legs lifted high in the air, and he laughed.

"Such beauty," said Hinkley.

He'd always loved young boys. So innocent. So easy to intimidate.

A siren sounded, and a teacher walked into the yard. Lunch time was over.

Hinkley sighed.

He started the car and pulled out from the kerb.

He didn't notice the Ford Explorer behind him.

Simon changed into his least stained T-shirt and was opening his fourth beer when there was a knock at the door of his apartment. Gizmo started barking.

"Quiet, Giz. We don't want to scare her off."

Simon checked himself in the mirror and patted down some wayward hair. Then he opened the door.

A large man stood in the entrance. He was wearing a long black leather coat and sunglasses. His jaw was shaded with stubble and his fingers were covered in heavy rings.

Gizmo growled at the stranger, who sneered at the little dog in return. Gizmo ran behind the couch.

"Simon?" said the man in a Russian accent.

"Um … yes."

"You wait for Sienna?"

"Who wants to know?"

The man leaned forward and cracked his knuckles. He repeated his question.

"Um … yes I am," said Simon. "Where is she?"

"I need four hundred dollars," said the man.

Simon swallowed.

"I need to see Sienna first."

The man hesitated, then took a step to the side. A young woman emerged, wearing a thick coat and a knitted hat.

Simon mentally compared her to the escort agency photos. There was a strong resemblance, but it was hard to be sure through the layers of clothes.

"The money is inside," he said eventually. "But I thought that I'd pay her afterward."

"You not pay *her*," said the man. "You pay *me* … for driving her here."

"Oh. I see."

Simon turned to go inside. "Let me get the money."

The man followed him into his apartment. Gizmo barked from behind the couch.

"You're not going to wait here the whole time are you?" said Simon.

The man shook his head. "I wait in car. In case there's trouble."

"There'll be no trouble," said Simon.

He found his wallet and counted out the notes. He handed them to the man who pocketed the cash and opened the door.

"You have one hour," said the man. He walked away.

"Come in," said Simon. He held the door open for the woman. "Sienna."

She smiled, and brushed against him as she entered the apartment.

"Can I take your coat?" he said.

"Thank you."

Simon detected a hint of a Russian accent, though not as strong as her minder's accent. She removed her coat and handed it to Simon. Underneath she wore a black négligée. Simon tried not to stare.

She had long dark hair and cheekbones that emphasised her pale blue eyes. Her legs seemed to linger as she walked.

"You have a lot of computers," she said. "And a cute dog." Gizmo had emerged from behind the couch and was sniffing her.

"I'm a programmer. Or at least I was. I suppose, technically, I still am."

"I bet you're very smart." She moved towards him.

"Um ... above average, I guess."

"I like smart men." She took his hand. "Come. We shower first."

"Shower? Is that necessary?" He couldn't remember the last time he'd cleaned his shower.

"Yes. You will enjoy, I promise. I'll soap you all over."

"Okay. It's through here."

She led him into the bathroom.

Gizmo tried to follow, but was stopped by Simon's foot in the doorway.

"No, Giz. I don't need any help."

Jerry Upton was playing with his daughter, Maddison, when the phone rang. It was her sixth birthday and Jerry had bought her a Shetland pony.

"When can I ride him, Daddy?"

"When the riding instructor gets here, darling. She'll be here at ten."

He walked over to his phone and picked it up.

"This is Jerry."

"Hey, Jerry. Mike. Just ringing to see if you'd heard the news."

"What news?"

"About Dick?"

Jerry groaned. "What's he done now?"

"He ... died."

"What?"

"Got caught in an avalanche up in Canada."

"Seriously?"

"Yep. Finally got into some trouble that he couldn't buy his way out of."

"The stingy bastard," said Jerry. "He'll be sitting in hell wishing he hadn't wasted that money on his lawyer."

"Ain't that the truth."

"What happened? Was he skiing alone?"

"No, he had a guide. They were skiing in the back-country. The guide survived."

Jerry laughed. "Maybe Dick didn't tip him."

"Yeah, probably. Anyway, the funeral's next Friday."

"Thanks."

He hung up the phone and shook his head. Just goes to show. All the money in the world doesn't guarantee you a long and happy life.

He sat down next to his daughter. "Where were we, darling?"

"You were about to read me a story. About a pony."

Sienna slipped out of her négligée. Simon didn't move. He stared.

He'd had sex before. After the work Christmas party. The woman from HR had been drunk and they'd shared a cab ride home.

She hadn't cared that he was a virgin, and he hadn't cared that she was fat. He hadn't known that she was married.

Sienna wasn't fat. She was hot.

Simon's body reacted to the beautiful woman.

Sienna moved toward him. "Let me help you with that," she said.

She removed his clothes and led him into the shower by his erect penis.

Stephen Hinkley drove home to the empty house on the outskirts of Moncton, New Brunswick. It was a large house that was the property of the Church. He was living there while the Archbishop decided what to do with him.

Over the course of his career, Hinkley had been moved several times. Whenever it became uncomfortable.

Unfortunately, it was becoming more and more difficult to start again. With social media and the Internet, it was almost impossible.

He parked his car in the garage and went inside to watch porn.

Hinkley replayed his favourite clips until the sun crept beneath the horizon. He fell asleep with an eerie light from the computer reflecting off his face.

He didn't hear the Ford Explorer pulling into his driveway.

Hinkley woke with a start and found it hard to breathe. There was a bag over his head. He tried to pull it off, but something grabbed his arms and forced them behind his body. He felt coldness on his skin as his wrists were handcuffed.

"What the hell?" he said. His voice was muffled by the bag.

His head lurched violently forward as it was stuck by an object from behind. "Silence," said a man's voice.

"Who are —"

He was struck again. The blow left his ears ringing.

"I said, be quiet," said the voice.

Hinkley closed his mouth.

"We're going for a little ride, Stephen," said the man.

The man waited to see if Hinkley would ask where they were going. He didn't.

"Good," said the man. "You're learning."

The man pulled Hinkley roughly to his feet, and pushed him toward the front door. Hinkley stopped suddenly when his forehead hit the wooden frame.

"If you make a sound, I'll hurt you," said the man.

They went outside, and Hinkley was forced to lie down in the back of the Explorer. The man hog-tied him, and covered him with a blanket.

His heart was pounding.

The man started the car and drove quietly along the icy streets.

"I suppose you're wondering who I am?" said the man.

Hinkley didn't respond.

"It's okay. You can talk now, Stephen."

There was a pause before Hinkley spoke. "Um … yes. Who are you?"

The man checked his rear-view mirror. No one was following.

"I used to know a priest, Stephen. He was just like you."

"Really?"

"Yes. I went to a boarding school where he taught."

"Where was that?"

"It doesn't really matter. What matters, are the things he did … to discipline me."

"Oh, I see," said Hinkley.

"Yes. He used to give me a choice. A lashing with his belt … or sex education."

The man paused.

"I chose sex education. I wish I'd chosen the belt."

"What happened to him?"

"He died."

Hinkley swallowed. His mouth was dry.

"How did he die?"

"That's not important," said the man. "What's important, is how you're going to die."

Hinkley moaned.

The man didn't speak for another twenty minutes. By the time they arrived at their destination, Hinkley was whimpering.

The man untied his legs and dragged him out of the car. Hinkley still wore the bag on his head. He couldn't see anything, but he heard the distant sound of water lapping against the shore.

"Walk," said the man. He pushed Hinkley in front of him.

Hinkley was still wearing his slippers, and they quickly became wet as he walked. Wet and sticky.

"Is that mud?" said Hinkley.

The man laughed.

"You're not from around here, Stephen. So you probably don't know where we are."

"No," said Hinkley.

"We're on the edge of the *Bay of Fundy*."

They walked for another fifty metres, before the man jerked him to a stop. Hinkley felt himself being pushed against something hard. It was curved and made of wood. The rope that had held him in the car was used to secure him to the pylon.

Hinkley strained against his bonds but he couldn't move. A few seconds later, the bag was ripped from his head.

A large man stood in front of him. The man's face was only inches away.

"I want to see the look in your eyes," said the man.

Hinkley tried to back away, but couldn't. He was tied to a white post. The post was seventy metres from the shoreline, on a tidal flat.

"Do you know what the *Bay of Fundy* is famous for?" said the man.

Hinkley shook his head.

The man smiled. "The biggest tides in the world." He paused. "And the tide is turning."

Hinkley's eyes widened.

"No," he pleaded.

The man ignored him. "Today's tide is predicted to be about twelve metres."

"I'll do anything," said Hinkley.

"You've done enough already, Stephen."

He punched Hinkley in the stomach, causing him to open his mouth. Then he stuffed some cloth into the opening and secured it with duct tape.

The man turned and walked back to his car, ignoring the groans behind him.

He sat in the front seat and opened his thermos. It was going to be a long night.

Simon was reminiscing about Sienna's visit when his phone started beeping. It had been a memorable evening — except at the start when she'd soaped him. She'd laughed at his premature excitement and he'd turned red. For a moment he'd thought about adding her to his list. But she'd redeemed herself.

Simon picked up his phone and read the message.

"Jesus," he said.

Another prize had been claimed.

He logged on to The App and checked who it was. Stephen Hinkley.

Damn. Why couldn't it be Upton?

He opened a web page to *The Vancouver Sun*, and checked the latest news. Nothing about Hinkley.

Maybe they haven't announced it yet.

He smiled.

Perhaps nobody knows. No one except the killer.

He examined the claim. The decrypt key was valid. He decoded the bet and started to laugh.

"You imaginative bastard," said Simon.

He memorised the deciphered text before clearing it.

"Stephen Hinkley. Sunday, 2nd March, 1:00 am ADT. Drowned by high tide in the Bay of Fundy, near Moncton."

Simon did a quick google to find an online news source for Moncton. *Times and Transcript*. He selected the link and examined the *Trending News* headlines. Still nothing.

He checked his watch and did a quick calculation. It was about eight o'clock in the morning in Moncton. He would need to give them more time.

Simon got back into bed.

Mabel Hunter was walking her dog along the water's edge. She'd been carrying out the morning ritual for the last ten years — ever since she'd moved back to New Brunswick. She particularly loved walking at low tide. The rock formations, created by the extreme tides, were a natural marvel.

She raised her dog ball launcher, and threw the tennis ball towards a white post in the distance. Her dog,

Maisie, tore off in pursuit of the ball, wet sand flicking up behind her.

Maisie had run about thirty metres before becoming distracted. She stopped next to the post and sniffed at something on the far side. She started to bark.

"What have you found, girl?" said Mabel. She'd been meaning to buy a new set of glasses, but hadn't gotten around to it.

As she neared the post, she could see something hanging there limply. "What is it Mais —"

She screamed.

An elderly man was tied to the wooden pylon. His skin was wrinkled and pale. A crab sat on his head, eating his right eye.

Maisie licked dried salt from the man's hand.

"Come away, Maisie. Come here. Now."

Maisie reluctantly obeyed.

Mabel pulled out her phone and dialled 911.

"Police. I need the police," she said to the operator.

She gave her location.

"Sit tight," said the operator. "An officer will be with you soon."

Mabel waited for five minutes, considering her options. Then she made another call. To her niece.

Christine had just started her new job, as a journalist for CBC News.

"It's Aunt Mabel, dear. There's something you might be interested in."

She gave her niece the details, then waited for the police to arrive. Mabel wanted to remove the crab, but decided against it. She didn't want to tamper with evidence.

Fifteen minutes later, a police car from the Royal

Canadian Mounted Police pulled up on the road side. An officer stepped out of the car. He was almost run over by the CBC News truck that skidded to a halt beside him.

Mabel waved to her niece.

CHAPTER FIVE

Recognition

Simon got out of bed and resumed his search for news about Stephen Hinkley. He eventually found an article on the CBC News website. It included a video clip featuring an attractive young reporter. She was standing on the shore of the *Bay of Fundy*.

"Police have confirmed they are treating the death of Father Stephen Hinkley as suspicious. He was found this morning by a woman from Moncton, who was out walking her dog."

The picture changed from the reporter to that of middle-aged woman with her dog. The woman's name was Mabel.

"It was terrible," said Mabel. "He was tied to a post in the bay. He must have drowned when the tide came in."

"Was that all you saw?" asked the reporter.

"No," said Mabel. "There was a … crab."

She paused, but the reporter urged her to continue.

"It was eating his eye," said Mabel, before turning away from the camera.

The reporter nodded sombrely. "That must have been terrible."

A policeman stepped in front of the camera and the video clip ended.

Simon brought up the tide charts for that part of the *Bay of Fundy*. High tide was at 2:04 am ADT.

Near enough to 1:00 am. Hinkley was probably dead

by then.

He logged on to The App and closed off the betting.

Detective Speed had received the call at about 8:00 am. He'd driven straight to the scene. A TV crew from CBC was already there.

He approached the young RCMP constable and asked him who they were interviewing.

"That's the lady who found him," said the constable. "That paedopile, Hinkley. I recognised him from the news. Plus his driver's license was in his tracksuit pants."

"You didn't tell them that, did you?"

"Um … only that Hinkley's death looked suspicious. Which was kind of obvious, given that he was handcuffed."

"Jesus Christ," said Detective Speed. "Go and stop them from filming. I'll deal with you later."

Bloody idiot. He shook his head. What were they teaching them at the Academy?

Speed pulled out his phone and called his partner. "We're going to need a full team on this one. Send me forensics and a couple of uniforms who know what they're doing."

He moved closer to the body. At the base of the post were multiple sets of footprints.

Speed growled.

The constable approached him.

"They're not happy, sir. The reporter wants to know if she can interview you."

Speed glared at him, and made a note of his name. "I don't give a shit. Go and set up a perimeter around the body. And don't let anyone else near it."

"What about forensics, sir?"

"What about them?"

"Should I let them near it when they arrive?"

Speed took a deep breath. "Constable Johnson, how long have you been a police officer?"

"This is my second week, sir."

"I'd never have guessed."

Speed walked over to the reporter and told her to get out of his crime scene. He asked the older lady to stay so he could interview her.

"Reporters. Bloody vultures," he said, after the news crew had retreated to the road side.

Mabel gave him an icy stare. "She's my niece. And she's very good at her job."

Speed closed his eyes and massaged his temples. Brilliant.

Dillon Black sat in his van on the side of the road. He was on the outskirts of Los Angeles, on the boundary of the semi-rural area of Hidden Hills. Sprawling estates with vineyards and stables were visible from his vantage point on the hillside. One of them was the property of Jerry Upton.

Dillon watched the house through binoculars, making notes on the pad beside him. A small girl was riding a tiny pony.

Dillon had been unemployed since he'd returned from Afghanistan, where he'd served as a Marine Corps sniper. He'd had trouble readjusting to life back in the States. He kept seeing the people he'd killed in his dreams. Lately he'd started seeing them when he was awake. His doctor said he had PTSD, but the Government refused to believe his diagnosis.

A week ago, an old Marine Corps buddy had come to his house in Seattle to cheer him up. They were having a beer in the backyard when Lance had mentioned The App.

As Dillon had listened to Lance's explanation, he'd felt something change inside his head. It was as if his brain had been rebooted.

Neurons flickered to life and the heightened activity produced a vision. But unlike his usual hallucinations, this one gave Dillon hope.

It also gave him a chance to use his specialised skills.

His skin tingled at the prospect.

Dillon had waited for Lance to leave, then he'd downloaded The App and begun researching. His first step was target selection.

The most valuable target was Jerry Upton. And Dillon knew what to do with High-Value Targets.

He'd carefully disassembled and cleaned his rifle. He'd also cleaned his pistol — just in case. Dillon didn't intend to use a handgun, but he'd remembered his instructor yelling about "the seven Ps"; Proper Planning and Preparation Prevents Piss Poor Performance.

Dillon packed his weapons and ammunition in his Chevy van, along with a pair of night-vision goggles. He added a two-week supply of MREs. No mission would be complete without mystery meals.

After loading his supplies, he'd driven south to Portland, where he stopped at an Internet cafe. He'd downloaded maps and photos of Hidden Hills. Dillon was amazed at the type of information available on the Internet. Satellite photos. Contour maps. Even photos of the target's house. It made planning his mission so much easier.

Once he'd gathered enough intelligence, Dillon had resumed his journey to Los Angeles. He'd arrived last night.

Today was his first day of reconnaissance. It had gone well. He'd surveyed the surrounding territory, and picked out potential firing positions. He'd also observed the target and his family.

He put down the binoculars and rubbed his eyes, then he drove back to the motel.

Christine Hunter was sitting at her desk at the CBC office when her phone rang. She was re-watching the interview that she'd done with her aunt. Her boss had been very impressed.

She paused the video clip and picked up the phone.

"Is that Christine Hunter?" said a man's voice. "The journalist who did that report about Stephen Hinkley?"

"Yes," said Christine. She smiled. She wasn't used to getting calls from fans.

"I have some information that you might find interesting."

Christine sat up straight and picked up her pen. "What have you got?"

"A possible motive," said the man.

Her shoulders slumped. "I already know he was a paedophile."

The man made a tut-tut sound. "That's not what I was going to say. I think he was killed for money."

She rubbed her forehead. "What makes you say that?"

"He was at the top of that list … on my phone."

Christine raised her eyes and shook her head. She should have expected some crank calls.

"Okay. Thanks for your call," she said.

The man sighed. "If you don't believe me, then check it out for yourself."

He gave her the details about The App and hung up.

Christine was less sure of herself after hearing what he'd said. She picked up her cell phone and searched for The App.

It was rated five stars. "What have I got to lose?"

She pressed the button and downloaded it.

Five minutes later she was in her boss's office.

"You have to see this."

Detective Speed was squeezing a stress ball when the phone rang. He leaned forward and picked it up with his spare hand. A woman's voice spoke.

"This is Christine Hunter, from CBC News."

He groaned. "I told you already, lady, I'm not going to be interviewed."

He leaned forward to disconnect the call, but her next sentence stopped him.

"Did you know that Stephen Hinkley was on a hit list?"

He sat back in his chair and paused mid squeeze.

"A hit list? What are you talking about?"

"I'll take that as a *no*," said Christine.

Speed coughed. "I didn't say that. Tell me what you know about a list."

"What's in it for me?"

"How about I don't charge you with obstruction."

"Really Detective? You're trying to bully a journalist?"

Speed gripped the stress ball harder. He paused. "What do you want?"

He could feel her smiling on the other end of the phone.

"Just an interview, and a couple of quotes, Detective."

He gritted his teeth. "Meet me here in an hour. But I'm not saying a word until you tell me what you know."

He hung up. Bloody journalists.

Simon was reading the news online when he saw the article. It was the same woman who'd broken the story about Stephen Hinkley.

"It's that pretty journalist again, Gizmo," he said.

Gizmo looked up briefly from his position on Simon's lap. He sniffed Simon's hand before closing his eyes again.

Simon pressed play on the video clip.

"The investigation into the brutal murder of alleged paedophile, Stephen Hinkley, took a bizarre twist today. In a CBC News exclusive, we can reveal that Stephen Hinkley's name was high on a potential hit list. A cell phone app, known only as 'The App', allows punters to bet on the time and manner of someone's death. Under the rules of The App, the winner is the person who correctly guesses the circumstances of someone's death. Yesterday, Stephen Hinkley was near the top of that list, with a prize pool in excess of $50,000. Today, betting has been suspended on Stephen Hinkley, possibly because someone has claimed the prize."

Simon logged on to The App, and checked the number of downloads. They had increased significantly from the previous day.

Dillon waited until most of the houses were dark before parking his van. Hidden Hills was a gated community, so it wasn't possible for him to drive any closer. He parked in an area he'd scouted the day before.

There were no surveillance cameras.

He'd replaced his license plates with a set he'd stolen from another van. It was the same model as his, and had been left in long term parking at the airport. It would be days, or even weeks, before someone noticed the missing plates.

Dillon climbed into the back of his van and changed into his camouflage gear.

His *ghillie suit* had been carefully handmade. Strips of tattered burlap and Cordura had been strung together with cargo netting. Then it was dragged through the mud and dung. Most *ghillie suits* stunk and Dillon's was no exception.

Dillon added the finishing touches to his outfit with some twigs and leaves. Then he smeared green and black paint on his face and checked the result with a handheld mirror. Satisfied, he lowered the night vision goggles and picked up his rifle.

He slowly opened the door and slipped into the cool night air. His goggles turned everything an eerie green.

There was no one around, so he climbed the fence and began the slow crawl to the top of the hill. It took him forty minutes to cover the one hundred yards.

From his vantage point, he could see Jerry Upton's house. More importantly, he could also see the backyard.

"Sierra one," he said to himself. "In position."

"What do you mean you can't tell me their names?" said Detective Speed. He was on the phone. He'd been trying all day to determine who'd created The App.

The server was hosted in Russia. But the names of the people who owned it were hidden behind a series of shelf companies. They were incorporated in different countries — Russia, Germany, Canada, and Australia — to name a few.

The Russian woman's voice was monotone and disinterested.

"That information is confidential. You do not have proper authority."

Detective Speed strangled his stress ball. "Well how do I get that?"

"You must contact Ministry of Foreign Affairs."

Speed groaned. "I already did that. They told me to call you."

He visualised the woman's face being eaten by a crab.

"Sorry. I cannot help you," she said.

She didn't sound sorry.

He hung up and drove to Tim Hortons. He ordered a four cheese bagel.

His cell phone rang while he was waiting. Speed recognised the ringtone for his father — a submarine dive alarm.

"What's up Dad?"

"How'd you know it was me?"

"A lucky guess." There was an awkward silence. "What can I do for you, Dad? I'm in the middle of an investigation."

"Oh. I see. Well … it's just that I'm in Moncton for a day or two and I thought we could catch up."

"You're here? Today? Jeez, Dad, you should have warned me. I could have made some arrangements."

"I didn't want to bother you. And there was some business that I needed to take care of. I booked into a motel. But I thought we might have coffee before I head back."

"Um … sorry, Dad. Not a good time. I promise to catch up with you soon though. Next time I'm in Fredericton."

There was another silence that was eventually broken by his father.

"Okay. I'd better hit the road in that case. Avoid the traffic." He disconnected the call.

Speed shook his head. His father had booked into a motel?

Simon checked his email account. There was one from a Detective Speed. The email had been routed anonymously to his personal account via a remote server.

"To the people who own The App — please call me," said the message. "It's in relation to an investigation." There was also a Canadian phone number.

Simon pressed delete. If anyone asked, he'd say that he thought it was spam.

He reached into a box on the table, and picked out a jelly-filled Timbit. He bit it in half.

Yum.

He gave the other half to Gizmo, who'd been camped under the box for several minutes.

Simon entered the detective's details into google and hit the Return key.

Dillon lay prone on the ground as he observed Upton's house through his trusted Unertl scope. His heels were lowered, as he'd been taught, to minimise his profile. His rifle, a customised suppressed Remington 700, rested on a bipod in front of him.

The morning sun struggled to reach him through a

layer of thick cloud.

He scanned the windows in Upton's house. The distance was three hundred yards. There was no visible activity.

His stomach grumbled, so he opened an energy bar. He stored the wrapper in his camouflaged bag.

As he chewed, he dialled the target range into the bullet drop compensator. Then he checked his body position. Everything was as it should be.

His breathing was relaxed, and his heartbeat steady and slow.

He smiled to himself. It was good to have a job.

After half an hour, there was movement behind an upstairs window. The little girl was jumping on her parent's bed.

Dillon flexed his fingers. Time to get up Jerry.

The girl was dressed in her riding clothes — jodhpurs and a helmet. She was keen to ride her pony.

An early morning horse ride suited Dillon fine.

Jerry Upton finally emerged from bed. His kissed his wife, and left her to sleep.

Dillon watched through his scope as Upton pulled on his jeans and a T-shirt. Over the top he dragged a grey sweater. The word Harvard was emblazoned across the front in crimson letters.

Upton headed downstairs to the coffee machine and pressed a few buttons. He tied up his sneakers while he waited for his morning kick-start.

His daughter bounced up and down on the balls of her feet. She was standing next to the door.

Finally, with his coffee mug in hand, Upton followed his daughter outside. Dillon chambered a round, and followed the target through his scope — crosshairs on the back of Upton's head.

The scope went black as Upton entered the barn with his daughter.

Dillon glanced at his watch. A quarter after eight. He picked up his cell phone and launched The App. It was time to place his bet. He allowed Upton five minutes to saddle the pony.

Four minutes later, Upton emerged from the stable. He was leading a grey pony with one hand, and carrying his coffee in the other. The girl sat on top of the pony. She grinned at Upton with pure white teeth.

Upton lifted his face to his daughter, and smiled back.

Dillon moved the crosshairs onto Upton's nose. He took a breath and exhaled slowly, waiting for his natural respiratory pause. Then he squeezed the trigger.

The suppressed rifle coughed, and a split second later blood splattered the girl's face. The coffee mug fell to the grass. White cappuccino foam spread across the ground, turning pink as it mixed with the blood draining from Upton's head.

Dillon picked up the empty shell casing and put it in his pocket. He retrieved a small plastic bag from inside his jacket. It contained particles of trace evidence that he'd picked off the floor of his motel room when he'd first arrived. He scattered hairs and fibres around the area where he'd lain.

Then he carefully crawled backwards down the slope, erasing his tracks with a small branch as he went.

By the time the little girl woke her mother, Dillon was already on the freeway heading north.

Back at Upton's house, Maddison grabbed her mother's hand and gazed into her tear-filled eyes.

"Mommy? When can I ride my pony?"

CHAPTER SIX

Unwanted Attention

Christine was having a late lunch in a diner, halfway between Saint Johns and Moncton. She'd driven down to the University of New Brunswick to meet with the chair of the Department of Computer Science, Professor Harris.

He'd given her a crash course in the fundamentals of cell phone apps. Although Christine had struggled with some of the terminology, she now had a better understanding of how they worked.

As she munched on her cheeseburger, her attention was drawn to a news bulletin on CNN.

"In breaking news, banker, Jerry Upton, was shot and killed this morning at his Los Angeles property. Police are still searching for the assailant. So far, they've refused to speculate on a motive. Upton was well known for his role in sparking the GFC."

Christine stopped chewing.

Upton. Jerry Upton.

She'd seen his name recently in The App. It was at the top of the list.

Shit.

She grabbed her phone and jabbed at the icon for The App. She drummed her fingers on the table while it loaded. Eventually the list appeared.

There it was. Jerry Upton. And betting was still open.

She saved a screenshot on her phone before racing

outside to her car. Her half eaten burger was left on the table next to a sizable tip.

She sped back to the office, not caring if she got a ticket.

Dillon continued north along I-5 until he reached Sacramento. He stopped at a *Super 8 Motel* to get some rest.

Once inside, he opened The App and claimed the prize for Jerry Upton. Then he lay back on the bed and replayed his mission.

Reconnaissance. Infiltration. Execution.

The moment of impact. Bullet meeting flesh.

Target crumpling, like a puppet without strings.

Dillon celebrated his success with a Jack Daniels from the minibar. Then he grabbed his phone and reviewed the most valuable candidates on the list.

"Who's next then?" He patted the rifle beside him.

Simon was walking Gizmo back from the shops when his phone beeped. Another bet had been claimed. He stopped on the corner of Broadway and Granville, placing his groceries on the ground. He pulled out his phone to check the name.

Jerry Upton.

"Yes," he cried, startling his dog and the people next to him. "How do you like them apples, Jerry?"

People walking past gave him a wider berth.

He picked up his bags and tugged on Gizmo's lead. They ran the rest of the way home. Once inside, Simon checked the news and confirmed the death. Then he closed off the betting.

He went to the fridge and opened a beer.

To Gelderman and Upton. May you rot in Hell.

Christine arrived back at her desk in the late afternoon. She'd phoned her boss from the car and told him she had another story.

The story got bigger the next time she loaded The App. The betting on Upton had closed.

She unlocked her computer and glanced at her watch. An hour before the main news bulletin. Plenty of time.

She began to type.

Twenty minutes later, she stopped and picked up her phone.

Detective Speed grabbed the receiver with a sticky hand and dropped the last piece of donut on his desk. He talked while he chewed. "Dud-egg-dove Speed."

"Is that Detective Speed?" said Christine.

He tried swallowing — too quickly — and erupted into a coughing fit. He fumbled for the coffee on his desk, knocking it into his lap.

"Fuck."

Speed grabbed his water bottle, emptying half of it onto his crotch. He drank the remainder, dislodging the donut from his throat.

"Who is this?" he said.

"It's Christine Hunter, from CBC News. Did I catch you at a bad time?"

"Yes," he snarled. Goddam journalists.

"Sorry to hear that, Detective, but I have some more information for you. I was hoping to get a response."

A low noise emanated from the back of Speed's throat. He imagined her wearing a set of handcuffs. "What?" he said.

"Another murder," said Christine. "From the list."

The image vanished and he pressed the phone hard against his ear. "I'm listening."

"The murders have gone international."

"What?"

"Jerry Upton. Los Angeles."

Speed hadn't heard about the murder. He'd been busy with his own investigation. But he knew the name.

Christine told him what she knew, then asked him some questions. He confirmed that he was investigating a possible connection between The App and the death of Stephen Hinkley. But he refused to speculate on any connection to Upton's death.

When he hung up, the first thing he did was check his cell phone.

He shook his head. "Holy shit."

The list was growing, and the leading prize pools had tripled overnight.

Simon sat on his couch, watching the evening news. The lead story was about Jerry Upton's murder and a possible connection to The App.

He'd been killed in front of his six year old daughter. There was a photo of the girl being held by her mother. She was wearing a blood spattered blouse.

Simon looked away.

The girl reminded him of his young niece, Amy. Blonde hair, pink ribbons, blue eyes.

Little Amy … who'd cut her finger at the family picnic. All that blood and all those tears. Until a band-aid and a kiss had made it better. She'd hugged her dad.

Simon shook his head. There were other kids *without* a father because of Upton. The world was a better place without him.

Except for the girl.

Simon turned off the TV. Hiding her face.

Perhaps it was better to shut things down — before it got out of hand. And before the police became too interested.

He finished his beer and logged on to The App. The summary page displayed automatically.

"Whoa," said Simon. He hadn't expected that.

The number of bets had exploded.

More than a million people. Looking for justice.

Ordinary people, whose pleas were no longer being heard.

The App had given them a voice. One that reverberated and couldn't be ignored.

Simon nodded.

His moment of doubt passed.

He logged out and grabbed another beer from the fridge. Then he opened Sienna's webpage and made an appointment.

Detective Speed's hand hovered over the keypad on his phone. Hesitating.

But he dialled the number.

A woman answered. "FBI. How may I direct your call?"

"I need to talk to someone in your Los Angeles office," said Speed. "About a murder. I'm a detective with the Royal Canadian Mounted Police."

"One moment, sir."

He was put on hold. He'd expected a recorded message explaining the virtues of the organisation's mission statement. Instead, he was subjected to some crappy elevator music.

"This is Special Agent Marks. How may I help you?"

Speed took his feet off the desk.

"My name is Detective Speed. I'm from the RCMP. In Canada." There was a pause. "The country to your North?"

The agent wasn't *that* special.

"Are you trying to be funny?" said Marks.

"No, just making sure," said Speed.

"What can I do for you, Detective? You mentioned something about a murder?"

"Yes. Jerry Upton's."

"Interesting. What have you got?"

"He was on a hit list."

Speed told him about The App, and about the two murders he was aware of. He briefly described the circumstances behind the death of Stephen Hinkley.

"Hmm, I think I've heard about The App," said Marks. "Fascinating idea. Crowdsourced assassins, enforcing the People's will."

Speed hadn't really thought of it like that. To him, it was simply murder.

"Who are the owners?" said Marks.

"I haven't been able to determine that," said Speed. "I know the server is hosted in Russia, but from there it's a bureaucratic maze."

"And you're hoping the FBI can help?"

"Exactly."

"I'll see what we can do."

An hour later, the phone on Speed's desk rang. It was Special Agent Marks.

"He's one of yours," said Marks.

"What?" said Speed.

"The developer. He's Canadian."

"You're shitting me."

"Afraid not. He lives in Vancouver. One Simon Simpson."

Speed didn't know whether to be happy or not. On one hand, it would give him more control over the investigation. On the other, it was a major pain in the ass.

He'd been hoping to blame the Americans. They were obsessed with guns. Nobody would have been surprised if an American had created The App.

But a Canadian? The local media was going to have a field day.

Speed sighed. "Okay. Thanks. I'll get Vancouver to follow the lead, and let you know what they find."

He hung up the phone and calculated the time in Vancouver. It was early in the evening.

He phoned Vancouver homicide. Eventually, he was patched through to a Detective at his home.

"Detective Kelly," said a gruff voice. "Make it quick, I'm watching the last period of the Canucks game."

"Sorry, but I'm hoping you can help me," said Speed. He introduced himself, and briefly explained the situation. In the background, he heard the crowd roar on Kelly's television.

"Damn," said Kelly. "Missed it. The Canucks scored on the Rangers."

"What's that make it?"

"Three apiece."

"Go Canada," said Speed.

There was a pause. Speed could hear Kelly swallowing a drink.

"Um. So you want me to go and quiz this guy, Simpson, eh?" said Kelly.

"Yeah. That would be great."

"No problem. First thing tomorrow."

"Tomorrow?" said Speed.

"Yeah, it's getting late," said Kelly. "He's probably not home."

Plus the hockey was on.

"It's not like they're going to get any deader," said Kelly.

Speed realised he wasn't going to get anywhere, so he thanked the detective and hung up.

In the meantime, he ran a background check on Mr Simpson.

Simon woke with the sun shining in his eyes. His head hurt from too much beer.

A small groan next to him brought him fully awake.

He froze for an instant before remembering what had happened.

Sienna. He'd paid her to stay the night.

He relaxed. She lay there with the sheet covering half her body. He stared at the other half. She was worth every cent.

The sheet covering Simon's waist began to rise like a circus tent. He slid his hand under the sheet, and was about to wake her when someone knocked at the door.

"Shit," he said. "Who the hell goes visiting at this time of the morning?" He glanced at the clock by the bed. It was after nine o'clock.

"Simon, this is the police," said a voice. "We'd like to ask you a few questions."

Police. Fuck.

Sienna sat bolt upright. "Just tell them I'm your girlfriend," she said. "They can't prove a thing."

"Um, okay. But that's probably not why they're here." Sienna frowned.

There was another knock on the door. "Come on Simon, open the door."

Damn. He got out of bed, and pulled on his pants and a T-shirt. He adjusted his shirt, trying in vain to cover the remnants of his erection.

"Don't answer their questions," said Sienna. "And demand to see a lawyer. Trust me, I've done this before."

Simon nodded.

"Coming," he said.

Gizmo was barking at the front door. Simon bent down and picked him up. "Shh, Giz."

He removed the chain from the front door and opened it. There were two people standing outside, a man and a woman. The woman's gaze slipped down to the bulge in his pants.

She smiled. "I hope we didn't catch you at a bad time."

Simon eyes danced around, avoiding the woman's face. They eventually settled on the man.

"What can I do for you?" said Simon.

"Do you mind if we come in?" said the man. "I'm Detective Kelly, and this is Detective Peters."

Simon hesitated. "Um … okay, I guess." He stepped back, and let them inside. "Have a seat." He cleared away the leftover pizza and empty beer bottles.

"Did you have a party?" said Detective Kelly.

"Um … just a small celebration."

"What were you celebrating?" asked Detective Peters.

Simon paused. "It's not important," he said. "What did you want to talk about?"

Just then, Sienna entered the living room from the bedroom. She was wearing Simon's 'I Love New York' T-shirt. She sat next to him on the couch and placed her hand on his thigh. "I'm Simon's girlfriend, Sienna."

Simon smiled. He'd never had a girlfriend.

The detectives exchanged glances.

Gizmo climbed over Simon's lap and licked Sienna's hand. Simon pulled him away.

"What do you do for a living, Simon?" asked Detective Kelly.

"I'm a computer programmer. Or at least I was, until I lost my job."

Sienna squeezed his leg lightly with her hand.

"And you?" said Detective Kelly. "Miss…?"

"Just Sienna. I'm a model," she said.

Detective Peters wrote something in her notebook.

"So would you say that you're unemployed then, at the moment, Simon?" said Kelly.

"I'm doing some work for myself."

There was an awkward silence, which was finally broken by the female detective.

"Would your work be related to a cell phone application?" Detective Peters made a show of checking her notes. "Something called, 'The App'?"

Sienna dug her fingers into Simon's leg. He grimaced.

"Why?" he said.

"We're just trying to establish what you do," said Kelly. "To help us with our inquiries."

Sienna interrupted. "And what inquiries are those?"

"Oh, just some minor things. Nothing to be concerned about."

"That's what the police always say," said Sienna. "Before they frame someone. That's what you're trying to do."

"Now there's no need to get defensive," said Kelly. "Nobody is accusing anyone of anything."

"Do you intend to charge Simon with something?" said Sienna.

"Good heavens, no," said Kelly. He glanced at Peters and raised his eyebrows.

"Do you have a warrant?" said Sienna.

"No, nothing like that. We just want to ask some questions."

"He doesn't have to answer your questions."

Simon's phone started to beep. He recognised the tone. Another prize had been claimed. He looked at it nervously.

"Did you want to check that?" said Detective Peters.

Simon shook his head.

"Are you sure?"

He nodded.

"Technically, you don't have to answer our questions," said Kelly. "But if you don't, it might look suspicious."

Sienna made a snorting sound. "We'd like you to leave now," she said. "And if you want to ask more questions, let Simon know in advance. So he can bring a lawyer."

Simon nodded, and placed his hand over Sienna's. "Yes," he said. "So I can bring a lawyer."

He stood and opened the front door.

"It was nice meeting you."

"Damn," said Peters, as she walked back to the car.

"We almost had him talking."

"Until she stopped him," said Kelly.

"Did you buy the girlfriend story?"

Kelly laughed, and shook his head. "More like a hooker."

"That's what I thought." Peters opened the driver's door of their unmarked police car.

"Drive us back to the station," said Kelly. "I'll call Detective Speed and give him the good news."

"He won't be happy."

"Maybe not. But there's something going on there." Kelly scratched his nose. "Did you see how nervous he was when his phone went off?"

"He's hiding something."

Peters started the car.

"On second thoughts," said Kelly, "I could use a coffee. Take a detour past that place on Oak. Detective Speed can wait."

Simon closed the door behind the detectives, and returned to the living room. Sienna was lying on the couch with her legs apart. Gizmo sat on the floor, watching.

"Have you been naughty?" Sienna smiled at Simon, beckoning him closer. "I like bad boys."

Simon hesitated, still processing the morning's events.

"You look tense," she said. "Let me help you relax." She glanced at her watch. "Besides, you've paid me for another two hours."

Simon took a step closer, and Sienna reached towards him.

His phone beeped. A reminder of the claim.

He stopped, considering his options. Then he turned

towards the computer.

"Do you want to know what I've done?" he said. "Why the police were here?"

Sienna sat up, placing her feet on the floor. She nodded quickly.

"Grab a chair, and come over here," said Simon.

He sat down at his computer and turned it on. Sienna rolled a chair next to him. She placed a hand on his knee, stroking it with her thumb.

"Tell me everything," she said. "Every wicked detail."

Simon's biggest regret since he'd developed The App, was that he hadn't been able to share it. Nobody knew what he'd done. Or what he'd achieved.

He craved some recognition.

And here was Sienna. Begging to be told.

Her hand moved further up his leg. Massaging.

Could he trust her? It was a risk.

She rubbed his groin, and began nibbling his ear.

What the hell, he had to tell someone.

"Give me your cell phone for a minute."

She grabbed it out of her bag and gave it to him. He searched for The App, then handed the phone back.

"Download this," he said.

"I want to know what it does first," said Sienna.

So he told her.

Detective Speed had spent most of the previous night learning about Simon Simpson. Simon was squeaky clean. No arrests. No speeding fines. He even paid his taxes on time.

According to Simon's LinkedIn profile, he'd obtained his Computer Science degree at the University of British Columbia. Since graduating, he'd worked for a single company.

Until last year.

His current occupation was listed as 'Self Employed'.

Simon's Facebook profile indicated that he had very few friends. He was also a member of an online chess club.

In short, he was boring. And probably a virgin.

Not a criminal mastermind.

Speed slurped his coffee, then plunged his fork into the large plate of bacon poutine. His eyes focused on the greasy mound, as he scooped up chips, bacon and cheese curd.

He was wiping gravy from his chin when his phone rang. He reached for it, careful to avoid his coffee.

It was Detective Kelly with news about Simon Simpson.

"What have you got?" said Speed.

"We paid him a visit," said Kelly. "Nervous motherfucker."

"I'm not surprised."

"Seriously. He looked like he was going to wet himself when his phone beeped. We probably would have had him talking, except for the girl."

"What girl?"

"Some Eastern European sounding broad. Gave her name as Sienna. We think she's a hooker."

Speed poked at his poutine. That didn't sound like the guy he'd been reading about.

"What happened?"

"We were about to press him on The App, when she tells him to lawyer up. She accused us of trying to frame him."

"Shit," said Speed.

"Exactly," said Kelly. "I'll tell you this though. Something is definitely going on. I think we should take another run at him, even if he *does* bring his lawyer."

"See if you can find out who the girl is," said Speed.

He hung up, contemplating what he was going to say to the FBI.

He loaded another mound of poutine onto his fork. Simon and a hooker, eh?

CHAPTER SEVEN

Something Unexpected

"So you're a broker?" said Sienna. "For assassinations?"

"Um ... I hadn't thought of it like that," said Simon. "I prefer to think that I help people who can't help themselves. When the courts have failed them."

"Very noble," said Sienna. She stroked Simon's leg. "And very clever."

Simon swallowed. "You think so?"

Sienna slid off the chair and onto her knees.

"I like smart men."

Five minutes later, Sienna traced her finger along the top of Simon's computer screen.

"You took longer this time," she said.

"Mmm," said Simon, nodding.

Gizmo yawned and walked across the room to his basket.

Sienna pointed at a red item on the screen. "What does this mean?" she said.

Simon opened his eyes and looked at the monitor. "That means that someone has claimed a prize."

"A murder?"

"Shh. Don't call them that," said Simon. "In case someone hears." He touched her arm. "They're prizes. For correctly guessing the circumstances of someone's death."

"Ah ... of course," said Sienna. "The death is just a —"

"Coincidence?" said Simon.

"Yes, that is the word."

Sienna leaned forward on her chair, pointing at the screen. "Aren't you going to open it and see who it is?"

She reminded Simon of his brother's kids on Christmas morning. Sitting in front of the tree. Can we open our presents now? Can we?

"Okay," said Simon.

He selected the red symbol, and the subject of the bet appeared.

"Clutz Becker," said Simon. "No idea who you are."

"He's German," said Sienna.

"I agree his name *sounds* German, but —"

"I know of this man."

Simon raised his eyebrows. "Really?"

Sienna nodded. "He's the leader of an anti-Islamic organisation in Germany."

Simon stared at her with his mouth open. "How do you know that?"

Sienna smiled. "Because I read the German news."

Simon shook his head. "I thought you were Russian."

She laughed. "I am. But I speak four languages. German is one of them."

Simon grinned at her. Not just a pretty face.

He checked the decrypt key, then decoded the bet.

"It says he'd die yesterday evening, in Berlin. Somewhere called, '*Unter den Linden*'. From poisoned coffee."

"*Unter den Linden* is a boulevade in Berlin," said Sienna. "It's very pretty."

She sat back in her chair, and gazed out the window at the North Shore mountains. "Clutz Becker was a racist pig. A good person to kill."

"Or to die accidently," corrected Simon.

Sienna chuckled. "Or that."

"But is he really dead?" said Simon. "I need to make sure before paying out on the bet."

Sienna moved her chair towards the computer. "Out of the way. I can help you with that."

Simon did as she asked. She navigated to the website for *Spiegel Online*.

"He's dead," said Sienna, after a brief search. "But they haven't confirmed the cause. We will have to wait."

"Thanks. You've saved me a lot of time." He put his hand on her thigh. "I wonder what we should do while we wait?"

Sienna smiled at him, and looked around the room. Her eyes locked onto a rectangular object on the table.

"I know," she said. "How about a little game?"

Special Agent Marks had just received the initial autopsy report. Jerry Upton had been killed by a single shot to the head. The bullet was a 0.308 Hollow Point Boat Tail. It had severed the spine from his brain.

Precision shooting.

Marks picked up the forensic report. The shooter had been three hundred yards away. Hairs and fibres had been found at the scene. They were still being analysed.

There were also some scrape marks leading back to the road, but nothing usable.

A sweep of the surrounding neighbourhood had drawn a blank. No witnesses and no surveillance cameras covering the road.

That wasn't a coincidence. The shooter knew what they were doing.

Marks scratched his head. Something bothered him.

He doodled with his pen on the blotter.

He was interrupted by a phone call. It was the Canadian detective.

"Detective Speed, what have you got for me?"

"Nothing concrete, yet," said Speed. "The Vancouver Police interviewed him, informally. Said he was acting squirrelly. But before they could crack him, he asked for a lawyer."

"Damn," said Marks.

"Yeah. That's not all," said Speed. "There was an Eastern European woman with him. She was the one who pulled out the 'L' word."

"Any idea who she is?"

"No, but the Vancouver detectives are going to push him again. Try and get some probable cause to search his computer."

"Good," said Marks. He gave Speed the details from the lab reports.

"*Your* killer sounds like a pro," said Speed. "A nice clean shot to the head. Not like mine."

Marks agreed. "Using someone as crab bait seems more personal."

"Check," said Sienna.

"Whoa," said Simon. He hadn't seen that coming. "Where did you learn to play chess?"

Sienna had forked Simon's king and rook in a twin pronged attack.

She grinned. "I haven't always been a call girl."

Simon nodded. "I'm beginning to appreciate that." He moved his king out of harm's way, but in doing so, sacrificed his rook.

"I come from a wealthy family," she said. "My father

is a doctor in Moscow. I was sent to the best boarding school money could buy."

"So how did you end up in Canada? In your current … occupation?"

"I got bored with school. I started sleeping with one of my teachers."

Simon raised his eyebrows.

"He got fired, and I was expelled. My father was humiliated."

She moved her queen, capturing the rook. "Check."

"Shit," said Simon.

Sienna stared at Simon's king. "He hired a full-time tutor to teach me at home. She was a bitch. I was never allowed to leave the house."

Simon blocked the queen with his bishop.

"So I ran away," said Sienna. "For an adventure."

She moved her queen again. "Check."

Simon shifted his king once more. He was running out of options.

"My father cancelled my credit card and froze my bank account. He disowned me. I was living on the streets of Moscow."

She clenched her jaw.

"Then I met someone who showed me how I could make money. He became my pimp. Eventually I was brought to Canada."

She attacked Simon's king once more with her queen. "Checkmate," she said.

When Christine first learned about The App, she'd asked for her boss's help to find its creator.

He'd made a few calls. The resources of the Canadian Broadcasting Corporation were brought to bear.

Two days later, he handed her a piece of paper. "Bingo," he said.

She scanned it quickly. "Simon Simpson? Not exactly Lex Luthor, is it?"

He shrugged. "It still has alliteration." He waved his hand toward the note. "There's a phone number at the bottom. Call it." He walked away.

She opened a web browser, and started her search. Who was Simon Simpson?

An hour later she'd formed an opinion. Intelligent and possibly shy. Probably a loner.

She dialed Simon's number.

Sienna glanced at her watch. "I'd better get ready. Ivan doesn't like to be kept waiting."

"Ivan? Is he your boss?"

"No, he's just the muscle. My pimp's name is Aleksei."

Sienna went into the bedroom to get changed.

Simon's phone rang. He didn't recognise the number.

"Is that Simon Simpson?" said a female voice.

"Um ... yes," said Simon.

"My name is Christine Hunter."

Shit. He recognised the name from the news.

"If you're selling something, I don't want it," he said. "And if you're calling to tell me that my computer has a virus, I can fix it myself."

Christine laughed. "I'm not selling anything, and I'm not a scammer. I'm calling from Moncton." She paused. "I'm a journalist, with CBC News."

"A journalist?" he said, acting surprised.

Sienna's head emerged from the bedroom. She frowned at Simon. He shrugged his shoulders.

"Yes," said Christine.

"From Moncton?" said Simon.

"Yes."

"Calling *me*?"

"Yes."

"Wow."

There was an awkward silence. Simon squeezed the arm of his chair.

"I was hoping you could answer some questions," said Christine.

"Questions?"

"Yes."

Another awkward silence.

"Would that be okay?" she said.

"What questions?" said Simon. He closed his eyes, and sat on his spare hand. It stopped shaking.

"What do you do for a living?" said Christine.

"Why do you want to know?" Something brushed his arm, and his eyes shot open.

Sienna was standing next to him. Arms crossed. Listening.

"I've been looking into your employment history," said Christine. "And your education."

"What?" said Simon. "You've been checking up on me? Why?"

"To help with my inquiries. For my story."

"Inquiries?" said Simon. "Jesus, you sound like those two cops."

"The police?" said Christine. "Have they been asking you questions? About The App?"

"The App?" said Simon. "What's that?" The pitch of his voice rose.

Sienna reached forward and grabbed the phone.

Simon didn't resist.

"This is Simon's girlfriend," said Sienna. "He can't talk now. He's busy."

"Wait," said Christine. "It's important —"

"Thank you. Goodbye." Sienna hung up the phone.

She turned to Simon. "You need to get a lawyer."

"A lawyer? But I don't know any lawyers."

She smiled at him. "I do."

She opened her handbag, and pulled out a business card. She gave it to Simon.

"He's good," she said. "But not very ethical."

Simon took the card. "Sounds perfect."

Christine slammed down the phone.

Bitch.

She banged her hand on the desk.

Damn. She needed to be in Vancouver. So she could speak to Simon in person.

But she'd never convince her boss. Not without more evidence.

She opened The App on her phone and explored the different menu options.

Closed bets. That sounds promising.

She began to read.

Ten minutes later, she found a name she recognised.

Dick Gelderman.

Christine opened a web browser, and accessed the Factiva database. She searched for recent news articles about Gelderman. There were several describing his recent death. In Vancouver.

She bit her lip. Ouch. She tasted blood.

The articles said his death had been an accident.

But was it?

According to the rules of The App, 'closed bets' meant that someone had claimed a prize.

A man had been skiing with Gelderman. Tom Roberts.

But he'd survived.

Christine printed the article, and made a few notes on the page. Then she knocked on her boss's door.

"I have to go," said Sienna. "Ivan just messaged me."

"I really enjoyed last night," said Simon.

"I did too. And our game of chess." She winked at him. "But now I have to work."

"Work?" said Simon. "Don't you get time off?"

Sienna looked away, then lowered her eyes to the floor. "Aleksei works us hard. To him, an overnight appointment counts as rest."

Jesus.

"Your boss sounds like a real bastard."

There was an awkward pause, before Simon took her hand. "When can I see you again?"

Sienna raised her eyes. "Anytime you want. But you'll have to book me. Aleksei doesn't let us have any friends."

"How about tomorrow? I'll book you overnight."

She moved closer to him and rested her palm against his face. "That would be nice. I can check the German news for you." She brushed his cheek. "And beat you in another game of chess."

She pulled away and opened the door. "See you tomorrow, Simon."

"Yes, tomorrow."

He closed the door.

"Sienna," he whispered.

"You need to send me to Vancouver," said Christine. She smiled at her boss. "Please."

He peered at her over his glasses, the fluorescent light reflecting off his head. "We don't have the budget to go chasing hunches," he said. "We're not CNN."

"It's more than a hunch. Vancouver connects to all these deaths. And I've found another one."

She told him what she'd discovered on Factiva.

"Gelderman?" he said. "You think he was murdered … with an avalanche?" He chewed on his pen. "That *would* make an interesting story."

"I don't have proof, but I think I can get it in Vancouver. I'll question Roberts. And follow up with Simon Simpson. I can even inspect where Gelderman was killed."

"Hmm," said her boss. He clenched his jaw, clamping down harder on the pen.

"I'll talk to the Vancouver police," said Christine. "Simpson mentioned something that makes me think they've questioned him."

"Do you realise how much hotels cost in Vancouver?"

"I'll stay with one of my aunts," said Christine. "You won't need to pay for a hotel." She leaned forward, gripping the edge of the desk. "Please. This is the story of a lifetime."

Her boss had ink on his lip, where he'd bitten through his pen.

Christine pointed to her bottom lip.

He rubbed his mouth, smudging the ink across his chin. He removed his glasses, and scratched his bald spot with one of the wire arms. "All right," he said finally. "Don't let me down."

"Thanks" said Christine. "You won't regret it." She

stood to leave, then pointed at her chin. "You might want to look in a mirror."

CHAPTER EIGHT

Legal Matters

Simon examined the business card. Eli Rabinovich. Lawyer.

He rubbed his fingers across the raised lettering.

Black letters on a white background. Ordinary letters. They looked harmless.

Simon hesitated. If he called, he was admitting that he needed help. That maybe he was doing something wrong.

Maybe.

A girl in a bloodstained blouse flashed through his mind. He shook his head.

He thought about another girl, whose father had killed himself when he lost his job. He thought about all the people who had placed their bets. Raising their collective voice.

Then he thought about a woman who smiled at him. And beat him at chess.

She'd said to get a lawyer.

He picked up the phone.

Christine threw her clothes into a suitcase. She squeezed the phone against her ear with her shoulder.

"Police Department," said a woman's voice.

"Could you put me through to Detective Speed, please?" said Christine. "I've lost his direct number. Tell him it's the Vancouver detective who's looking into the matter of Simon Simpson. He'll know who it is."

There was a delay while she was put on hold. She hoped her ruse would work. She'd assumed that Speed would have the same geographical problem as her. He would need someone on the ground in Vancouver.

The phone clicked.

"Detective Kelly, that was quick. Have you re-interviewed him already?"

"Actually, it's Christine Hunter," she said.

"What the fuck?" said Speed. "You can't do that. Shit. You've made me spill my coffee."

"Sorry, detective. But you've been holding out on me." She twirled her hair with her finger.

"What do you mean?"

"Simon Simpson."

"Who's he?"

Christine smiled. He'd make a terrible poker player.

"I thought we were friends, Detective."

"Hah. Like the lion and the zebra," said Speed. "And I'm the one with stripes."

"Now, now, Detective. Our relationship is mutually beneficial."

"Friends don't pull the shit that you just pulled."

"I want to make a trade."

She heard Speed groan on the other end.

"What?" he said.

"I have some information you'll find interesting. I'll give it to Detective Kelly … when I meet him."

"Meet him? Why would he meet with you?"

"Because you're going to give me an introduction."

"Shit."

Christine smiled. She closed the lid on her suitcase.

Special Agent Marks doodled furiously on his notepad. The most recent lab report didn't make sense.

The hair samples came from different people. Five of them.

He'd been sure that the shooter had worked alone, and five people should have been noticed. Something wasn't right.

The lab was checking the DNA, to see if they could find a match. It would take a while.

He finished the picture he was drawing of a little girl. And her pony.

"Sounds like an interesting cell phone application," said Eli Rabinovich. "And potentially very lucrative." He didn't mention the moral issues. "But I think you are wise to engage a lawyer."

"Sienna said you were good," said Simon. "That you'd be able to help me."

"I'm sure I can," said Eli. "In fact I can see this being the start of a long and fruitful relationship."

"Do you think that I'm breaking the law?"

Eli laughed. "That's an interesting question. The law is a malleable thing." He paused. "A lawyer is a bit like a blacksmith, Simon … a good one is able to craft a legal defence that will blunt the sharpest attack. A bad one, on the other hand, will give you a rusty defence that is full of holes."

"What kind of defence will you give me?"

"I'll need to hear all of the details before I can start to build your defence. Come to my office tomorrow afternoon, and we'll discuss things." He smiled. "We'll also discuss my fee."

Eli cleared his diary for the following afternoon. He

made a note to thank Sienna the next time he saw her.

Dillon Black had arrived back in Seattle with a sense of pride. He'd waited a day before checking his bank account. The digital cash had been transferred.

It felt good to be employed again — in the profession he'd trained for.

Dillon was determined to make the most of his opportunity. He wanted to be the best.

For inspiration, he turned to some people with a proven track record.

The Beltway Snipers.

In 2002, John Allen Muhammad and Lee Boyd Malvo had gone on a three week killing spree around the Washington, DC area. Their actions had resulted in the deaths of ten people. A key to their success was the method they used.

They'd built a sniper's nest in the trunk of their Chevrolet Caprice. The back seat had been modified to allow the shooter to lie in the trunk, and fire through a specially created hole near the licence plate.

Dillon had a van. It would make an excellent shooting platform. No one could see him if he blacked out the windows.

He drew up plans to modify his van. Then he drove to Home Depot.

Simon rolled over in his tangled sheets. His thoughts racing. He gave up trying to sleep around 3:00 am.

Simon turned on his computer and started his favourite chess program. He changed the difficulty level to Advanced and began to play.

He needed to practice. For Sienna.

Christine wheeled her hand luggage into the baggage collection area of Vancouver Airport. A middle aged woman waved frantically at her from behind the low stone wall. The woman had greying hair, which was tied in a bun. Christine headed towards her.

"Thanks for picking me up, Aunty Joan. You didn't have to."

"Nonsense." Christine's aunt ambled sideways through the gap in the wall, and squeezed her tightly, like a bear embracing a hiker. "Of course I'm going to pick up my famous niece."

Christine's neck flushed red. "I'm not famous, Aunty Joan."

"I just saw you on TV. And Mabel told me all about it."

Christine frowned at the mention of her other aunt. "How is she?"

"Still having nightmares, I'm afraid."

"About the body?"

Joan nodded. "Something about an eye. But she refuses to talk about it."

Christine's aunt's home in Kerrisdale was an elegant two story house, with stone pillars and a white gate. Joan parked her Lexus between a Mercedes and a BMW on the verge of her tree-lined street.

"You can have Johnathan's old room," she said. "At the top of the stairs, on the left."

Christine unpacked her clothes then made her plans for the following day.

"You're a genius," said Eli. And he meant it. He

examined the young man sitting opposite him. Average height. Pale complexion. Slender build. He shook his head. "A goddamn genius."

"Um ... thank you," said Simon.

"In all my years as a lawyer, I've never seen anything like this enterprise of yours." He shook his head. "And I've seen a lot of things."

"Really?" said Simon.

"Yes. And you've given me so much that I can work with."

"How do you mean?"

"Well, for starters, you've hosted the back-end servers in Russia. A truckload of legal impediments there. And then there's your company structure, which is spread across the globe."

Simon smiled. "I thought it might be prudent."

"It was," said Eli nodding. "But who did you use to set things up?"

"My accountant handled it. Steven Batty."

Eli made some notes. "I'll need to talk to him. Probably transfer the administration of your companies to my office." He tapped the side of his nose. "The less people who have access to your information, the better. One less chink in the armour."

Simon nodded and gave him the accountant's phone number and address.

"And then there's the way you've designed The App," said Eli. "Brilliant. Any potentially incriminating information is encrypted. You have no way of knowing who placed a winning bet until that person sends you their decryption key ... *after* the death has occurred. You know nothing in advance. You don't know when. You don't know how. You don't know where."

"I thought it might be —"

"Prudent," said Eli. "It was. Believe me." He flashed his salesman's smile at Simon. "And in addition to all your precautions, there's still the concept itself."

Pink circles bloomed on Simon's cheeks.

"Don't be embarrassed, Simon. Your creation is a work of art. The potential to generate income … and to reform society, is immense. I'm not even sure that you're breaking any laws."

"Seriously?" said Simon. "So I might not need a lawyer?"

The smile disappeared from Eli's face. He shook his head. "I didn't say *that*, Simon."

Eli stared at him for several seconds, and Simon lowered his eyes.

"Police from multiple jurisdictions will come after you. They've already started." Eli paused. "Trust me, Simon, you need a lawyer."

"That's what Sienna said."

"She's a clever girl," said Eli. And very beautiful. "One more thing, Simon."

"Yes?"

"The cell phone application? That people download? You said it's made available through an online store. Where are the online stores based?"

"Um … they're in the United States. But they don't hold any data on their sites. Only the apps themselves."

Eli rubbed his chin.

"You might want to prepare for the day when you can't use those online stores anymore."

"What do you mean?" said Simon.

"The US authorities might eventually exert some pressure on them. To stop people downloading your app."

"Oh, I hadn't thought of that."

"There's been precedents with other types of vendors."

"I suppose I could look at creating a web-based app. One that doesn't rely on third party vendors."

"That's a good idea."

"Is there anything else?" said Simon.

Eli smiled. "Just my fee." He wrote down some numbers on a piece of paper and pushed it across his desk.

Simon looked at the clock again. It had only moved forward by one minute. He walked to the window and peered outside. His apartment opened directly onto the street. From his window, he could see up and down the moonlit road. Nothing.

He breathed into his cupped hand, and shook his head at the smell. He went to the bathroom and cleaned his teeth. On the way back, he checked on Gizmo in the spare room.

"Sorry, Giz. But it's a bit weird with you watching." Gizmo whined as he shut the door.

Simon glanced at his watch. One minute to eight.

There was a knock at the door. He stumbled over a computer cable as he rushed to open it.

"Sienna," he said.

He froze, mouth open.

"Oh my god. What happened?"

Sienna stood in the building's shadow. Her makeup failed to disguise her swollen eye. Her bottom lip quivered, and a tear etched a trail through her mascara.

"It's nothing," she whispered. "Can I come in?"

"Of course." Simon took her arm and guided her to a chair. "Can I get you anything?"

She nodded. "A drink. Something strong."

"Of course." He retrieved a bottle of Smirnoff from his freezer, and poured her a glass. "Here."

Sienna took the glass, and gulped it down in a single shot.

"Another?" said Simon. She nodded.

He refilled her glass. "What happened? And don't say it's nothing."

She took a sip from the glass. "It was Aleksei. He hit me … for yawning on the job."

"For yawning?"

She nodded. "After I left you yesterday, I had to entertain one of his important clients. I was so tired that I yawned … while we were doing it. The client was offended."

"So your boss beat you?" Simon clenched his fists. "You're safe with me." He sat down, and put his arm around her. "You can sleep all night if you want to. We don't need to do anything else."

How could any man beat a woman? Let alone Sienna? He pulled her closer. He'd do anything to protect her.

Sienna smiled at him. "Thank you, Simon. You're very kind." She finished her vodka, and handed him the glass. "Let me check the German news for you."

"You don't have to do that now."

"But I want to."

She sat down at his computer and opened the web page for *Spiegel Online*. She quickly found what she was looking for.

"The police have confirmed that he was poisoned."

"That was fast," said Simon. "Thanks."

She turned to face him. "Are you going to pay the winner now?"

He shook his head. "I have to close the bets off first, and give potential claimants twenty-four-hours notice." He took her hand. "But I'm more worried about you at the moment."

"I'm okay. This isn't the first time he's beaten me." She raised Simon's hand to her lips and kissed it. "Seriously, I'm fine. Send your notifications, then we can talk."

Simon hesitated. "Okay," he said finally. "But I wish I could help you."

"Me too." She kissed Simon's hand again. "But I'm not sure how."

She tapped the keyboard. "Send your messages, Simon. While I fix my makeup." She stood and went to the bathroom.

Simon did as he was told.

She returned ten minutes later.

"You look much better," he said. The make-up concealed the colour of the bruising, but the puffiness remained.

Sienna gave him a small smile. "I feel better. Being here." She sat down next to him and rested her hand on his leg.

"Did you call the lawyer?" she said.

He told her about his meeting with Eli Rabinovich. She laughed when he mentioned Eli's fee.

"Don't worry," she said. "That's only his initial offer. Leave it to me, I'll get you a better deal."

She stood and held out her hand. "I'm tired now. Why don't you come to bed and keep me warm?"

CHAPTER NINE

Breadcrumbs

Christine opened the blinds, revealing the view through her bedroom window. The sun shone brightly on the North Shore Mountains. A crown of snow glistened on each of the peaks; Cypress, Grouse and Seymour.

If things went well, maybe she'd have a chance to ski.

She planned to visit Simon after breakfast. Her boss had given her the address. If she was lucky, she'd catch him by surprise. Maybe even meet that foreign bitch who'd hung up on her.

Christine walked downstairs to the kitchen, where her aunt was making breakfast. Joan looked up from the stove.

"I've made pancakes for you, dear."

"Thanks, Aunty Joan. But I could have made my own breakfast."

Joan shook her head. "Do you normally even eat breakfast? You're as skinny as a rake."

"Of course I do," said Christine. Usually just a piece of fruit.

"Well, I'll not have you starving in my house. Now eat those pancakes, while I cook you some bacon and eggs."

Simon woke with a mouth full of hair. He was lying on his side, facing Sienna's back. Spooning. His arm was draped protectively around her.

Their naked bodies pressed together, and he became

aroused.

A few minutes later, Sienna stirred. She stretched and pushed her buttocks into him.

"Morning," she said into her pillow.

"Sorry," said Simon. "I didn't mean to wake you."

Sienna chuckled. "That's okay. I couldn't think of a better way to wake up." She rolled over on top of him, and stuck her tongue in his ear.

Simon responded by moving his hands down to her hips.

She grinned at Simon, and began to rub against him.

Twenty minutes later she collapsed on top of him. Her breathing was erratic as she panted in his ear. "You made me come before you, Simon. Definitely improving."

They lay there for several minutes.

"I wish I could stay like this all day," she said. "But Ivan will pick me up soon ... for another job." She shook her head. "God, I hate living like this."

Simon stroked Sienna's hair, pulling her tight with his other arm. "Then quit," he said "I'll support you while you look for another job."

Sienna didn't say anything for almost thirty seconds. Then she sat up and rubbed her eyes. When she took her hands away, Simon saw she was crying.

"What is it?" he said.

"You don't understand. I'm Aleksei's property. I can't just quit." She wiped her eyes with the back of her hand. "Wherever I go, he'll find me. And drag me back."

Simon twisted the sheets tightly with his hands. "He's evil. Someone needs to do something about him."

She nodded. "He's been running prostitution rings for decades. He's even *killed* some of his girls who tried to escape." Fresh tears ran down her face, smudging her make-up. "I wish *he* was dead."

Simon pulled her close, and whispered in her ear. "Maybe it could be arranged."

He told her what he had in mind. "There's only one problem, though," he said.

"What's that?"

"Finding the money."

Sienna looked at Simon with a determined expression, and wiped away the remnants of her tears. "You let me worry about that. I'll think of something."

Christine pulled up outside Simon's apartment in one of her aunt's three cars — the Suzuki. Her aunt used it for shopping because it was small and easy to park — and she didn't mind the doors getting dinged in car parks.

Christine was applying her lipstick in the rear-view mirror, when the front door of Simon's apartment opened. A woman emerged.

Christine turned her head to get a better look, smearing her lipstick in the process.

Bitch.

The woman had long dark hair, and high cheekbones. She was also sporting a swollen eye. Christine reached for her camera, and snapped a couple of photos.

The woman got into the passenger side of a car parked outside. A heavyset man sat in the driver's seat. Christine took some more photos before they drove off in the direction of the Granville Street Bridge.

Christine repaired her lipstick, then knocked on Simon's door.

Simon stopped when he saw the young woman in the doorway. She was attractive. But not Sienna.

She *did* look vaguely familiar.

The woman stepped forward, holding out her hand. "Simon, isn't it? My name's Christine Hunter."

Simon recoiled. He recognised her now. "What are you doing here?"

"I came to talk to you. About The App. Do you mind if I come in?"

"I've got nothing to say to you." He started to close the door.

"Wait." She wedged her foot in the gap. "Don't you want people to hear *your* side of the story?"

He hesitated. "What story?"

"About a cell phone app that's used to murder people."

He opened the door a fraction.

Christine continued talking. "If you don't tell people *your* side, the only thing they'll hear is what the police tell them."

Simon shrugged his shoulders. "Why should I care about that?"

"Because the police are saying that you're a madman. Someone who enjoys killing people. And I don't think you are."

Simon shook his head. "I'm perfectly sane," he said.

"But that's not what people will think. If nobody contradicts what the police say."

He bit down on his bottom lip, weighing up what she'd said. There might be some truth to it.

But then he remembered his lawyer's warning.

"I can't talk to you," he said. "My lawyer told me I shouldn't speak to anyone without him present."

Christine frowned. "Does that include your European girlfriend?"

Simon's eyes narrowed. "Leave her out of this."

"That's a nice black eye she's got. How did that happen?"

Simon shook his head. "It wasn't me, if that's what you're thinking."

Christine shrugged. "I won't know what to think if you don't tell me."

"It was her boss," said Simon. "He's an asshole." He looked at Christine's foot. "And now I'm going to take my lawyer's advice."

She pulled out her business card, and held it through the gap. "Think about what I said. I'd like to hear your side. You can even bring your lawyer."

Simon took her card. "Okay. I'll think about it. Thanks."

She removed her foot and he closed the door.

Christine was pleased with the outcome of her first meeting. True, Simon hadn't admitted to his involvement. Not directly. But he hadn't denied it either. She'd also started to build rapport. And that was half of what being a good journalist was about. Making people trust you.

He'd said enough to make her believe that she was on the right track. The way he'd reopened the door to listen, and the fact he had a lawyer. Both good indicators.

In addition, she had a photo of his girlfriend with her driver — and a licence plate. Something to trade with the police.

Christine smiled.

Her next meeting was a two hour drive away. In

Whistler. She was going to pay Tom Roberts a visit.

The drive passed quickly on the *Sea to Sky Highway*. Christine stopped for coffee at a diner in the town of Squamish. Through the window of the diner, she could see several tiny people suspended precariously from a rock face by their ropes. The sheer wall of granite cast a shadow over the town. Christine shivered.

She resumed her journey, and an hour later parked in the Whistler car park. It was full of skiers' cars. Christine had to park a long way from the administration office, and it took her ten minutes trudging through slush and snow before she reached the reception.

"I'm a journalist from CBC News," she said to the receptionist. Christine showed the girl her credentials. The girl looked suitably impressed. "I was hoping I could interview one of your ski guides."

The girl asked Christine to wait, and a short while later a man in a business suit approached her. He had presidential hair and a smile to match.

"I'm John Simkins, from the resort's public relations department," he said. "How can I help you?"

Christine explained how she was doing a story on the recent avalanche, and that she wanted to interview the guide who'd survived.

Simkins frowned. "I'm terribly sorry, but that won't be possible at the moment."

"If he's out with a client, I'm happy to wait," said Christine.

"It's not that," he said. "I'm afraid, Mr Roberts, has gone to Switzerland."

"Oh." Christine's shoulders sagged. "Is he working there as a guide now?"

Simkins shook his head. "He's heli-skiing in Zermatt

for a few weeks." The public relations man moved closer and lowered his voice. "I believe he suddenly came into some money. Something about a death in the family?"

Christine's head shot up. "Really?"

She pulled out her notebook.

CHAPTER TEN

Takedown

Special Agent Marks had just gotten off the phone with the commander of the Hostage Rescue Team, the FBI's elite counter-terrorism unit. They were planning to assault the home of Randy Lee, a white supremacist, who was currently on parole for armed robbery. Lee's DNA had popped up as a match for a sample retrieved from the scene of Jerry Upton's murder.

When Lee had been arrested years earlier, they'd found unlicensed weapons in his home. One of them was a hunting rifle. There'd been several shooting targets pinned to his wall, as a testament to his ability with the weapon.

HRT were taking no chances. Assault and sniper teams prepared to move.

Marks called Detective Speed to give him an update.

"How confident are you that he's your guy?" said Speed.

"That's just it, I'm not. The guy who killed Upton feels like a pro. Not some redneck, white supremacist."

Marks drew a series of concentric circles on his pad, and put a cross through the middle of them. "We also got a DNA hit from a hooker. But she has an alibi."

"Yeah?" said Speed.

"She was at her regular motel, doing business. The clerk and security cameras confirmed it. Interestingly, the motel is on the same highway that leads out to

Upton's house."

"Does she know Randy Lee?"

"She said she didn't think so. But I think she was lying."

"Could be one of her Johns."

"Maybe. I'll let you know what we get from Lee."

He hung up, then drove to the staging point for the assault.

After John Simkins had answered her questions about Tom Roberts, Christine asked him for a tour of the avalanche site.

"As long as you're not going to say anything bad about the resort," he said.

Christine gave him a reassuring smile. "The article is more about Dick Gelderman and the events preceding his death."

Or his murder.

Simkins smiled back. "Perhaps we can use the publicity from your story to market a ski package? For people who want to see where he died. I understand he was quite the celebrity."

"I'm sure you *could* do that," said Christine. "If you wanted to."

Simkins beamed. "I'll arrange a tour for you in one of the resort's helicopters. Come with me and we'll get you kitted out."

An hour later, Christine's tour guide, Norman, pointed at some rocks through the helicopter's window. "The avalanche started just to the left of those," he said. "We'll set down behind them and hike to the top. Then we'll ski down through the avalanche zone."

Christine wore ski clothes the resort had provided.

They'd also lent her some skis.

She inspected her equipment. Although she hadn't been skiing for nearly two years, she was confident in her ability to navigate the slope.

The helicopter descended, turning everything white as the snow was flung around by its blades. They landed, and Christine followed Norman through the door. The cold air stung her nostrils and her nose began to run.

They moved a short distance away and covered their heads as the helicopter lifted off from the ground.

The air churned and ice particles whipped against Christine's cheeks. The deafening noise receded as the helicopter disappeared over the ridge.

"Follow me," said Norman.

They shouldered their skis, and slowly made their way up the slope.

Christine was puffing by the time they reached the top of the short climb. Norman laughed. "Don't get much exercise in your job, eh?"

"It's hard to when you're chained to a desk," she replied.

The guide nodded. "That's why I do this." He pointed behind him, at the white mountains and blue sky. "How do you like my office?"

"I hate you," she said.

She jammed the end of her skis into the snow, and retrieved the camera from her backpack. She took a few shots from different angles, before turning to Norman. "So where exactly did the avalanche start?"

"Over here." He walked about twenty metres to the edge of a precipice, and pointed. "This whole section broke away. The snow accelerated down the slope, and converged on that narrow chute below. Gelderman's body was found in there."

"Where was Tom Roberts?"

"He was standing pretty much where you are. He let his client have the first run on the untracked snow." Norman frowned.

"What?" she said.

"Well … evidently, Gelderman was a real prick. He'd been pressuring Tom to take him places that no one else was skiing."

"Did Tom tell you that?"

"Yeah. Over beers at the pub … the night *before* it happened." Norman didn't mention the rest of their conversation.

"Do you think that might have contributed to his death?" said Christine.

Norman shook his head. "Tom's an experienced guide. He'd never knowingly endanger a client." He waved his hand at the precipice behind him. "This area is known for avalanches, but Tom assessed the risk and concluded it was safe."

"So what happened?" said Christine.

He shrugged his shoulders. "It's not an exact science. Backcountry skiing is hazardous. Gelderman knew the risks and signed a waiver."

Christine walked towards the edge of the precipice. The snow around her had been disturbed by the wash from the helicopter. A small piece of orange material caught her eye.

"What's this?" She picked up the object, and handed it to her guide.

"Looks like a fragment from one of our avalanche charges," he said. "We sometimes trigger them on this slope. For safety."

Christine raised her eyebrows. "Interesting. Did anyone think it was worth triggering an avalanche on the day Gelderman was killed? For safety?"

"Obviously not," said Norman. "Or he'd still be alive."

Randy Lee was smoking weed in his living room. A portable television provided the only light. It flickered quietly in the corner.

Randy wasn't concerned about his upcoming drug test. He'd bought a clean urine sample through a friend. It was sitting in his fridge in a plastic cup.

There was a scraping sound outside the front door.

Must be the pizza. Quicker than expected.

He pushed himself to his feet, and took two steps towards the door. He was fumbling in his pocket for his wallet when the door burst inward.

There was a loud bang, and an intense flash of light. He stumbled backwards as white smoke filled his lungs.

A voice yelled at him, "Freeze motherfucker. FBI."

Randy screamed and jerked his hand out of his pocket. It was holding something black.

"Gun," yelled another voice.

There was a burst of noise. It was the last thing Randy heard before his head exploded.

The assault team stormed past him and cleared the rest of the house, then somebody turned on the lights.

"Shit," said the operator closest to Lee's body. "It was only his wallet."

As the assault team stood around looking at the bloody mess, there was a cough at the front door. They spun towards the noise with their weapons raised.

A young man stood in the doorway, scratching his

head. He was carrying a red bag. "Er … did somebody order a pizza?"

The team leader stifled a laugh. He nodded to the man who'd found Lee's wallet. "Give the guy a twenty, Hank."

Simon added Christine's business card to his growing collection. Perhaps he should mention her visit to his lawyer.

When he picked up Eli Rabinovich's card, he remembered his lawyer's warning about US app vendors.

Shit. Must get on to that.

He phoned his former work colleague, Pete Madden.

"I was wondering if I could trouble you for a bit more code?"

"Given up on the app development?" said Pete.

"No, I've already got some clients. But I want to expand into web-based apps."

"Awesome."

Simon described what he was after. "I want to build web applications that look good on any device."

"You mean an application that changes its layout, depending on the device's size and orientation?"

"Exactly. A responsive web app."

"I know just what you'll need," said Pete. "I'll make a copy and send it to you."

"Thanks. You're a good friend, Pete."

"I still feel bad about what they did to you, man. Hopefully there's some karma in this world. What goes around, comes around."

Simon laughed. "Let's hope so."

CHAPTER ELEVEN

Collision

Christine drove carefully back from the ski resort. The warm air from the car's heater made her drowsy. She opened the window and let in some cold air.

The roads were icy, and the lights from the oncoming traffic caused her to squint. As she rounded a bend just outside Squamish, a dark shape darted in front of her car. Christine stamped on the brake — too hard — and began to skid. There was a thud and a small bump as the shadowy figure disappeared under the wheels. The car spun before coming to a halt on the edge of the highway, its lights pointing into the trees.

Christine stepped out of the car, shaking, and walked around to the front. The first thing she noticed was the smell.

She knelt down on the ground and peered under the bumper. The lights of the passing vehicles were enough to show the crushed body of a skunk, its white stripe stained with blood. Christine gagged.

She got back inside the car and wound up the window, then drove into Squamish to recover her nerves.

While she waited at the diner for her coffee, Christine pondered what she'd been told about Mike Roberts. He'd died suddenly, and supposedly left his brother, Tom, a lot of money.

Christine drank the coffee in silence then resumed her

journey. She eventually reached the Lion's Gate Bridge around eight o'clock. The background lights of Vancouver's high-rise buildings were punctuated by the darkness of Stanley Park.

Christine drove over the bridge and through the park. She detoured through a car wash on Broadway. Fifteen minutes later, she arrived at her aunt's well lit house.

Aunty Joan was serving a roast when she entered the kitchen. "Perfect timing," said Joan. "You're just in time for dinner."

Christine didn't tell her that she wasn't hungry.

"Sit down and start on that, dear. I'll just pop your apple pie in the oven."

Christine's stomach groaned in protest when she climbed the stairs an hour later. She sat down gingerly on the bed and turned on her laptop. She searched for information about Mike Roberts.

Christine found a small article in the archives of *The Vancouver Sun*. Mike Roberts had invested his life savings in some bad investments. He'd lost everything and then taken his own life.

He was penniless when he died.

Simon worked most of the day on the design for the web application, only stopping to open an email from Pete Madden. It had a large attachment containing some zipped up source code.

Pete had done well. The code snippets would save a lot of time in the development phase.

Simon was about to return to his design work, when the phone rang.

"This is Detective Kelly. We met the other day at your house."

Simon's heart rate increased.

"Um … I told you to leave me alone. I'm not going to speak to you without a lawyer."

"We'd like you to come in to the station. For a chat. You can bring your lawyer."

Shit. Simon swallowed, his mouth suddenly dry.

"Um … I'll talk to him, and see what he says. Give me your number."

Simon hung up and phoned Eli Rabinovich.

"Don't worry," said Eli. "I'll speak to them."

Simon gave him the Detective's name and number.

"We'll probably still need to go in to the station. But just do as I tell you, and you'll be fine."

Simon thanked him, then hung up and checked his bank balance. Between Sienna and his lawyer, he was spending some serious money.

He needed a bigger income.

Simon opened The App to review the latest bets. He snorted when he saw the name at the top.

Dillon Black stared through his Unertl scope at the face of Cecil Muller.

It was ironic, Dillon thought, that the hunter had become the hunted. He laughed, causing the image to shake.

Cecil Muller had rocketed to the top of the The App's betting in less than two days, after an unprecedented social media campaign against him. He was a rich American business man who enjoyed big-game hunting in his spare time. His latest kill had been a lion in Africa. Unfortunately, for Muller, he'd made the mistake of killing one of Kenya's national treasures.

The adult male lion had been lured out of its

sanctuary with some bait. The gruesome death had been filmed and uploaded to Facebook, where it had rapidly become the biggest trending news item.

Dillon lay on his stomach, in the back of his specially modified van. It was parked in a car park on the outskirts of Portland, Oregon. The parking area overlooked the tennis courts where Cecil Muller played each week. The specially designed hatch next to the van's licence plate was open, giving Dillon a perfect view of the target.

He relaxed his breathing and checked his posture as he'd been taught. The wind was blowing harder than it had been on his last mission. But he used the flags on the roof of the tennis club to help gauge its speed and direction. He made some minor adjustments.

Dillon positioned his eye behind the scope. Muller was dressed in a white shirt and shorts. He was about to serve. Dillon counted, as Muller bounced the ball, preparing for the toss. Once, twice, three times. His ritual. Dillon waited for the moment when Muller was fully extended with his racquet, eyes high, focusing on the ball. Then he pulled the trigger.

Muller missed his serve and collapsed to the ground. Blood slowly pooled around him and seeped into the grass, reminding Dillon of the video he'd watched of the lion being killed.

A woman screamed at the other end of the court.

Dillon closed the hatch in back of the van, and stored his rifle. Then he slid in to the driver's seat and headed back to Seattle.

Simon wasn't surprised when he heard about Cecil Muller. His death was leading most of the news bulletins. Simon also wasn't surprised when his phone beeped to announce that someone had claimed the prize. It was a large amount. The biggest so far.

He shook his head. The prize for Cecil Muller was triple that of the prize for an African dictator. But the dictator killed people.

Simon did a quick calculation to determine his cut. Then he opened the *Erotic Playmates* web page and booked Sienna.

CHAPTER TWELVE

Bargains

Detective Kelly sat next to his partner. Christine Hunter was facing them. Kelly looked at her warily. Like a boxer, sizing up his opponent.

"Detective Speed said you might have some information," he said.

Christine smiled back. She'd worn a slightly revealing skirt, and a blouse that was a fraction too tight.

"I do have something you'll find interesting, Detective." She paused. "But nothing's free in this world."

He stared at her. His female partner, Detective Peters, scowled at the split in Christine's skirt.

"What do you want?" he said.

Christine leaned back in her chair and recrossed her legs. "Just to be kept informed about your investigation."

Detective Peters snorted.

"What would that entail?" said Kelly.

"Keeping me up to date on your progress. Letting me know when you discover anything new."

"We can't tell you anything that might damage the investigation."

"What if I promise not to publish anything without your permission … unless I get it from another source?"

Detective Kelly shook his head. "That's a loophole you could drive a truck through."

Christine brushed her knee lightly with her fingers.

"You might want to hear what I know before making a decision. About another murder in your own backyard. That someone has gotten away with."

Kelly glanced at his partner, who shrugged her shoulders.

"We can give you a heads-up on anything we release to the media," he said. "Possibly twelve-hours notice."

Christine pursed her lips. Then she sat forward, and held out her hand. "That will do. For now."

They shook hands.

Christine opened her notebook, covering her knees.

"Have you ever heard of Dick Gelderman?"

She told them what she'd discovered about him and his guide, Tom Roberts.

Both detectives were very quiet by the time she stood to leave.

"One more thing, Detective Kelly." Christine flicked through her file, and retrieved a photo. "Do you think you could run this licence plate for me?"

Eli Rabinovich leaned back in his red leather chair, with his feet resting on his desk. He cradled the phone with his shoulder, while he filed his nails.

"I talked to the police, Simon. We're meeting them tomorrow at noon." He picked at one of his cuticles with the pointy end of the file. "I chose that time because they'll be hungry and eager to stop for lunch. They'll be less likely to drag things out."

"Should I meet you there," said Simon.

Eli's feet came off the desk and he grabbed the phone.

"Under no circumstances are you to enter that building without me. You hear me? Meet me at my office at eleven thirty."

He hung up.

He needed to control things with the police. They seemed excessively confident when he spoke to them on the phone. As if they knew something he didn't. That bothered him.

Eli bit the nail on his thumb.

Simon was waiting by the door when Sienna arrived. He took her coat, then led her to the couch.

"You're looking much better," he said. He touched her cheek. The swelling had gone down. The bruising was barely visible beneath her make-up. "You look good."

"Thanks." She smiled at him. "How have you been?"

He told her about his conversation with Eli and about his upcoming meeting with the police. He didn't tell her about Christine Hunter. She mightn't like another woman coming to see him.

"I've also started developing a web-based version of The App. It was something Eli said I should do."

Sienna touched Simon's hand and moved it on to her leg. "That reminds me," she said. "I've been giving some thought to my problem with Aleksei. And how to raise enough money."

Simon nodded. She would need to raise a lot. A difficult task. He stroked her leg. "Any luck?"

"Maybe," she said.

His hand went further up her leg. "Really?"

"It would require you to make some code changes."

He stopped rubbing her thigh and withdrew his hand. Her pale blue eyes followed the movement.

"What do you mean?" said Simon.

Sienna moved closer, until their legs were touching.

She placed her hand on his thigh.

"Well, all these people are placing bets. Thousands of them."

"Millions, actually."

"Even better. Millions." She smiled at him. "But how do they know what's been bet on a given subject?"

Simon frowned at her. "The App tells them. It keeps a tally."

"Exactly. The App tells them. You tell them."

"What do you mean?"

"Well, if you told them something different, how would they know?"

Simon chewed his bottom lip. "Um … you mean lie to them?"

"That's one way of looking at it. But it's for a good cause, remember?" Her fingers lightly brushed his groin.

"I'm still not sure I quite understand your idea."

Sienna grinned. "It's simple really. You skim some of the other bets into a reserve fund, and then use the money from that fund to place a very large bet on Aleksei. Then we sit back and let The App do its thing."

Simon stared at her, his eyes straining. "Wow. You've really thought this through."

Sienna's smile fell away and she dropped her eyes. "Of course I have. You can't imagine what it's like. To be somebody else's property." She raised her chin. "You'd give it a lot of thought too, if you were in my position."

Simon blinked. "Sorry. Of course I would. You're right."

There was an awkward silence.

"Can it be done?" asked Sienna.

"I don't see why not." Simon frowned. "I could make the changes in such a way that no one would notice. I'd only skim the bets if more than one person was betting at approximately the same time. If I only took the minimum bet in the cluster, the total pool would always increase by at least the right amount."

Sienna touched his cheek. "I knew you'd think of a way to protect me." She kissed him and moved her hand further down. "You deserve a reward."

Detective Speed agreed with Special Agent Marks' earlier assessment. The murder of Stephen Hinkley was personal.

He kneaded his stress ball like a piece of dough. Perhaps he'd been approaching this investigation the wrong way. Until now, he'd been concentrating on finding the killer through a connection with The App. But in doing so, he'd neglected other potential leads.

What if the killer had a reason for hating priests? Priests who had a thing for little boys? What if he'd killed before?

Speed walked back to his computer and opened the database search program. He entered the criteria for unsolved homicides involving priests. Three records were returned.

The first was for a murder from sixteen years ago. Speed discounted that as too old.

The second was in Toronto, three years before. There was a suspect in that murder but the police had been unable to build a case against the man. Speed ran a background check on the suspect and discovered that he'd been in jail for the last eighteen months — for a different crime. He couldn't have killed Hinkley.

The third murder was more promising. It had occurred eight months previously, near Fredericton in

New Brunswick. When Speed read about the method that was used to kill the victim, he released his grip on the stress ball. The rapidly decompressed ball flew out of his hand, narrowly missing his cup of coffee. Speed didn't notice.

The victim had been staked to the ground. Naked. In the woods. Honey had been spread over his genitals.

An autopsy confirmed that the priest had still been alive when the bear found him.

The killer had wanted to make a statement. Not unlike the one made in the *Bay of Fundy*.

Speed pulled up the contact details for the investigating detective.

Simon put his clothes back on and checked the time. His reward had lasted an hour.

He sighed and arched his back.

"You should probably let your dog out," said Sienna.

Shit. He'd forgotten about Gizmo. He'd put him in the spare room before Sienna arrived.

Simon cautiously opened the spare-room door and peered inside. Gizmo was sitting in the middle of the room.

"Sorry, Giz. You can come out now."

Gizmo stood slowly and ambled past Simon with his head down. Simon tried to pat him, but Gizmo turned his head away.

"I think he's sulking," said Sienna.

"Hm. I'll make it up to him later. In the mean time, I'm going to modify the code to skim the bets."

Sienna was laying on the couch in her underwear. "Is there anything I can do to help?" she said.

"Actually, there is."

"Really?" She grinned at him.

Simon nodded. "There have been three more prizes claimed, and I haven't had a chance to confirm the deaths. Do you think you could handle the verification?"

Sienna sat up. "Of course. But which computer should I use … if you're using that one?"

"You can use the laptop." He carried it to her on the couch. Her breasts squeezed together as she reached for it.

"You could also do something else," he said.

"What's that?"

"Put some clothes on."

Sienna pouted.

"So I don't become distracted," he said.

"Oh, I see." She smiled and picked up her clothes from the floor. She went into the bedroom to get changed.

Simon's eyes followed her until she disappeared. Then he turned back to his desk with a sigh.

It was time to do some serious coding.

Simon sat down at his computer and launched his integrated development environment. While it loaded, he opened a can of Coke. After swallowing a mouthful, he selected some music and stretched his arms high above his head.

Then he lowered his hands to the keyboard and started to type. He didn't notice when Sienna returned from getting dressed.

Sienna picked up the laptop and began her task of verifying the killings. Occasionally she looked up at Simon, who was swaying backwards and forwards with the music. She chuckled at his method of working.

When she'd finished confirming the deaths, Sienna

picked up a book from the coffee table and started to read. She hadn't heard of *The Day of the Triffids*, but the cover said it had sold over a million copies. Couldn't be too bad. She quickly became engrossed in the tale of human calamity.

The last piece of music on Simon's lengthy playlist was the *William Tell Overture*. By the time it had reached its climax, Simon was on the final stretch. His body heaved in unison with the horns and violins.

As the last horn faded away, he looked up and saw Sienna staring.

"What?" he said.

She smiled. "You. I was admiring your performance."

"Performance?"

"To the music."

"Oh." He hadn't realised he'd been that entertaining. "I was engrossed in what I was doing."

Sienna laughed. "I noticed. You've been working for almost five hours."

"Shit. Sorry." He rubbed his eyes. "I'm almost finished. Just a little more testing to do."

"That's okay. Do you want to know what I found?"

"Please."

She sat next to him with the laptop and showed him the relevant web pages. "I've confirmed the deaths of these three people, but only two of the causes. The authorities haven't said yet how the third person died."

"Where did they die?"

"One in France and one in Australia. The outstanding death was in Israel."

Simon's hand shot out and he squeezed Sienna's arm. "We've gone totally global."

Sienna nodded and placed her hand on his leg. "If you

want, I can send the notifications while you finish your testing?"

"Sure." He showed her how to close off the bets and send the notification message, then went back to his work.

Twenty minutes later, he sat back and stretched. "Finished," he said. "I've deployed it remotely to the server in Russia."

"Wow, that was quick," said Sienna.

Simon grinned. "It was for a good cause, remember. Do *you* want to make the first bet on Aleksei?"

"Seriously?"

"Yes. We'll start with a dollar, but you'll need to enter Aleksei's details. Because it's the first bet. Do you have a photograph of him?"

Sienna nodded. "I can get one from his company website."

"Okay. Let's do it."

Sienna opened The App on her phone, and followed the instructions for creating the first bet on a subject. Fifteen minutes later, she was finished.

"Let's check it in the database," said Simon. He opened the database window and searched for records on Aleksei Volkov. A single row was returned.

"What's that?" said Sienna, pointing at a large number on the screen.

"121657669 is your unique identifier in the system, as the creator of the bet."

"Really?" Sienna's eyebrows narrowed. "I thought it was anonymous?"

"Don't worry, it is. There's no readable information stored in the system that identifies you. The ID just links your encrypted bet and account in case you claim a prize."

"Oh, I see." She relaxed. "Is that it then?"

"Almost," said Simon. "Now we just wait for the reserve fund to build up enough cash. And then we place another bet. A big one."

Sienna stood and straddled Simon. "Thank you, Simon. You have no idea how much this means to me." She kissed his cheek and then his mouth. He slid his hands along her thighs and under her dress.

She wasn't wearing any underwear.

Marks sat in the interrogation room across the table from 'Bambi.' She was the prostitute whose DNA had been found at the Jerry Upton murder scene.

"Are you sure you don't recognise this man?" He placed Randy Lee's drivers licence photo on the table in front of her.

Bambi sat back with her legs crossed, chewing her gum with an open mouth. Her fishnet stockings had holes in several places. "Like I told you guys before, I'm not sure. Probably not."

Marks had thought she was lying in her original statement and assumed he'd discover the truth when they questioned Lee. But Lee's untimely death made that impossible. So he was back to interrogating the woman.

"I think you can do better than that," said Marks.

Bambi chewed her gum and blew a bubble. She shrugged.

Marks reached into his file and pulled out another photo. He placed it on top of Lee's drivers licence photo. It was the scene photo from Randy Lee's death at the hands of HRT. Part of his head was missing and blood was all over the floor.

"How about now? Do you recognise him in this photo?"

Bambi swallowed her gum. She coughed violently.

"What the fuck? Jesus, what happened?"

Marks shook his head. "Mr Lee was killed recently during his apprehension, on suspicion of murder. And both *his* DNA and *yours* were found at the scene of that crime. With him dead, the DA is going to start looking at the next person to prosecute. Bambi."

The blood had drained from her face. She reached for the glass of water on the table.

"He told me he was a truck driver, who was on parole."

Marks picked up his pen. "So you did know him?"

She nodded. "He was one of my clients."

"How often did you see him?"

"About once a month."

"Always at the same motel?"

She nodded.

Marks reached into his file and pulled out several more photos. They showed different angles of the *Hollywood Stars* motel. "Can you show me which rooms you used with him?"

Bambi nodded again. "I always use one of two rooms, at the end of the block. Management prefers me to be discreet." She pointed to the rooms in the photo.

Marks picked up his phone and called forensics. "Get a team to the motel, and check out rooms 103 and 105. I want fingerprints and trace evidence."

He raised his eyes at the response.

"I know it's a motel room. Just do it."

He hung up.

"Thank you, Bambi."

She tilted her head. "You mean I can go?"

"Yes, for now. We're not interested in your business activities." He stood and opened the door for her. "Just make sure you're available if we have any more questions."

She left the room, and Marks was about to do the same when his phone rang. It was an agent working another case. In Portland.

"We just got a ballistics match that I thought you'd want to hear about," said the agent.

"Shoot," said Marks.

"We had a guy murdered in Portland with a weapon that matches the murder weapon used to kill Jerry Upton. Same MO. Single shot to the head."

"When?"

The agent told him. It was *after* Randy Lee's death.

Damn.

Upton's killer had claimed another victim.

Marks disconnected the call and started The App on his phone.

CHAPTER THIRTEEN

Winds of Change

Zimbabwe was reaching the end of its rainy season. The mild temperature meant conditions were pleasant for the large crowd. They cheered enthusiastically for the president of their country. For some, it was a genuine display of affection. For most, it was because they'd been paid.

Flags flapped above their heads, and the green and gold of their T-shirts rippled in the afternoon breeze.

Jonathon Mtembo stood sweating in front of the stage. He was wearing an unbuttoned suit, and his head turned from side to side while he scanned the crowd. As far as the crush of people were concerned, he was just another bodyguard protecting their aging leader.

The president was a huge man, with a double chin, and eyes set deep within tunnels created by his cheeks. He raised his meaty fist in the air. Spit flew from his mouth as he derided his political opponent's courage and virility. The crowd roared and his supporters beat the air with their flags.

Jonathon ran through the list in his head.

His wife and children were in South Africa with his brother. They would be taken care of. *Check.*

His brother had been given instructions on what to do. *Check.*

A letter had been posted to the media. It would arrive tomorrow. *Check.*

Jonathon pressed his damp palms against his trousers. He couldn't back out now, even if he wanted to. But his resolve was firm.

As a member of the president's protection detail, Jonathon had seen how the man behaved in private. The corruption and extravagance. The brutality towards those who opposed him. Jonathon had personally witnessed unspeakable acts of torture.

He'd come to the conclusion that his country didn't have a future. Not under its current leader. And it looked like he was going to be re-elected. Bribes and intimidation were powerful tools.

But Jonathon had a tool of his own. One he could use to help his country. And his family. His children would be able to afford an education. They could go to university.

Jonathon thanked his God for showing him The App.

He prayed his wife would understand.

The president's speech reached its raucous conclusion and a path was cleared for his exit. He walked down the stairs from the platform. He was wearing a white business shirt and a red tie. One of the bodyguards supported him, to prevent another embarrassing fall. The video of *that* incident had gone viral.

The worker who'd incorrectly laid the red carpet was severely punished. He'd never do it again. Not without his hands.

The grinning face of the president walked towards Jonathon. He waved clasped hands above his head. Confident of victory in the upcoming election.

Jonathon breathed deeply. Preparing.

As the president walked past his position, Jonathon pointed into the crowd. "Gun," he yelled. He drew his weapon, as if to protect his leader. The bodyguards looked to where Jonathon was pointing. Some of them moved to protect the president. Including Jonathon.

He moved in close behind his leader and whispered in his ear. "Our country deserves better."

He pulled the trigger. Once. Twice. He would have pulled it a third time, but the other bodyguards reacted. They aimed their weapons and fired.

Jonathon fell to the ground, the bullets hammering his chest. He landed beside the president.

The president's eyes stared at him. Lifeless.

Jonathon smiled.

Simon's phone beeped while he was getting ready for his interview with the police. Another claim.

It was from Zimbabwe. Someone had killed its president. He checked the online news and discovered that the assassin had also died.

He shook his head.

The prize was modest in comparison to the one for the lion killer, Cecil Muller. But despite this, someone had given their life to stake a claim.

Simon's skin prickled. For some people, it wasn't about the money.

CHAPTER FOURTEEN

Interrogations

"Don't answer that," said Eli.

Detective Kelly glared at the lawyer. He leaned towards him, pressing his hands into the interview table.

"It's a simple question," said Kelly. "I just want to know if he owns The App." He turned towards Simon.

Simon sat silently, staring at a spot on the wall.

"It may be a simple question," said Eli. "But my advice to my client is to remain silent. All you have is supposition. If you have any tangible proof, then show us."

Eli paused for several seconds. "Well, do you? Are there any documents in your possession that prove Simon's ownership of this so called application?"

Kelly breathed out slowly. "We were hoping to accelerate the process, by letting Simon just acknowledge the fact."

"That's very generous of you," said Eli. "But we're not in a rush. We'd prefer things to be done by the book."

Detective Peters cleared her throat. "Surely it's in Simon's best interest to get this thing resolved as quickly as possible."

Eli smiled and shook his head. "You let me worry about Simon's best interests."

Kelly looked at the clock. It was half past twelve. His stomach rumbled.

This line of questioning was getting them nowhere, so

he tried a different angle. "Simon, what do you know about the death of Dick Gelderman?"

That got a response. Simon's head turned sharply towards Kelly.

Kelly smiled. "You recognise that name, do you?"

Simon smiled back. "He was a banker, wasn't he? From New York?"

"Yes."

Simon took a sip of his coffee. "I read about him in the news. It said he died in an avalanche."

Kelly nodded. "That's the one."

"A terrible accident," said Simon. He shook his head slowly.

Detective Peters leaned on the table. The metal frame creaked. "That's the thing," she said. "We're not sure it *was* an accident."

Simon's head stopped moving. "No?"

"We're thinking Gelderman had a little help. That maybe the avalanche wasn't an act of God."

Eli interrupted them. "That's all very interesting, Detective, but what does this have to do with my client?"

"Maybe nothing," said Kelly. "We're not sure at this stage."

Detective Peters sat back and cracked her knuckles. "How did you lose your job, Simon?"

Simon was staring at the wall again. "I got laid off."

"Because of the GFC?"

Simon nodded.

"The GFC that Dick Gelderman helped create?"

"I suppose so."

Peters drummed her fingers on the table.

"Does that mean you're happy that he's dead?" said

Kelly.

"Don't answer that," said Eli. He waggled his pen at Kelly. "I hope you're not insinuating that my client had something to do with Mr Gelderman's death."

Kelly smiled at the lawyer. "Of course not, Mr Rabinovich."

Simon pushed forward on his chair. "I'd never want anyone to die like that. Not even that bastard."

Eli looked at the clock on the wall. "It's lunch time, detectives. My client has answered enough questions for one day." He stood and ushered Simon towards the door.

Kelly knew he couldn't stop them. "Enjoy your lunch," he said. "I'm sure we'll be meeting again."

Eli chuckled. "You might try having some evidence next time."

Kelly watched as they left the room.

He shook his head. Goddamn lawyers.

His job would be a lot easier without them.

Eli drove out of the police station and over the Cambie Street Bridge. He turned to Simon in the passenger seat. "What was that about? With Gelderman?"

Simon bit his fingernails.

Eli reached forward and turned down the music.

Simon paused. Then he told him what he knew.

Eli waited until Simon had finished before speaking. "I wonder why they suddenly think it was murder? The avalanche ... after saying it was an accident."

Simon shrugged.

"Very unusual," said Eli. "They must have found something. Possibly to do with the ski guide." He made a mental note to have his investigator look into it. "In the meantime, say nothing to the police. And continue working on your web-based version of The App. Something tells me you're going to need it."

"I'll make it my priority," said Simon.

A few minutes later, they pulled up in front of Eli's office. Simon noticed the address on the red-tiled facade; 666 Burrard.

He stifled an involuntary laugh. "Does it get hot in your office, Eli?"

Christine Hunter adjusted the focus of her camera's long range lens.

The image of a man sharpened in the viewfinder. He was tall and muscular, with close cropped hair that was beginning to turn grey at the sides.

She took several photos as he climbed into his Mercedes SL Roadster.

The licence plate that she'd given to Detective Kelly was registered to an import/export company. The company's sole owner was a Russian named Aleksei Volkov.

Christine sat in her car, watching his house in Gleneagles on Vancouver's North Shore. It was a massive property, overlooking the picturesque bay. Evidently, Aleksei's business did extremely well.

Detective Kelly had also run a background check on the owner. He was suspected of having ties to Russian crime gangs. Kelly warned Christine to be careful.

The Mercedes drove towards her.

She picked up a map and pretended to look for directions. The car drove past without slowing. It turned the corner at the end of the street. Christine followed the Mercedes in her aunt's Suzuki.

She didn't notice the dark sedan following her.

"Things are starting to get interesting," said Kelly. He was in his office, talking to Detective Speed on the phone. He played with the autographed hockey puck he kept on his desk.

"How so?" said Speed.

He told Speed about his meeting with Christine Hunter, and its implications for Dick Gelderman's death.

"I think Vancouver should take the lead in the investigation," said Kelly.

"Agreed," said Speed. "The first death looks like it was in your jurisdiction. And Simpson lives in Vancouver as well."

Detective Peters was sitting on the other side of Kelly's desk. He gave her a thumbs up.

"Besides," said Speed, "I'm looking at Hinkley's murder from another angle."

"What have you found?"

"Another murder of a priest. Eight months ago. Also in New Brunswick." Speed launched into a coughing fit. It continued for several seconds. Kelly looked at Peters with concern.

"Are you okay?" said Kelly. The coughing fit ended, and he heard Speed swallowing a drink.

"Sorry. A piece of cake got stuck in my throat," said Speed. "Anyway, the deceased used to teach at a boarding school, where he evidently abused the kids. We're thinking one of them got some revenge. Goddamned priests, eh? My father always warned me about them."

Kelly nodded. "That's understandable." He'd never trusted priests either, despite his Irish heritage. There was something unnatural about choosing to be celibate. Evidently their vow didn't extend to little boys.

"Let me know if you catch the guy," said Kelly. "In the meantime, I'll need to liaise with the FBI."

Speed gave him the contact details for Special Agent Marks.

Kelly thanked him and hung up. He nodded to Detective Peters. "I think we should chat with Tom Roberts."

Christine followed the Mercedes along the Upper Levels Highway, then over the Ironworkers Memorial Bridge. They turned off the Trans-Canada Highway when they reached Burnaby.

She was three cars behind the Mercedes when it entered the parking lot for a small industrial park. She drove past the entrance, and executed a three point turn further down the road. Her Suzuki momentarily blocked the path of another car, and one of the men inside it gave her the bird. Christine smiled and waved.

The Mercedes was in front of a small warehouse. A sign on the building said *Matryoshka Import and Export*. Christine parked in front of another building that advertised computers in its window. She took some photos of Aleksei's office with the long range lens.

Then she waited. She checked her watch every five minutes. Then every two.

Finally, she'd had enough. She walked up to Aleksei's office, and went around the back. She peered into the dumpster near the loading dock. What she saw surprised her.

There were used TV dinners and water bottles piled in the back. There were also empty jars of cosmetics.

She took a photo with her phone.

The loading bay doors were open, so Christine climbed up the stairs alongside the dock and entered the building. She heard voices coming from further inside. Women's voices. They were speaking a foreign language.

The warehouse was filled with shelves that were stacked high with pallets. They created a complex maze. Christine wandered through the passageways, trying to locate the voices. After several minutes, she reached a wire fence. Her path was blocked.

The wire fence formed a cage, with four sides and a roof.

Inside it, she caught a glimpse of several bunk beds. Some of them were occupied by women.

Christine was about to take a picture on her phone when someone forcefully grabbed her arm.

"What are you doing in here?" said a large man. He was dressed in a long black coat and his fingers were covered in heavy rings. Christine recognised him as the man who'd picked up Sienna.

"Is this *Chow's Computer Supplies*?" she said. "I need to buy a new printer. I saw your advert online for a laser printer, and wanted to check it out."

"No, it isn't," said the man. "You have no business being here."

"You're hurting my arm," said Christine.

"What are you doing here?"

"I told you, I want to buy a printer."

Another man appeared. Aleksei. "What is the problem, Ivan?"

"I found this woman in the back of the warehouse."

"I'm looking for *Chow's Computer Supplies*," said

Christine. "I told this oaf that I need to buy a printer."

Aleksei looked Christine up and down. He paused to stare at her legs. He smiled. "You have a nice figure. You could be a model."

"Thank you, but I already have a job. I'm a writer … children's books … which is why I need a new printer. My last one broke."

Aleksei stared at her for several seconds, then nodded to Ivan. "Let her go."

Ivan released Christine's arm, and she rubbed it.

"Sorry for the misunderstanding," said Aleksei. "*Chow's Computer Supplies* is two buildings further down. Ivan will show you the exit."

He walked back into his office, which was actually a caravan. It looked like something a movie star would use.

The trailer was parked in the front section of the warehouse and his most profitable girl was waiting for him inside.

"Who was that?" said Sienna.

"Just some woman who got lost. She was looking for a printer."

He sat on the double bed, and beckoned Sienna closer.

"I'm pleased with your recent work. You've been making a lot of money."

Sienna smiled. "One of my clients likes all night sessions. What can I say? He likes what I do."

Aleksei laughed. "Of course he does. We all do."

He leaned back on the bed and undid his belt. "Come here and remind me."

Christine walked past her car and into *Chow's Computing Supplies*. In case they were still watching.

The man behind the counter beamed at her. "Ah, how can I help you, beautiful lady?" He walked around to where she was standing. "Are you looking for something in particular?"

"Thank you," said Christine. "But I'm just browsing."

The doorbell rang, indicating another customer had entered the store. It was Ivan.

"Actually," said Christine. "I was hoping you could show me your laser printers."

"Excellent," said Chow. "I have many fine models."

He proceeded to extol their virtues. Christine nodded her head. She used her peripheral vision to look at Ivan. He stood by the computer games, pretending to browse.

After ten minutes, Christine realised that he wasn't going to leave until she'd bought something. Damn.

"I'll take that one," she said.

Chow's face sagged. She'd pointed to the cheapest model in his store.

"Would you like to buy the extended warranty," he said. "With this model, you might need it."

Christine shook her head. "Just the printer will be fine."

Chow scowled at her. "Very well." He picked up a box from under the shelf, and carried it to the counter. Christine reluctantly gave him her credit card. She didn't think she'd be able to claim it as a work expense.

When she turned to leave with her new purchase, Ivan had gone.

Asshole.

She walked outside and placed the printer on the back seat of her car. She was leaning inside to secure it when something tapped against her hip.

"What the hell —"

Christine twisted her head, and found herself looking at the man who'd given her the bird on the road. She stiffened. "Who are you? What do you want?" Adrenaline fueled her as she reached into her handbag.

"Quiet," said the man. He squeezed into the back seat beside her. "Detective Kelly sends his regards."

"You're a cop?" She relaxed her grip on the pepper spray.

The man nodded. "Kelly said that he warned you to be careful. But I see you chose to ignore him."

"I'm a big girl," said Christine. She manoeuvred herself onto the other seat.

"You were lucky to get out of there. Volkov isn't a nice man."

Christine lifted her chin. "Did you follow me here?"

The man smiled. "Not exactly. We followed Volkov from his house. You were an added bonus."

"I haven't done anything wrong," said Christine. "You can't stop me doing my job."

"We're not trying to, Miss Hunter. But don't push your luck. No story is worth dying for."

He got out of the car and walked away.

Christine waited until her breathing had returned to normal, then she drove back to her aunt's house.

Christine could smell her aunt's cooking when she walked through the door. Some kind of seafood.

She dumped the printer down on the kitchen table.

"Guess who's dropped in for a surprise visit?" said her aunt.

"Who?" said Christine.

"Your Aunt Mabel."

Christine's mouth widened into a broad smile. "Aunt

Mabel's here? In Vancouver?"

Joan nodded. "She flew in this afternoon. Isn't that wonderful? She's upstairs unpacking."

"How is she?" said Christine.

Joan shrugged. "She seems okay. Perhaps a little quieter than usual. But nothing a good dinner won't fix."

Christine laughed. Food was her aunt's solution to every problem.

"Can you set the table for me, dear?"

"Sure," said Christine. She picked up the printer.

"What's that?"

Christine held out the box. "I bought you a printer. To say thanks for letting me stay."

Her aunt sighed. "You shouldn't have."

Christine shook her head. "It was the least I could do. You've been so good."

Aunt Joan stepped forward and enveloped her in a hug. "No, I mean you really shouldn't have. I don't have a computer."

"Oh," said Christine. "I didn't realise."

"It's okay. Perhaps Mabel can use it."

As if on cue, Christine's other aunt walked into the kitchen. She wrapped a thin arm around her niece.

"Hello, dear. How's my favourite niece? Has Joan been trying to fatten you up?"

Christine laughed. "You know she has."

"Speaking of which," said Joan. "Dinner is ready."

They sat down at the table, while Joan removed the pot from the stove.

"What's for dinner, Aunty Joan?"

"One of my specialties." She whipped off the lid, revealing the contents. Crab claws floated in a seafood

broth. "I hope you like it."
   Mabel shrieked.

CHAPTER FIFTEEN
Oregon Trail

Marks had flown into Portland on a regular domestic flight. He was met at the airport by the agent he'd spoken to earlier.

"We have a ballistics match with the bullet from the Jerry Upton murder," said Agent Wilkie.

"What else have you found?" said Marks.

"Nothing much. There's no sign of the shooter. No shell casing. No body imprints."

Marks nodded. "We're dealing with a pro."

Agent Wilkie's Crown Victoria was parked in the passenger drop off area. The traffic cop on duty gave them a nod.

They left the airport and turned onto the freeway. Marks looked out the window.

"Where's that enormous snow covered mountain I saw from the plane?" he said.

"You mean Mount Hood?"

"Yeah."

"It's behind us. A bit hard to see from here."

Marks swiveled his head around anyway. "The pilot said it's volcanic."

Wilkie nodded. "People say it will explode like Mount St. Helens one day."

Marks' thoughts returned to the investigation. The pressure mounting with each murder. Upton's killer was just getting started.

"Are we going straight to the crime scene?" said Marks.

"We can if you want."

"Let's do that."

The car picked up speed. Dark fir trees whizzed past his window until they eventually became a blur.

Marks closed his eyes and contemplated his opponent's next move.

Dillon Black was watching a movie about a sniper. It was one of his favourites.

Except he didn't like the ending. He felt sorry for Eddie, the former Marine who'd killed the movie's hero on a gun range.

Like Dillon, Eddie had struggled with life after leaving the Corps.

But unlike Dillon, Eddie hadn't found a purpose.

Dillon scrolled through potential targets on his phone. So many to choose from.

The ballistics experts were mapping the crime scene when Wilkie and Marks arrived. The agents badged their way through the surrounding cordon.

Wilkie approached the lead tech. "What have you got, Bob?"

The tech was dressed in jeans and a windproof jacket. He introduced himself to Marks.

"We've reconstructed the positioning of the victim and we're trying to calculate where the bullet was fired from."

He pointed to a model of a skull that was perched on top of an adjustable tripod.

"The vic was playing tennis. Evidently he was serving,

with his head tilted back, looking at the ball."

The model skull was tilted backwards on the tripod, and there was a hole the size of a quarter on one side.

"We've recreated the entrance wound from scans of the deceased's skull." He walked over to a laptop computer next to the tripod. "Want to see something cool?"

The agents looked at each other. Agent Wilkie mouthed the word 'cool'. They joined Bob next to the laptop.

On the screen was an image of the surrounding landscape, with multiple red lines emanating from a single point. Each line was annotated with a yardage marker.

"We've mounted a camera and a laser in the skull, and we're reverse engineering the shot."

Marks nodded. Very impressive. He pointed to the line that was annotated with three hundred yards. "Can you zoom in on the endpoint of this one?"

"Sure," said Bob. He fiddled with the keyboard, and a section of the carpark grew larger.

"Why three hundred yards?" said Wilkie.

"Because that's the range Upton was shot at. The killer might prefer that distance."

The tech shook his head. "Nobody saw anyone shooting from over there. And they would have."

"Not necessarily," said Marks.

Wilkie nodded. "Are you thinking what I'm thinking?"

Marks smiled. "Yeah."

"What?" said Bob.

"Do you remember the Beltway Sniper?"

Two hours later, Marks was back at the airport waiting for his return flight to Los Angeles. His phone rang.

"This is Detective Kelly. I'm calling from Vancouver. Detective Speed gave me your number."

Kelly explained that he was taking the lead in the Canadian investigation, and raised the possibility of another American being killed. Dick Gelderman.

"Are you serious?" said Marks. "I thought his death was an accident."

"Yeah, so did we initially. But now we're not so sure."

He explained.

"Have you spoken to this Tom Roberts yet?"

"We're working on tracking him down. Seems he's on a skiing holiday in Switzerland. Any progress on your end?"

Marks updated him on the Portland murder.

"Jesus," said Kelly. "This thing is getting out of hand."

Simon had worked long hours for the last two days. He wanted to finish the web-based version of The App. The interview with the police had highlighted its importance.

Eli was right, it was only a matter of time before they tried to shut him down. But he'd be ready.

He was progressing well on the updated version. His new task was much simpler than the original task of developing The App. All of the back-end code was already done. Only the user interface needed to be replaced.

Simon stretched his neck.

To clear his mind, he logged on to the database and checked the total of the skimmed bets. More than

$50,000 so far. Impressive. Even *he* might kill Aleksei for that.

But then again, he'd probably have killed him for free.

As Dillon scrolled through the list of targets, he noticed that many of them were outside of the United States. The prospect of overseas travel was appealing.

But he'd have problems with his gun. It would be difficult to transport through customs.

Buying a new one would also be an issue. Most countries weren't as accommodating as his when it came to purchasing weapons.

He thanked God for the Second Amendment. At least *his* government wouldn't try to stop him from owning a sniper's rifle.

The United States was a great place to live. Plenty of freedom, and the right to defend yourself against whack jobs. It was incredible how many of them owned guns.

Dillon refined his search for targets in the United States. There were hundreds. He sorted the results by value.

Hello Senator Quaid.

The senator's brief bio said that he'd repeatedly thwarted legislation designed to tighten the regulation of the finance industry. The biggest contributors to his election campaign were the investment banks and brokerage firms.

Dillon smiled. He'd never been to Washington, DC. It would be a road trip to remember.

CHAPTER SIXTEEN
All In

Simon took Sienna's coat. "Have a seat," he said. "I've got some news."

She flopped onto the couch and patted the space beside her. "Something good?"

He sat where she'd indicated. "The bet-skimming plan worked better than we thought."

"Tell me," she said.

Simon turned his body so he was facing her. "The total has reached fifty thousand. We should place the bet."

Sienna frowned. "Do you think it will be enough?"

"Should be," he said. "Prizes have been claimed for less."

Sienna moved closer to him and placed her hand on his thigh. "I've got a better idea. Why don't we wait until tomorrow morning? The total will be even bigger then."

Simon shrugged. "We could do that."

She pouted and moved her hand higher. "I can think of plenty of things we can do until then."

"Ah," said Simon. He looked down at her hand. "You're probably right."

Sienna stood and grabbed his hand. She led him to the dining table and pushed him firmly onto a chair.

She licked her lips as she leaned forward, whispering in his ear. "Why don't we start with a game of chess?"

Detective Kelly stood at the end of the airplane gantry. He was waiting for the passengers from a Swiss International Airlines flight to disembark. He held a photograph of Tom Roberts in his hand. Detective Peters stood about twenty metres away, resting against a pillar.

Kelly nodded to her as the First Class passengers began to file past him.

The flight manifest said that Roberts was seated in 29A. The emergency exit. Kelly wasn't surprised. According to his information, Roberts was six foot four inches tall and weighed two hundred and twenty pounds. A big unit.

Kelly eyeballed each passenger as they disembarked, comparing them to the photo in his hand.

He saw a head poking up above the others.

Roberts.

Kelly gave Detective Peters a discreet nod.

He pulled out his credentials and stepped in front of Roberts with his hand up. "Excuse me, sir, do you mind if I have a word with you?"

Roberts stopped and looked at the credentials. "Sure. But I haven't got anything to declare. I've just been skiing."

Kelly motioned Roberts to one side. "I'm not from Customs. I'm a detective with the Vancouver Police Department. I was hoping you could accompany me down to the station to answer some questions."

Roberts placed his knapsack on the ground. "Questions?" he said. "What about?" He looked at the line of passengers heading to immigration. "I'm in a bit of a hurry."

"It's about one of your clients. Dick Gelderman."

Roberts didn't react. He stared impassively at Kelly. "*Gelderman*? He's *dead*. Haven't you heard? Died in an avalanche."

Kelly nodded. "That's what we wanted to talk to you about."

"I've already given a statement to the police."

"I know," said Kelly. "But that was before we received new information."

"New information?" said Roberts.

"It would be easier to discuss that at the station. Would you mind?"

"Um … sure," said Roberts. He turned and picked up his hand luggage, pausing to adjust the strap. Then he spun back violently, using the knapsack as a weapon. It swung in a wide arc, hitting Kelly hard on his left cheek.

Kelly staggered, clutching his head. A ringing sound filled his ears. Roberts bolted past him and ran towards the pillar.

Roberts was looking over his shoulder. He didn't see Detective Peters as she stepped in front of him.

Peters dropped her shoulder and braced herself for the hit. Just like she'd been taught by her ice hockey coach.

The air exploded from Roberts' lungs as Peters drove through his solar plexus with a perfect body check. He flopped to the ground like a half dead fish, gasping for air.

Peters gave a satisfied grunt. She rolled Roberts on to his stomach and cuffed him while leaning on him with her knee.

"Didn't your coach teach you the golden rule?" she said. "Always keep your head up when skating through centre ice."

Kelly walked up to them with his hand pressed against his head. He nodded to Peters.

"I'll have to come and watch you play some time."

Simon sat at the dining table in his boxer shorts. The rest of his clothes lay in a pile on the floor.

"You're quite good at strip chess," he said.

Sienna nodded. "I've had some practice."

She'd won three games straight. She sat opposite him, fully clothed.

The current match had lasted longer than the others. For the first time, Simon had a real chance of winning.

Simon advanced his queen. "Check."

Sienna studied the board closely. "Nicely done. You're learning."

He nodded.

She eventually blocked him with her bishop, but Simon quickly responded with his rook. He winked as he removed her bishop from the board.

Sienna countered by capturing Simon's rook with her queen.

But it was futile.

Simon lifted his own queen and tapped Sienna's piece on the side of its crown. Her queen toppled over.

"Check," he said.

Sienna cursed in Russian. She stared at her remaining pieces for several minutes before knocking her king off the board. "I resign."

Simon grinned. "Did you see that, Gizmo?"

Gizmo looked up from his basket and made a noise that was half bark, half yawn. Simon threw him a Pringle. Gizmo moved his head a few inches and snapped it up.

Simon started to reset the pieces for another game. "What's it going to be? Shoes or dress?"

Sienna stood and walked to the pile of clothes on the floor. She frowned as she reached under her dress and removed her panties.

"I think we've played enough chess for tonight."

Detective Kelly and Detective Peters were watching Tom Roberts through the one way mirror. Roberts was holding an icepack against his ribs.

"I'd better be the good cop," said Kelly with a grin.

Peters laughed. "You think?"

They opened the door to the interrogation room. Roberts looked up. His eyes narrowed when he saw Detective Peters.

"Can I get you something to drink?" said Kelly.

Roberts shook his head.

Peters walked behind Roberts. She stopped when she was out of his field of view. "You killed Dick Gelderman," she said. It was a statement, not a question.

"I didn't," said Roberts.

Peters ignored him.

"Was it for the money? Or to avenge your brother's death?"

"Neither," said Roberts. "It was an accident. An avalanche." He turned his head, trying to see Peters.

Kelly sat in front of him, across the table. "If you tell us the truth, we might be able to help you," he said.

Roberts turned to face Kelly. "I *am* telling you the truth, I swear."

Kelly nodded. When a suspect said 'I swear' they were usually lying.

Peters lifted a metal bin above her head and dropped

it on the floor. Roberts jumped in his seat.

"We found fragments from the explosive charge you used to trigger the avalanche," she said. "That's no accident."

She picked up the bin and banged it against the back of Roberts' chair. "It's murder."

Roberts shook his head.

"If you tell us everything, perhaps we can find some extenuating circumstances," said Kelly. "Get the charge downgraded."

Roberts stared at him. He took a deep breath. "If you're charging me, I want a lawyer."

"We're not charging you yet," said Kelly. "We're just trying to understand what happened."

"I didn't kill him," said Roberts.

"Then why did you assault a police officer?" said Peters. She walked around to where he could see her. She leaned forward on the desk and looked him in the eye. "Why did you run if you're not guilty?"

"I panicked. You made me nervous. I'd smoked marijuana while I was away and I thought you were going to swab my clothes for residue."

"Is that the best you can do?" said Peters.

"What? It's the truth."

"Where did the money come from, Tom? For your little ski trip to Switzerland?"

"I inherited it from my brother."

"Bullshit," said Peters. "Your brother died penniless. He didn't leave you squat."

They were interrupted by a knock at the door. Kelly looked at Peters and shrugged. Nobody would interrupt them at this point unless it was important.

Kelly opened the door. "What?" he said to the young

policewoman outside.

"Sorry to interrupt," said the woman. "It's just that there's a man out here who claims to be Mr Roberts' lawyer. He's asking to see his client. Now."

"Shit," said Kelly. He slapped his palm against the wall. "Fucking lawyers."

"What should I tell him, Detective?"

Kelly sighed. "You'd better send him in."

He walked back inside the interview room.

"When did you have a chance to call a lawyer?" said Kelly.

"I didn't," said Roberts.

"Well there's someone outside who's claiming to represent you."

At that moment, the door was flung open. Eli Rabinovich stormed into the room.

"Not another word," said Eli. "I'd like to talk to my client now. In private."

"Fancy seeing you here," said Kelly.

"What can I say?" said Eli. "My services are in demand."

Kelly shook his head then slowly walked to the door.

Detective Peters followed. She turned in the doorway. "How are those ribs, Tom?"

Eli had been about to sit down to dinner when he'd gotten a phone call from his private investigator, Sam McCain. Eli had asked him to find out everything he could about Tom Roberts.

One of the things he'd discovered was Roberts' flight details.

McCain had been waiting for Roberts at the airport when he saw him being escorted away by police. He followed them to the station and called his boss.

Eli was concerned about the implications for his lucrative client, Simon Simpson. So he took action.

"I'm here to represent you," said Eli. "I'm familiar with your case. A little bird told me you might be in trouble."

"What?" said Roberts. "How did you even know I was here?"

"A long story," said Eli. "But not nearly as interesting as yours."

Eli leaned forward and lowered his voice.

"On the morning of Thursday, 27th February, at approximately 10:00 am, you artificially created an avalanche that killed your client, Dick Gelderman. You did so, to avenge the death of your brother, Mike, who'd lost all of his money on worthless investments that Gelderman had helped to set up. You also placed a bet on the time and manner of Gelderman's death using a cell phone application known as The App. You were lucky enough to win that bet and subsequently received a payout of $65,628. You celebrated your win with a skiing trip to Switzerland and on your return were arrested by police. I'm told you assaulted a police officer in the process. How am I doing so far?"

Roberts stared at him with eyes like fried eggs. "Who *are* you?"

Eli smiled. "A friend."

Sienna was already dressed by the time Simon awoke.

"Good morning, sleepy head," she said.

Simon stretched. "You wore me out."

Sienna laughed. "Well … you *did* beat me at chess." She pulled back the covers. "Now get up, so we can place the bet. I have to go soon."

Simon groaned but did as he was told.

"Where are my pants?" he said.

"On the dining room floor where you left them."

He grinned. "I like that game. We'll have to play it again."

Sienna whacked his bare bottom with her hand. "Stop dawdling. We have to place that bet before I leave."

He walked past, Gizmo, who gave him a strange look, and sat down at his computer naked.

"Wow," said Simon. "The skimmed bets have reached sixty thousand."

"*See.* I told you." Sienna slid her hand across his shoulder. "Why don't you put some clothes on and make us a cup of coffee? I can place the bet. Just give me the details for transferring the funds."

"I thought you were in a hurry?"

Sienna patted his arm. "I have enough time for coffee."

Simon shrugged. "Okay." He gave her the account details and picked up his clothes. Then he went into the kitchen.

He returned ten minutes later and found Sienna standing by the door.

"How did you go?" he said.

"All done. I've bet the entire account balance on Aleksei." She looked at her watch. "But I have to go now. Another job."

She pecked him on the cheek.

Simon watched her leave then looked at the two cups of coffee he was holding.

He shook his head. "Women."

Gizmo gave a single yelp.

Simon sat down at his computer and opened the source code for The App. He drank both coffees while he deleted all traces of the bet skimming. Then he redeployed the updates to the server in Russia.

After verifying the results, Simon went back to bed and fell asleep. He dreamed about shooting Sienna's boss.

Christine woke up early and called her boss in Moncton. They discussed her proposal for a story.

By the time they'd finished, Christine could smell breakfast being cooked downstairs. She looked at her waist and groaned. If she ate much more, she'd need to start buying new clothes.

Christine delayed her encounter with breakfast by checking the current betting in The App. The first few names had been on the list for several days. The dollar amounts next to them had increased steadily.

When Christine reached the eighth name on the list, she dropped her phone. Aleksei Volkov.

Son of a bitch.

She picked her phone up off the carpet and dialled Detective Kelly. His frosty demeanour changed once he heard what she had to say.

"You're telling me that someone has bet more than sixty thousand dollars on Aleksei Volkov?"

"That's what it looks like. He wasn't anywhere near the top last night. But this morning, he was suddenly number eight."

"Shit," said Kelly.

"Yeah, someone should probably warn him."

"Thanks. We'll take care of it."

Kelly hesitated. "There's something else," he said.

"What?" said Christine.

"We found Tom Roberts last night. He was taken into custody at the airport."

"Really? So you have him there now?"

"Um. Not exactly. Some meddling lawyer mysteriously showed up and sprung him."

"A lawyer?"

"Yeah. Eli Rabinovich. And get this ... he's also representing Simon Simpson."

"Now that *is* interesting," said Christine. "Did you charge Roberts with Gelderman's murder?"

"Not yet. But we did charge him with assaulting a police officer." He gave her the details of what had happened.

"Thanks for the information, Detective."

"Likewise."

She hung up and slowly made her way downstairs. Her Aunt Joan was in the kitchen.

"Where's Aunt Mabel?" said Christine.

"I just took her breakfast in bed. She's still feeling a bit poorly."

Christine frowned at her aunt and made a tutting sound.

Joan held up her hands, defensively. "How was *I* supposed to know?"

CHAPTER SEVENTEEN

Warnings

Detective Kelly rang the doorbell of Aleksei Volkov's mansion on Vancouver's North Shore. He'd checked with the surveillance team and been told that the target was inside the house.

Kelly stared into the camera above the door and held up his credentials. He'd noticed several other cameras dotted strategically around the grounds.

After a couple of minutes the door opened slightly. Aleksei Volkov peered through the gap.

"What can I do for you, detectives? If you've got any questions, I'd like to call my lawyer."

"That won't be necessary," said Kelly. "We've just come to warn you about a possible threat to your safety."

"Really?" said Aleksci. "Then you'd better come in." He opened the door wider.

Kelly stepped into a large entrance hall. He was followed by Detective Peters.

Aleksei led them past an indoor pool and into his living room. The wide window framed a magnificent view of Bowen Island.

Detective Peters gave a low whistle. "I could get used to that."

Aleksei chuckled. "Not unless you're supplementing your income, Detective."

"Why, how much did this place cost?"

"A little under eight million."

"Jesus."

Kelly cleared his throat. "If we could talk about the threat to your safety?"

"Certainly," said Aleksei. "Please have a seat."

They sat down facing the water. Kelly explained to Aleksei about The App.

Aleksei remained silent. When Kelly had finished, he lit a cigarette and took a long drag.

"Let me get this straight. You think my life is in danger because my name has appeared on a list on someone's cell phone?"

"Not just any list," said Kelly. "A hit list. And people who appear on it have a nasty habit of dying."

"But who would want to kill me? I'm just the owner of a little import/export business."

Detective Peters looked around the room at the grand piano and the chandelier. "Your business seems to do pretty well."

"I admit I'm very successful," said Aleksei. "But that's hardly a reason to kill me."

"Regardless, we think you'd be wise to take some precautions," said Kelly.

"My house is very secure. I have an excellent security system."

"Just the same, you should be careful. Call the police if you see anything suspicious."

Aleksei smiled. "Perhaps I could phone the surveillance team that is watching my house? They'd be in the best position to respond."

The detectives looked at each other. Peters lifted a hand to her face and rubbed her eyes. She pinched the bridge of her nose.

"Thank you for coming," said Aleksei. "If you need to talk to me again, you should probably call my lawyer."

"Let me guess," said Kelly. "Eli Rabinovich?"

"Ah, you know him?"

Kelly clenched his jaw. "We've recently become acquainted."

They left the house and walked up the driveway to their car. "Drive past the surveillance team," said Kelly. "We'll give them the good news."

Simon listened to the message on his phone for the fourth time.

"This is Christine Hunter. I'm putting together a piece for the six o'clock news. I'd like to give you another opportunity to tell your side of the story. Please call me." She left her number.

The clock on the wall showed one minute to six.

Simon had thought about calling her several times during the day. But each time he'd heard Eli's voice in his head. Don't talk to anyone.

It was too late now.

Simon turned on the television and switched it to CBC News.

After several news items about the economy and the threat of terrorism, Christine Hunter appeared on the screen.

"There have been significant developments in the investigation that started with the death of priest, Stephen Hinkley. As was reported in a CBC News exclusive, Hinkley was murdered after his name appeared on a global hit list. Since then, more than thirty people on that list have died. The deaths have been widespread. From Australia to Zimbabwe. And

Germany to the United States."

The camera zoomed out, revealing the snowcapped peak of Grouse Mountain in the background. A gust of wind shook the camera, causing the picture to wobble.

"In a major development, the circumstances surrounding the death of banker, Dick Gelderman, are now being re-examined. The police had previously described his death as an accident. However, it has since been determined that Gelderman's name was at the top of the list. His ski guide, Tom Roberts, was reinterviewed by police yesterday.

"In another exclusive, CBC News can reveal the name of the man behind The App. Vancouver resident, Simon Simpson — shown here in a photo from his Facebook profile — is a software engineer. He was laid off from his job last year as a result of the GFC; a crisis that was in large part caused by the actions of Dick Gelderman. Simpson has so far refused to comment.

The camera zoomed in, tightening on Christine Hunter's face and framing her auburn hair.

"Police are urging anyone on the list to take precautions. The person currently at the top of the rankings is US Senator, David Quaid. The highest ranked Canadian resident is Aleksei Volkov. Volkov is a wealthy businessman who runs an import/export business in Burnaby. This is Christine Hunter in Vancouver, for CBC News."

Simon turned off the television. He sat on the sofa with his head in his hands.

Shit.

"Ivan, have you seen this video?" said Sienna. "It mentions Aleksei. He's being talked about on the national news."

"What are you talking about?" said Ivan.

Sienna showed him the video on her phone. She'd received a warning message from Simon about the news segment.

"What is this thing she mentions?" said Ivan. "The App?"

"Here," said Sienna. "I've downloaded it on my phone."

She opened The App and handed her phone to Ivan. "See? There's Aleksei's name. He's currently number eight on the list."

"I recognise this journalist," said Ivan. "She was the woman I caught snooping around the other day. She said she wanted to buy a printer."

"Obviously she was poking around for a story."

Ivan nodded. "I'll call Aleksei and let him know."

Sienna put out her hand to stop him leaving. "Do you think Aleksei will be safe in his house? There are so many windows and doors to guard. Maybe he'd be safer *here* … with only two doors and no windows. If he stayed inside, no one would even know he was here."

Ivan tilted his head to the side. He stroked his chin as he digested what Sienna had said.

"You may be right," said Ivan. "I'll suggest it to Aleksei."

Sienna smiled and brushed Ivan's arm. "You can tell him it was your idea."

Senator Quaid squirmed in his black leather chair. He tugged at his tie in an attempt to get more air into his lungs. Beads of sweat dribbled down his forehead.

"What do you *mean* someone is trying to kill me?

Who? Why don't you arrest them?"

The Assistant Chief of the United States Capitol Police shook his head. "We're not really sure who wants you dead, sir."

The inspector sitting next to him cleared his throat. "That's not entirely true, sir. At least eighty thousand people want you dead — if we assume each person bet a dollar."

Assistant Chief Stubbs glared at his subordinate. "What Inspector MacPherson is trying to say is that we aren't aware of any specific plots to kill you. However, based on the information provided to us by the FBI, we believe an attempt on your life is likely."

"But why?" said Senator Quaid. "What have I done?"

"It's not because of anything you've done, Senator," said Stubbs.

"Actually, sir," said Inspector MacPherson, "According to The App, it's because you repeatedly thwarted legislation that might have prevented the Global Financial Crisis."

Stubbs snapped his head around. "Inspector, didn't you have an urgent meeting to go to?"

MacPherson looked at his boss and shook his head. "No, sir. I cleared my calendar specifically for this meeting. As ordered."

Stubbs face changed colour from its usual white to a pale crimson.

"Are you okay, sir?" said MacPherson. "You look a bit flushed."

Senator Quaid wiped his forehead with his handkerchief. "What are you doing to protect me? I'm a United States Senator for God's sake."

"Rest assured, Senator, we've already taken

precautions to protect you," said Stubbs.

"But there's no guarantees," said MacPherson.

"What?" said Senator Quaid.

"Nobody can guarantee your safety," said MacPherson. "We can only try our best. And hope the killers don't know what they're doing."

"What? You said killers? Plural?"

MacPherson nodded. "Bound to be more than one attempt. That amount of money is a big motivator."

Assistant Chief Stubbs rose from his chair and put his hand firmly on MacPherson's shoulder. "We'll leave you to do your work now, Senator. And we'll get back to doing our job of *protecting* you. There's no need to worry." He squeezed MacPherson's shoulder and pulled him towards the door.

When they were outside, Stubbs turned to MacPherson. "What the hell was that about? We were supposed to be reassuring the Senator. Not scaring the crap out of him."

MacPherson shrugged. "I voted for the other guy."

Stubbs glared at him. "That's not very professional."

MacPherson lifted his head, meeting his boss's stare. "Maybe not … but then again, I lost my house in the GFC."

Aleksei sat in the caravan inside his warehouse in Burnaby. He took a sip of his vodka.

"The police already warned me about the list. But I didn't know about the woman. Sneaky journalist bitch."

Sienna was perched on the end of the couch. "Do you know who wants you dead?"

Aleksei shook his head. "I'm not sure. Probably one of the Chinese gangs. They had a monopoly until we arrived." He took another sip of his drink. "But you can be sure I'm going to find out. Even if I have to torture that guy who created The App. What was his name?"

Sienna coughed. "Um … Simon Simpson," she said.

She moved closer and touched Aleksei's shoulder. "What are you going to do until then? Your house has all those windows. It would be very easy to shoot you."

Aleksei nodded. "Ivan had a good idea. He suggested I move into the warehouse for a while. Easier to protect."

Sienna smiled at Ivan. He smiled back.

"It's a good suggestion," she said.

Aleksei laughed. "I'm glad you are so concerned about my welfare." He put his hand on her leg and slid it under her dress. He frowned when he reached her underpants. "I told you not to wear those here." There was a ripping sound as he yanked them away.

Sienna lowered her eyes. "I'm sorry. I forgot."

Aleksei grunted. "It seems you need reminding."

She gasped as he slapped her face.

Aleksei looked up at Ivan. "Go and check that the building is secure."

An hour later, Sienna limped down the stairs of the caravan. Ivan stood outside the door. He said nothing as she hobbled back to her private room outside the wire cage. Her room was a disused office with a bed. It was a privilege she enjoyed for being Aleksei's favourite girl.

Ivan stepped inside the caravan and closed the door. He checked it was secure.

Aleksei was watching *Canada's Next Top Model*.

"I'll stay inside with you," said Ivan. "For extra protection."

Aleksei nodded. "Good idea."

Ivan put two guns on the table. He cleaned them one at a time. When he was finished, he reloaded the second weapon and looked up at his boss.

"What?" said Aleksei.

"Well … when I was standing outside the caravan earlier, it got me thinking."

"Careful, Ivan. You don't want to strain yourself."

Ivan ignored the remark. He sighted along the pistol. "I spent an hour staring at the caravan and it made me wonder."

"Really?" said Aleksei. "An independent thought?" He stared at Ivan who was eyeing him down the barrel.

Ivan nodded. "I am wondering why caravans are always painted white."

Aleksei laughed and shook his head. "Ivan, my friend. You ask some very strange questions."

When the explosion came, it was louder than Sienna had expected.

She ran outside and unlocked the cage with the keys she'd stolen while Aleksei was in the shower. He'd left her alone after sex and she'd used the opportunity to do several things; like opening the valve on the main gas bottle; and lighting a candle on the shelf above the stove.

She'd watched from her room as Ivan had sealed the caravan door. She'd already sealed the windows.

The pressure wave from the exploding gas was violent. Acrid smoke filled the air.

The girls were screaming as Sienna pulled open the door of their cage.

"Fire," shouted Sienna. "Grab your belongings. You are free."

"Free?" said one of the girls.

Sienna nodded. "Aleksei and Ivan were in the caravan when it exploded. They cannot hurt you anymore."

The girl nodded and grabbed the hand of another girl from her village. "Come Anya. We must leave."

Sienna picked up her bag. It was already packed.

Flames rose from the burning caravan. They reached to the roof of the warehouse. Thick smoke billowed from holes where the windows had been before the explosion.

Sienna grabbed the spare key for Ivan's car and ran to the front door. She was about to throw her bag onto the passenger seat when she noticed a pistol. Sienna picked it up and put it in her bag.

She took a final look at Aleksei's funeral pyre. *Do svidaniya*. Asshole.

Then she jumped in the car and drove away.

CHAPTER EIGHTEEN

Guests

There was a loud knock at the front door. Gizmo barked and ran around the room.

Simon looked at his watch. 3:00 am. Who could it be at this hour?

He flicked on the external light and peered through the peephole.

Sienna. Jesus.

He fumbled with the chain and opened the door. "What are you doing here?" he said.

She pushed past him. "It is done. I need a place to stay."

Simon shut the door.

"You mean he's dead? Already?"

She nodded. "Yes. He burned to death in an explosion."

Simon put his hands on her shoulders, examining her gently. "What? Who?"

Sienna shook her head. "I don't know. I was in bed when it happened."

She pulled away and sat down on the couch. Simon remained standing.

"How did you get here?" he said.

"I drove Ivan's car. He's dead too. Don't worry. I didn't leave the car out front. I dumped it on East Hastings with the keys in the ignition. Then I caught a cab. I had the driver drop me a few blocks away."

"Wow," said Simon. "That's very efficient. And careful."

"Necessary precautions."

Simon went to the window and peered out through the venetian blinds.

"The street is empty," he said. "No need to worry."

"Can I stay with you until I find somewhere else?"

"Of course," said Simon. "But you don't need to find anywhere else."

She raised her eyebrows. "No?"

Simon shook his head. "You can stay with me."

Sienna smiled. "Really?"

"Yes."

She stood and hugged him.

"You're safe with me," said Simon. "I'll protect you."

Sienna nodded. "I know you'll do your best. But just in case —"

She let go of Simon and reached into her handbag. She pulled out Ivan's gun.

"Jesus," said Simon.

"Don't worry. I know how to use it."

Simon was woken by the familiar beeping of his phone. He'd forgotten to put it on silent.

The toilet flushed. The bathroom door opened and Sienna walked out. She was wearing his U2 shirt.

"Was that your phone?" she said.

"Yes. Just someone claiming another prize."

He rolled over and stuck his head under his pillow.

"Aren't you going to check it?"

"It can wait," he said. His voice was muffled by the pillow.

She reached over and pulled the pillow away from his

face. Simon groaned.

"What?" he said.

"It might be important. It might be the claim for Aleksei."

"So?"

"I feel like I owe them. For saving me."

Simon sighed. "Okay. Pass me the phone."

Sienna handed it to him.

He checked the message. "You were right," he said. "It's for Aleksei."

Sienna pulled back the sheets. "Let's check it." She took Simon's hand and hauled him to his feet. "Here are your pants." She handed them to him.

She pushed him into the living room and he sat down at his computer. He validated the decrypt key and decoded the bet.

"It says he would die in a gas explosion," said Simon. "Last night. In Burnaby."

Sienna leant over his shoulder and examined the bet.

"Those details are correct. You don't need to wait for confirmation." She smiled. "Trust me, I was there."

Simon shrugged. "Okay. If you say so."

He froze further betting on Aleksei and sent out the notifications.

In the bathroom, Sienna's phone vibrated inside her handbag. She'd remembered to put it on silent.

Christine checked her missed calls. She had two. Both from Detective Kelly.

Shit.

She called him back without getting out of bed.

"I've been trying to reach you," said Kelly. "In keeping with our agreement."

"Sorry, my phone was off. What have you got?"

"Are you sitting down?"

She adjusted her pillow. "Near enough."

"Aleksei Volkov was killed last night. Along with his driver, Ivan Romanov."

"Shit. How?"

"In a gas explosion at Aleksei's warehouse."

"Was anyone else hurt?"

"We haven't found anyone … though there were a lot of beds out back. It looked like the occupants left in a hurry."

"They were women," said Christine. "I saw them the other day."

"Probably hookers. Illegals most likely."

Christine got out of bed and turned on her laptop. "Do you know if the two men were murdered?"

"It's too early to tell from the forensics. The damage was extensive."

"How long until you know?"

"A couple of days, maybe. It's possible that we'll never know for sure."

Christine rubbed some sleep from her eyes. "Thanks, detective. I appreciate the information."

"It's a two-way street," said Kelly.

"I won't forget."

They hung up. Christine looked at her warm bed then turned away.

She had another news story to prepare.

Senator Quaid sat in his favourite club, drinking from a large brandy balloon. His hand shook as he lifted the glass to his mouth.

"I can't believe this is happening to me," he said.

"You'd better believe it," said Senator Chisholm. "People on that list are dying. I just heard a news report that another one died in Canada."

Senator Quaid spluttered as liquor went down his airway. He coughed several times to clear his lungs. "Really?" he said eventually.

"Yes. Burned to death in an explosion."

Senator Quaid put his glass down and dabbed at his forehead with a handkerchief.

"I wish I'd never accepted those damn donations. From the banks. I had no option after that."

"You mean the financial reform legislation?"

Senator Quaid nodded. "That was their price. They wanted the legislation blocked. Too many regulations."

"You couldn't have predicted what would happen."

Senator Quaid stood and looked out the window nervously. Two police cars were parked outside on the street. Just a precaution they'd told him.

"Who would have thought you could crowdfund assassinations?"

Senator Chisholm shrugged. "Some people are saying that it's true democracy."

Senator Quaid shook his head. "If I could do things again, I wouldn't touch the money." He looked at Senator Chisholm. "You believe me, don't you?"

"I believe you, David. But it's not me you need to convince."

Senator Quaid picked up his glass and drained the brandy. He reached for the bottle.

"We've run out of milk," said Simon. "I'll walk down to the corner store and get some."

A morning without coffee wasn't an option.

"Okay," said Sienna. "I'm going to get changed." She walked past him, naked.

His eyes followed her into the bathroom. He decided he could get used to living with another person.

"Come on, Gizmo," said Simon. "Let's go for a walk." Gizmo leapt out of his basket and ran to Simon.

Simon attached Gizmo's lead and opened the front door. He was unprepared for the assault.

Shoulder mounted cameras zeroed in on his stunned expression and bulbous microphones jostled in front of his face. Reporters lobbed questions at him like grenades.

"Simon. Mr Simpson. Why did you do it? Why did you create The App? Are you a murderer? What have you got to say to Jerry Upton's widow?"

Simon stood speechless, like a teenager discovering his naked grandparents in the living room.

Gizmo barked loudly and pulled against his lead. He bit a male reporter on the leg.

Christine Hunter waved at Simon from the back of the scrum. She held up her hands and shrugged. "I tried to warn you," she mouthed. She mimed holding a telephone to the side of her head. "Call me."

"Do you have anything to say?" said the reporter with torn trousers. His microphone had a CNN logo.

"I … I … have to go," said Simon. He pulled Gizmo back inside his house and slammed the door.

Fuck.

"Are you okay?" said Sienna. She stuck her head out of the bathroom. "What was all that noise?"

"Er … you probably don't want to go outside."

CHAPTER NINETEEN

Competition

Dillon Black had reconnoitered the best shooting positions outside Senator Quaid's club. There were two possibilities.

The first position was on the roof of a building. It offered the best angle, but wouldn't allow him to shoot from his van.

The second position was on the third floor of a multi-story carpark. The angle wasn't as good, but his van could still be used as a shooting platform.

He'd opted for the second location.

When Dillon had modified his vehicle, he'd created two firing ports; one at the rear near the licence plate, and another one in the side of the van.

He was glad he'd taken the time to prepare properly.

A magnetic sign covered the side firing port. It said 'Bright Spark Electricians' in large black letters. To a casual observer, it looked like a normal sign.

However, the dot in the first 'i' had been neatly cut away. Dillon looked out through the hole.

The door to the senator's club was painted a glossy black. An American flag hung limply above the steps.

Dillon smiled. No wind.

There were two police cars parked on the street, but he wasn't concerned. They wouldn't hear the suppressed gunshot from that distance.

He went through his escape route in his head. The

carpark's exit was on the other side of the block. Away from the police cars. It was only a short distance from there to the freeway.

Dillon rubbed his eyes as he lay inside his van. He rechecked the adjustments on his rifle that compensated for his downward firing angle.

He centred the crosshairs of his Unertl scope on the black door and consciously relaxed his breathing.

The door opened. Two men walked outside. They were deep in conversation.

Dillon's finger tightened on the trigger.

Wait. Hold.

He relaxed his grip.

Neither man was his target.

A movement flickered in the corner of his eye. It came from the roof of a different building. The other shooting position.

Shit.

Dillon swung his scope towards the roof, searching for a counter-sniper team. His heart rate increased and his breathing became shallow.

Think Dillon. Focus.

The doors of both police cars opened. Uniformed officers jumped out. They looked up and down the street. One of the officers scanned the buildings. Searching. The officer's eyes swept across the carpark. They didn't stop.

The man spoke into his radio. All clear. Dillon's target was on the move.

Dillon quickly inspected the roof of the other building through his scope. The only person visible was an antenna repair man with a Washington Redskins cap. A false alarm.

He swung his scope back to the club's front door and forced himself to breathe deeply. His heartbeat slowed.

A black limousine pulled up next to the kerb. A minute later the front door opened again. A large man in a business suit staggered down the steps.

The man was drunk. He was being supported by a small man with white gloves. A steward.

Dillon exhaled and sighted on the bridge of Senator Quaid's nose. He could see the veins in his face.

Dillon's trigger finger tightened. It was halfway to the required pressure when a red cherry blossomed on the senator's chest. A second later, another cherry appeared.

The senator had been shot. Twice.

But not by Dillon.

He swung his scope back to the roof and was just in time to see the antenna repair man running away. With a rifle.

Mother fucker.

Dillon adjusted his aim and fired, but he missed the repair man. Different angles. The man disappeared into the stairwell.

Damn. He hadn't expected that.

Dillon hurriedly stowed his rifle and slid into the driver's seat of his van. It was time to leave.

After retreating inside his apartment, Simon had done the only thing he could think of in the circumstances.

He called his lawyer.

"You didn't say anything to them, did you?" said Eli.

"My exact words were 'I … I … have to go,'" said Simon.

"Good," said Eli. "Stay inside and I'll be right over."

Thirty minutes later he was knocking on the front

door of the apartment. Simon hid behind the door to let him in. Gizmo growled at the lawyer.

"It's okay, Giz," said Simon.

"Damned reporters," said Eli. "Circling like a pack of vultures."

Sienna appeared from the bedroom. She grinned at Eli. "Some people say the same thing about lawyers. Except the correct term is a 'kettle' of vultures."

Eli looked at Sienna. His gaze slid down to her legs. "Hello to you too. I see you escaped the fire at the warehouse?"

She inclined her head. "Of course."

"Do you have a place to stay?"

She nodded and placed her hand gently on Simon's shoulder. "Yes, thank you."

Eli grinned. "I see."

He turned to Simon. "I think you should lie low for a few days. Don't step outside the apartment." He glanced at Sienna. "Either of you."

"Suits me," said Simon. "But we need to eat."

"I can get one of my secretaries to pick up some groceries. Email me a list."

"Okay. Thanks."

"In the meantime, how's that web-based thing coming along?"

"Almost done," said Simon. "A couple of more days."

"Good," said Eli. "Put your time to good use then." He nodded to the door. "I have a feeling we'll be hearing more from the authorities soon … with all the publicity. Unless you want the money to stop, you should finish your contingency plan."

Sienna reached up and ruffled Simon's hair. "Don't worry," she said. "I'll make sure he finishes the job."

"Um —" said Simon. He was interrupted by his cell phone's familiar beep. Another claim. He checked the message.

"Hmm … that's unusual," he said.

"What is?" said Sienna.

"That was someone claiming a prize for Senator Quaid."

Sienna reached for Simon's phone. "I thought you said that someone had already claimed that prize an hour ago."

Simon nodded. "I did."

"Well, there must be a mistake in your software. The person shouldn't be allowed to make a second claim."

Simon stepped away from Sienna and stared at her. "There are no mistakes in my software."

She pouted. "Well how do you explain the fact that someone claimed the senator twice?"

"I never said the *same* person made two claims. Only that two claims had been made."

"Two *different* people?" said Sienna. "But that's impossible."

"Not impossible. Just highly unlikely."

Simon moved to his computer and sat down. "It's easy to check."

He started the database application and typed in an SQL query. A few seconds later, a long list of text was displayed on the screen.

"What's that?" said Sienna.

"That's a list of every claim that has been made, sorted in reverse time order. The most recent claim is at the top."

He pointed to the topmost item.

"See? The first line shows the claim just made for

Senator Quaid. You can see the ID of the claimant. 134684427."

"What does that prove?"

"The claimant's ID is different to the other database record for Senator Quaid." He pointed at the record from an hour earlier. "See?"

Eli had been listening to the conversation with interest. He stepped up to the computer.

"So if I understand this correctly, you have two winners for the bet on Senator Quaid?"

"It would seem so," said Simon.

"And they'll split the prize money? Just like if two people win the lottery?"

"Yep. That's what the Terms and Conditions say. Except each person's share is dependent on how much they bet. For example, if Person A bets two dollars and Person B bets one dollar, Person A will receive twice as much from the prize pool."

Eli smiled. "Excellent."

"Why?" said Sienna. "What's so good about that?"

"It might help Simon's legal position," said Eli. "If more than one person wins a prize, it suggests there's an element of chance. Just like normal gambling. It will make it harder for anyone to prove conspiracy. How can there be a conspiracy if the winner is random?"

Simon nodded. "Nice."

"What do you mean there were two assassins?" said Special Agent Marks. "The senator can't have been killed twice."

"Sorry, that's not what I meant," said Special Agent Dorner. "I meant to say that there were two *shooters*. But only one of them hit the senator."

Marks sighed. "Okay, but what's so important you had to phone and wake me at 5:30 am?"

"Sorry about that. I forgot about the time difference. It's actually 8:30 am in Washington, DC."

Marks heard Dorner shuffling through some papers.

"Um … the ballistic analysis has been done and it raised a red flag," said Dorner. "The techs found similarities between a bullet from our scene and the bullets from a couple of your cases. Jerry Upton and Cecil Muller."

Marks sat up straight in his bed.

"Sorry? What? You're telling me that my killer from the West Coast also shot Senator Quaid in Washington, DC?"

"Er … not exactly."

Marks rubbed his eyes. "Look, it's early in LA and I'm half asleep. You'll need to spell it out."

Dorner cleared his throat before continuing. "Well … from the evidence collected at the scene, it looks like your killer tried to shoot the guy who shot Senator Quaid."

Marks pulled the phone away from his ear and looked at it. Maybe this was a dream.

"Say what?" said Marks.

"I know. Weird huh?" said Dorner. "Just bear with me." He proceeded to explain what the forensics experts had discovered.

"Jesus," said Marks.

"One more thing," said Dorner. "From the angle of his shot, it looks like *your* shooter was on the third floor of a car park."

"A car park?"

"Yep."

Marks felt his scalp tingle.

Another car park. Just like with Cecil Muller.

They needed to look for the vehicle.

Dillon Black was taking his time driving back to Los Angeles, thinking about Senator Quaid.

He'd spent the previous night in Oklahoma City, and it was there that he'd received the bad news. Two winning claims.

Dillon tightened his grip on the steering wheel and pushed down on the gas. He'd be better prepared next time.

No one would be allowed to interfere.

After Eli had left, Simon had checked the database for other duplicate claims. He didn't find any.

But he did find something else.

He stared at the screen for a full minute.

Sienna interrupted his thoughts. "Are you going to finish off the web-based app now? You'd better do what Eli suggests."

Simon quickly shut the window he was looking at.

"Um … do you think it's important?"

She moved closer and sat down on Simon's lap. She kissed him.

"I think it's very important. If the authorities stop people from downloading The App, it will cripple your business. We don't want to run out of money … not with all those legal bills."

Simon nodded. "At least I won't have to pay Aleksei for your services anymore."

Sienna kissed his neck and traced her hand along his thigh. "Perhaps you could pay me an allowance?"

Simon leaned back and looked Sienna in the eye. "An allowance?"

She smiled. "I can make myself very useful."

Simon nodded his head slowly. "I guess we can think of something for you to do."

Sienna stood up and spun Simon's chair around to face his computer.

"You'd better get to work then. I'll let you know when you can have a break."

Simon worked solidly on the web-based app for two days. He didn't have much choice.

"Can I stop now?" he said.

"Have you finished?" said Sienna.

"Almost. I just need to deploy the WAR file."

Sienna shook her head. "After you've done that."

She was lying on the couch with her feet up, reading a book.

She raised her eyes. "What is a … WAR file anyway? It sounds dangerous."

Simon laughed. "It's a Web Application Archive file. Though I guess you could say that this file *is* dangerous … to people on the list."

"So what does it do?"

"In simple terms? It will let you use a web browser to access The App."

"So people won't need to download a specific app for their phones anymore?"

"Exactly. And the WAR file is deployed on a server in Russia, so the authorities in the US can't touch it."

Simon entered a few commands via the keyboard. "It's done."

Sienna got off the couch and walked over to Simon at

his computer. "Show me."

He held out his hand. "Give me your phone."

She gave it to him. Simon navigated to the web page and saved it as an icon on her home screen.

"There you go." He handed the phone back.

"Is that all?" said Sienna. "How do I log on?"

"The same way you did before. You'll need to re-enter your user ID the first time."

"I can't remember —"

"It's 121657669," said Simon.

Sienna's eyebrows jumped. "How did you remember that?"

Simon shrugged. "I have a good memory."

She entered the number and her password. The App's main screen appeared. "Hey, it looks almost exactly the same."

"That's the idea," said Simon. He pushed his chair back from the desk. "Can I go to the bathroom now?"

Sienna leaned forward and kissed him on the cheek. "Yes, you may."

CHAPTER TWENTY
Let Them Eat Cake

"How was your day?" said Joan. She was in the kitchen baking a cake when Christine arrived home.

"It was terrible, Aunty Joan, but thanks for asking."

"Why, what happened?"

"I spent the entire day waiting outside Simon Simpson's apartment. For nothing. He never came outside, and he's not answering his door or his phone."

"Maybe you should take him some cake? Everyone likes to eat." She patted her large stomach.

Christine shook her head. "I think that he's got his food needs covered. A woman came today with some groceries."

Although …? Christine had just realised the woman hadn't looked like a delivery person.

Christine thought about that and sifted through some ideas. She was about to go upstairs when she noticed a news bulletin on the television.

"Can you turn that up please, Aunty Joan?"

Her aunt adjusted the volume.

A CNN reporter was standing in front of the Capitol building in Washington, DC.

"… as you've just seen, Senator Chisholm has thrown his considerable political weight behind the proposed legislation. If the bill passes, the new laws will tighten the regulations on the finance industry significantly."

The camera switched to the anchorman in the studio.

He managed to smile and look serious at the same time.

"That's quite a turnaround for a man who has been widely regarded as a cheerleader for the banks. Why the sudden change, Kirsty?"

"Good question, John. Although Senator Chisholm didn't mention it, he's obviously traumatised by the death of his close friend, Senator Quaid. Some have suggested that Senator Chisholm wants to avoid the same fate."

John nodded his head. "Interesting. What was the reaction from the financial institutions?"

"They're *not* happy, John. They stand to lose big time if the legislation passes. Their lobbyists are working overtime to try and prevent that from happening."

"Are they likely to succeed?"

"I don't know, John. Before *The App*, I would have bet on the lobbyists every time. But things have changed, and anything seems possible now."

Christine shook her head. Maybe *The App* wasn't totally bad after all.

After eating a slice of cake, Christine went upstairs to work on the idea that was sparked by her aunt's suggestion. She turned on her computer and searched for takeout food places in Simon's neighborhood. There were plenty.

She chose four restaurants before racing downstairs and jumping in her aunt's Suzuki.

Fairview Slopes was a ten minute drive away.

She returned an hour later with four takeaway menus and a prepaid phone.

"Do you mind if I use that printer I bought you, Aunty Joan?"

"Of course not, dear."

Christine grabbed the printer and went upstairs. It was a cheap model, but she hoped it would do the job.

After connecting the printer to her laptop, Christine scanned each of the four menus; Japanese, Indian, Thai and Pizza.

All the major food groups.

Next, she opened a free graphics program that allowed her to manipulate images. She replaced the phone number on the menus with the number from the prepaid cell.

Lastly, Christine printed the modified menus. She inspected them closely and nodded her head. They would do the job.

She hoped no one would notice that the numbers were all the same.

A rustling sound made Simon look up from his position on the couch. Someone had shoved some papers under his front door.

Gizmo ran to investigate.

Simon walked over to where Gizmo was sniffing and picked them up.

"What is it?" said Sienna.

"Some takeout food menus. Japanese, Pizza, Indian and Thai."

"Good, I could use a change from what we've been eating."

Simon frowned. "Don't you like my cooking?"

"Um … it's not that. It's just that a change is good."

Simon stared at her. "You've only been here a few days."

Sienna shrugged. She jumped off the couch and

grabbed the menus. "I love Thai food."

Five minutes later she handed the menus back to Simon. "I've marked the dishes I want with a pen. Can you place the order? I'm going to have a shower. And tell them *not* to make it too spicy."

Simon watched as she disappeared into the bathroom. He shook his head. "Sure.

Christine barely made it back to her aunt's house before the prepaid cell phone rang. She answered it.

"I'd like to order some takeout," said the male voice.

"Hi Simon."

"Wow. How do you know my name? I didn't think I'd ordered from you before."

"It's Christine Hunter, from CBC."

"Er … what? Seriously? Your a journo and you need a second job?"

"You haven't called a restaurant, Simon."

There was a long pause. "Oh," he said eventually. "Sienna's going to be pissed."

"*Sienna*?"

"Yeah. She *really* wanted something from Mai Thai. And now I'll have to tell her I fell for a scam."

"Um … I can place your order for you if you like. To make up for deceiving you."

"Really? That would be great."

"Let me find a pen." She ran and grabbed the Mai Thai menu and a pen.

Simon gave her the order. Six dishes, plus rice. And an appetizer.

"Jesus," said Christine. "How many people are you feeding?"

"Only two. Sienna really likes Thai food."

Christine nodded. "Evidently."

"Can you ask them to make the dishes mild, please? She doesn't like them too spicy. Not like me." There was disappointment in Simon's voice.

Christine's lips curled upward. "I can do that. I'll phone it through in a few minutes." She placed the marked up menu on the table. "Um … aren't you mad at me?"

"No. Not really," he said. "The deception was actually pretty clever. It's what I'd expect from a good journalist." He paused. "I got your message the other day. You wanted to hear my side of the story. I almost called you. Several times."

"What stopped you?"

"My lawyer's advice."

"You mean Eli Rabinovich?"

"Yes. Do you know him?"

"I know *of* him. Did you know he's *also* representing Tom Roberts? *And* the late Aleksei Volkov?"

"Er … no, I didn't."

"I saw something on television tonight," said Christine. "A leopard changing its spots, you might say. It made me rethink what you've done."

"I never said I did anything," said Simon.

Christine bit her bottom lip. "Um … what if we went off the record, Simon?"

"What does that mean?"

"It means I can't use anything you tell me. At least, not without your permission."

"Is that a CBC thing?"

"It's a journalist thing. But at CBC, we honour it."

There was silence for about ten seconds. She waited. Eventually Simon spoke.

"Okay," he said. "But first, tell me about your leopard."

She told him about Senator Chisholm and the bill he was sponsoring. "They're tightening the regulation of the finance industry," she said. "Because of The App. Because of you."

This time Simon didn't deny it.

"I *also* saw something that made me consider The App in a different light," said Simon. "In Zimbabwe. The bodyguard who shot the president must have known it would cost him his own life. But he pulled the trigger anyway. Presumably he sacrificed himself for his family. And his country."

"I'm starting to understand," said Christine. "At least part of it. But I'd like to hear it from you."

"I have to go," said Simon.

"Don't you *want* to tell me your side?"

"It's not that. Sienna has finished her shower. She won't be happy with me talking to you."

Christine clenched her teeth. *Bitch.*

"Okay," she said, squeezing the phone. "But you'll tell me later then?"

"Maybe," said Simon. "Don't forget to order the food."

"I will, but call me. You have my number."

The line went dead.

Shit.

She sat motionless for five seconds then picked up the menu. She dialled the proper number for Mai Thai.

"I'd like to place an order, please. And could you make it *extra* spicy?"

"Certainly," said the man.

Sienna sat down at the dinner table. She was wearing a black kimono.

"I know it's not Thai," she said. "But it's the closest thing I've got to set the mood."

Simon eyed the kimono appreciatively. "You look lovely," he said. He raised his beer in a toast.

Gizmo eyed the food.

Simon had laid out all the food containers in a large circle. On each of their plates was a beautifully symmetrical bed of rice.

"Do you want me to serve you?" Simon asked.

"No, I can manage." She snatched at the largest serving spoon on the table.

Simon watched as she heaped generous amounts of Thai food onto her rice. The result was an overlapping river of sauces. The mixture contrasted sharply with his evenly divided portions.

She dug her spoon into the wet mound then guided it into her mouth.

"Fuck," she said. "This chicken dish is hot."

Sienna threw back her chair and reached across the table for Simon's beer. There were tears in her eyes as she chugged the bottle.

"It shouldn't be hot," said Simon. "I explicitly asked them to make it mild."

Sienna couldn't speak. She fanned her mouth with her hands.

Simon dipped a spoon into the sauce and carefully sipped the edge. "Mmm," he said. "It *is* spicy, isn't it?" He licked the spoon.

CHAPTER TWENTY-ONE

Back to School

Detective Speed drove through the gates of St. Anthony's boarding school for boys. It sat on a large property on the outskirts of Fredericton. The wrought iron gates were painted black and they hung between aging stone pillars. A pockmarked angel stood at the top of one pillar and a devil stood on the other. A warning to students about consequences and choices.

Speed parked his car in a visitor's bay next to some wide stone steps. The steps led to a corridor in the main building that was lined with photos. Each photo was marked with a different year. There were at least fifty of them.

At one end of the corridor the photos were black and white. At the other end they were printed in colour.

An attractive woman sat behind a desk at the coloured end of the corridor. She looked up through dark rimmed glasses as Speed approached.

"I'm here to see the headmaster," he said.

"Have you been naughty?" she said.

Speed reached into his pocket for his credentials. "I'm a police officer."

"I know who you are, Detective." The woman grinned. "I was just having a bit of fun. No need to put me in handcuffs." She looked him up and down. "Unless you want to."

Speed nodded and cracked a smile. "I see."

"The headmaster is expecting you." She indicated a closed door behind her.

Speed thanked her and knocked on it.

"Come in," said a loud voice.

The headmaster's office wasn't what Speed had expected. There were no leather chairs. No heavy wooden desks. No portraits of old men in academic gowns.

Instead, the room was sparsely furnished. The headmaster sat in a modern office chair. A computer with two screens sat on a desk made from glass and steel. Speed's initial impression was of a stockbroker making his trades.

"Have a seat, Detective. Can I get you anything to drink? Coffee?"

"Coffee would be brilliant."

The headmaster made the coffee himself using a machine hidden in the corner. He handed it to Speed.

"What can I help you with, Detective?"

"Some ancient history, actually. A boarding master by the name of Stiles. He was also the school's priest."

The headmaster nodded. "And a paedophile from all reports."

"Yes," said Speed. "That's what I'd heard. He also died last year."

The headmaster winced. "I know. Very unpleasant from all accounts."

Speed nodded.

"Still," said the headmaster. "If anyone deserved to die like that, it was probably Stiles."

"You didn't like him?"

"He left before I started teaching at the school. Mandatory retirement, I've been told."

"So the school knew?"

"It's not something they'll admit to. But I believe they forced him out. To prevent a scandal."

"Your honesty is refreshing."

"I've worked hard to rebuild the school's reputation. We're steadily making progress. If Stiles had been working for me, he would have been properly dealt with."

"Dealt with? You mean like feeding him to a bear?"

"No. I would have personally dragged him to the police."

"I wonder if his former students felt the same way? Would they have turned him in? Or would they have smeared him with honey?"

"I'm afraid I can't answer that one, Detective. It was a long time ago. Most of his students would be in their fifties or sixties now."

"Do you have any photos of Stiles? I saw all those photos on the wall coming in."

"The Reverend Stiles is in many of those. It's a tradition. Every year, the entire school is photographed. He was here for more than twenty years. I'll show you."

They walked outside. The headmaster's secretary winked at Speed. He tried to wink back, but only succeeded in closing both his eyes. She laughed when he bumped into the wall.

Speed rushed to catch up to the headmaster. They walked along the chain of coloured photographs, and into the school's dark past. They stopped near the beginning of the black and white section.

"There he is," said the headmaster. He pointed to a man with dark hair. He looked to be in his late twenties and had big hands, one of which rested on the shoulder of a young boy. Stiles was smiling at the camera. Unlike the boy.

"This photo was taken the first year Stiles was here."

Speed leaned closer, examining the picture. "Would it be possible to get a list of all the students for each year that Stiles was here?"

"Certainly. My secretary, Miss Anderson will be able to help you with that."

"*Miss* Anderson?" said Speed. "Excellent. I appreciate your help."

The headmaster excused himself, leaving Speed to look at the other photos. Speed moved slowly back down the corridor. He noticed that in each successive photo, Stiles had his hand on the shoulder of a different boy. None of the boys were smiling.

Speed stopped in front of one photo. He was drawn to it by a young face. He leaned closer, gently touching the glass. The layer of dust couldn't hide the misery in the boy's eyes.

Speed's thoughts were interrupted by Miss Anderson. She was carrying a stack of paper. "Here's that list of all the students you wanted, Detective. I've written the appropriate year on each page." She smiled. "I've also written my phone number."

It took Speed half an hour to drive from the boarding school to his father's house.

His dad was sitting on the porch carving a wooden figure with a knife. He was wearing faded blue jeans and a checked shirt under a jacket with a woolen collar. He stood when Speed's car pulled into the driveway.

"Did you get lost, boy?"

"Very funny, Dad. Is that a new car?" Speed pointed

to the Ford F350 parked beside the house.

"Yep. Traded in my old one. It was time for a change."

Speed nodded his head. He'd wanted to buy a new car for years, but couldn't afford it.

"So what brings you to Fredericton?" said his father.

"Can't a son come to visit his old man?"

His father raised his eyebrows and remained silent.

Speed chuckled as he lifted his hands up in the air. "Okay, you got me. I'm on a case. But I *did* promise you I'd visit the next time I was in town. So here I am."

"Well, now that you're here, you may as well come inside … and tell me what's important enough to drag you back to your old home town."

They walked up the front steps into the house. It had always seemed emptier to Speed since his mother died.

"Can you stay for dinner?" said his father.

"Sorry. I have a date."

"In Fredericton?"

Speed nodded. "I just met her. A secretary at the school."

Speed winced as his father squeezed his shoulder with one hand.

"Atta boy."

William Childs hadn't heard of The App. It wouldn't have mattered if he had. His actions would have been the same, regardless.

He was carrying a long black bag. Inside, was an AR-15 rifle he'd taken from his father's gun cabinet. In total, he had two hundred and forty rounds of ammunition in four high-capacity magazines. More than enough.

William opened the bag and pulled out his father's gun. He shifted his headphones over his ears and pressed play.

There was a moment of silence, followed by a hiss. And then it began.

Highway to Hell, by AC/DC.

He kicked open the door to the school cafeteria. His boot left a black footprint on the white door.

The first table he chose was full of players from the football team. He started with his chief tormentor, Buck Edwards.

Buck looked up. Initially he didn't notice the gun. His mouth started to form its customary sneer. But it stopped short and formed a wide O-shape instead.

William had never seen that shape on Buck's mouth before. It made a wonderful target.

Boom.

He shifted the rifle to a wide receiver who'd previously stolen his books.

Boom.

A running back.

Boom.

A linebacker dropped his tray and charged towards him. The linebacker was screaming, "I'm going to fucking kill you, Childs."

Boom.

Guess not.

After that, the football players became harder to hit. They were running away.

William moved on to the cheerleaders.

They looked beautiful. Cowering under the table.

Boom.

They didn't move. Another O-shaped mouth.

Boom.

The homecoming queen was missing half her face.

Beautiful.

He turned to the next table. It was full of geeky looking girls. They were screaming.

William spoke calmly to them. "Due to unexpected vacancies, the school will be holding another round of try-outs for the cheer squad. You're encouraged to apply."

After that everything was a blur. His shots became less discriminating.

There was one exception. His science teacher, Miss Lyons, was cowering under a table like a cheerleader. She froze as William approached. "Why?" she screamed.

He shrugged and uttered a single word. "Run."

She did. He let her go.

His physical education teacher wasn't so lucky.

Boom.

William looked around for more targets. There were none. Only dead bodies among the blood and broken glass.

He stared at those he'd killed. They'd learned to respect him. That's all he'd ever wanted.

He sat down on one of the chairs as the strains of Angus Young's guitar faded in his ears.

Police sirens wailed in the distance. He checked his watch.

A reasonable response time, but still too slow.

William rested his chin against the end of the barrel and took a deep breath.

Then he closed his eyes.

Boom.

CHAPTER TWENTY-TWO

Reaction

Journalists are opportunists. And they weren't going to let a good name go to waste.

"Billy the Kid shoots up school cafeteria in Texas," read one headline. There were other similar captions.

William Childs' parents went into hiding. His Uncle Tom was left to talk to the media.

"Billy was a lovely boy," said Tom. "He'd just been bullied one too many times."

Uncle Tom got tetchy when asked a leading question by a reporter.

"*No, Madam*. William's father doesn't think it's wrong to own five assault rifles. He keeps them locked up. It was just that Billy knew where he kept the key."

There were the usual calls from victims' groups to ban assault weapons. These were followed by the usual howls of protest from other groups about Second Amendment rights.

A senator from Kentucky claimed fewer people would have been killed if students had been armed.

The president of the National Right to Bear Arms Association, Bob Cutter, stood on the steps of the Capitol building, a clenched fist held above his head. "I'll give you my gun," he said, "when you pry it from my cold, dead hands."

Preston Shade sat in the leather chair smoking a

Cohiba cigar. He'd taken it from Senator Chisholm's humidor without asking. Smoke wafted across the desk and into Chisholm's face.

"Senator," said Shade, "Who helped you when you needed to fund that television advertising?"

Senator Chisholm shook his head. "You don't understand the position I'm in."

"Perhaps *you* don't understand, Senator. I don't *care* about your position. The group I represent invested a lot of money in you and now they expect a return."

"But there are people who want to kill me," said Chisholm. "They've already killed David Quaid."

Shade flicked ash onto the senator's desk. It smouldered on a lobbyist's report. *The Benefits of Global Warming.*

"Last time I looked," said Shade, "the price on your head was only ten thousand dollars. You're not even in the top one hundred yet. Stop being a baby."

Senator Chisholm brushed the ash into his *Bear Stearns* coffee mug.

"The only reason the bounty is still that low is because I sponsored the Finance Regulation Bill," he said.

Shade slammed his hand on the desk. "A bill that will cripple our business."

"I'd hardly say cripple, Preston. So you'll only make ten billion this year instead of twelve. You'll still be making money."

"That's not the point. We should be making twelve. Our shareholders expect twelve. And that's what our bonuses are tied to."

Senator Chisholm leaned forward. "I won't be much good to you dead."

"You're not much good to us now." Shade stood. He

stubbed out his cigar on the senator's desk. "Don't fuck with us, Chisholm. You'll regret it."

He turned and strode out of the office.

Senator Chisholm shook his head. Asshole.

The intercom on his desk buzzed. It was his secretary.

"Bob Cutter, the president of the National Right to Bear Arms Association is waiting to see you."

Brilliant. Just what he needed. Another lobbyist.

He picked up the file marked *Federal Assault Weapons Ban* from his desk and stuffed it in a drawer.

"Send him in, Carol."

Ten seconds later, the door opened and Bob Cutter strode into the room. He was wearing his ten-gallon hat.

"Afternoon, Senator."

"What's up, Bob?"

Cutter laughed and shook his head. "Now, ain't that interesting?"

"What's interesting?"

"Well, normally you say, 'What can I do for you, Bob?'" He pointed a finger at Chisholm then tapped the side of his nose. "But just then you asked, 'What's up, Bob?' Do you see the difference?"

Chisholm shrugged. "Not really."

Cutter sat down in the chair that Preston Shade had just vacated. He put his boots up on the desk. They were pointy and made of snake skin. Senator Chisholm stared at them.

"Rattlers," said Cutter. "Killed the little bastards myself."

Chisholm remained silent.

"Anyway, your question implied that I might have a problem. Do I have a problem, Senator?"

"I don't know. You tell me."

Cutter removed his hat and twirled it in his hands. "I've been hearing rumours, Senator. Rumours that you might be sponsoring another bill. A bill entitled *Federal Assault Weapons Ban*."

Chisholm continued his silence. His eyes were fixed on the hat in Cutter's hands. Twirling.

"Please tell me it isn't so?" said Cutter. He raised his hand up high in the air then brought it crashing down against the desk. The photo of Chisholm's wife jumped. "Please tell me we didn't pay you all that fucking money so you could sponsor a bill to ban assault weapons?" Spit flew from his mouth and landed in droplets on Senator Chisholm's face.

Senator Chisholm cleared his throat. "Er ... there's been a huge community backlash against the AR-15 and other military style rifles."

"So? There's *always* a bunch of moaning after a mass shooting. That's what we pay you for, numbnuts. To wear earplugs."

"It's not just that. There's also the list to consider."

"The list?"

"In The App."

Cutter burst out laughing. "You're afraid of a computer game?"

"It's not a game. It's deadly serious. And *my* name's on the list."

"You spineless jellyfish. What kind of a man are you? Scared of a little attention from some computer geeks?"

"Your name is on there too."

"I know," said Cutter. "But you know what the difference between you and me is?" He stabbed his finger at Senator Chisholm. "*You* want to get off the list. But not me. I want to see how high I can go. Just like the

Good Ol' Days. If someone's putting a bounty on *my* head, I want it to be a big one."

Cutter dragged his feet off the desk and dropped them onto the floor. He returned his hat to his head and stood.

"You make me sick, Senator. You're pathetic."

He walked out and slammed the door. A picture of the President fell off the wall and smashed.

Senator Chisolm closed his eyes and massaged his temples.

Pathetic maybe. But still alive.

Preston Shade flew straight back to New York after his meeting with Senator Chisholm. He used the phone in his private jet to schedule a meeting of The Committee.

The Committee was a select group of influential bankers and financiers. They shared common interests. Interests they defended vigorously.

Through its members, The Committee had access to significant resources, which in turn provided them with enormous power. Power to influence. Power to promote. Power to destroy.

Shade rode in his limousine from the airport to his office. He caught the elevator to the top floor. His personal assistant, James, was waiting for him when he arrived.

"Everything is ready for you, sir," said James.

Shade headed straight into his private boardroom.

Unlike normal boardrooms, this one only had a single chair. Behind the chair stood an aquarium containing Shade's prized collection of *Pygocentrus nattereri*.

He preferred their common name. Red-bellied piranha.

Shade sat in the chair. In front of him was a round

table. The table was divided into ten segments. Shade's chair occupied one of the segments.

He touched a button on the control panel in front of him. Lights flashed in each of the remaining segments. One after another, holographic images appeared around the table. Six men and a woman. They all had silver hair and unnatural tans.

The men wore dark suits with ties in varying shades of blue. The woman wore a grey pants suit.

The holograms looked around the table. Two of its segments remained empty.

One space was for the late Dick Gelderman. The other was for the president of a bank that had recently gone bust.

Both men were casualties of war. But no one had shed a tear. Tears were for the weak.

The piranhas circled in their tank behind Shade. He drank a mouthful of water and cleared his throat.

"As you know, I met with Senator Chisholm earlier today in Washington, DC. I expressed The Committee's position strongly. Unfortunately, I'm not convinced that he'll honour his obligations." Shade paused. "Chisholm is evidently more scared of this cell phone application than he is of us."

"What do you propose?" said the man to Shade's immediate left. Position number two.

"Obviously, we will cease to fund him. And we'll plant stories about him in the press to discredit him."

"Do you think that will be sufficient?" said the woman.

"If that doesn't work, we'll use our man to frame him. An affair with an intern, or possibly a school girl. No one will take his bill seriously after that."

"What about increasing our funding to some other senators?" said the man in position number six. "Get them to actively fight the bill in the meantime."

"Who did you have in mind?" said Shade.

"I was thinking of that senator who has been helping the gun lobby. The one who said our schools would be safer if all the students had guns."

Several of the holographic figures laughed.

"I think you're referring to Senator Nash," said Shade. "A perfect candidate. I'll make the arrangements." He looked around the table. "Any other suggestions?"

Two more names were put forward. Then the meeting was adjourned.

One by one, the holographic images flickered and disappeared. Shade rose from his seat and walked to the aquarium. He reached into the container next to it and pulled out two large goldfish. He enjoyed the sensation as they wriggled and squirmed in his hands. He slowly opened his palms and turned them over. They made a plopping sound as they hit the water.

The piranhas launched themselves upward from the bottom of the tank.

Detective Kelly was sitting with his feet on the desk and his phone pressed against his ear. He waited until Special Agent Marks had finished speaking.

"It's weird," said Kelly. "Why would *your* shooter travel all the way to Washington, DC, only to try and save Senator Quaid?" He rolled his autographed Canucks' puck backwards and forwards along the desk.

"It mightn't be as weird as it seems," said Marks. "How's this for a theory? What if *both* shooters were trying to kill the senator? Except they didn't know about each other until one of them took a shot."

Kelly stopped rolling the puck. He put his feet back on the floor.

"You mean your guy was trying to take out the competition?"

"Exactly."

Shit.

"You know what this means?" said Kelly.

"It means this is just the beginning. Pretty soon we're going to have people queuing up to kill anyone near the top of that list."

Kelly stood and carried his phone to the window.

Down on the street, ordinary people were going about their daily routines. Shopping. Jogging.

Killing people for money?

He shuddered at the thought.

"We have to bring this guy down," said Kelly. "Him and his computer program."

"Agreed," said Marks. "But how?"

"We need a search warrant for his computer. But to get that requires evidence linking him to The App."

"I'll talk to the State Department and see if they can put some pressure on our Russian friends to hand over Simpson's corporate documents."

"While we wait, can we do something to slow things down?" said Kelly. "Like stopping people from downloading The App? The platform vendors *are* US based."

There was a long pause. Finally Marks responded. "It might be possible with pressure from Washington. The senators are suddenly taking an interest ... now one of their own has died."

Kelly snorted. "Never bet against a horse called Self-

Interest."

"Don't worry about Tom Roberts," said Eli. He was sitting at a table on Granville Island, overlooking the water. His Bluetooth headset allowed him to tackle his plate of ribs while talking to Simon on the phone.

"But he's been arrested," said Simon.

"He's only been charged with assaulting a police officer. And he's out on bail."

"But they suspect he killed Gelderman. And they know I lost my job because of that bastard. They'll try and connect the two."

Eli wiped his mouth on his napkin and took a sip of his wine.

"Relax, Simon. I'm on top of the Roberts' situation. I'm more worried about what they'll find if they search your computer."

"Do you think they will?"

"It's the next logical step. Should I be worried about what they'll find?"

"None of the *data* is stored locally. That's all kept on the servers in Russia."

"Good," said Eli. He attacked another rib.

"All they'll find on my computer is the source code for The App."

"Hmm. Tell me about that. I need to understand exactly how it works."

Simon's explanation lasted forty-five minutes. By the end of it, Eli had several pages of notes that were covered in barbecue sauce.

He also had a plan.

"The Russians sent us some documents," said Special

Agent Marks. "Linking Simon Simpson to The App. It should be enough for a search warrant."

"That was quick," said Kelly.

"A little motivation goes a long way. And our political masters are more than a little motivated when it comes to The App."

Kelly gave a clipped laugh. "It seems a pity to shut it down in a way."

"I know what you mean," said Marks.

Simon's phone beeped. He recognised the tone.

Sienna's head popped up from its prone position on the couch. "Is that another claim?"

Simon shook his head. "It's to remind me to do something."

"What?" she said.

"It's nothing important."

Sienna sat up. Her eyes narrowed. "We shouldn't have any secrets, Simon."

"It's not a secret."

"Well, what is it then?"

He shifted uncomfortably on his feet. "It's embarrassing."

Sienna leaned forward. "Tell me. I promise not to laugh."

He sighed. "Okay. It's something my over-protective mother makes me do."

"Your mother?"

"She's a nurse at a private blood clinic. And she makes me store my own blood."

Sienna laughed. "Seriously?"

"You promised not to laugh."

"I'm sorry. It just sounds a bit weird."

"It's not *that* weird. It's called an autologous blood donation. Some people do it before surgery. Others do it in case of an accident."

"An accident?"

"Yeah. Especially if they have a rare blood type."

"*You* have a rare blood type?"

He nodded. "O-negative. I can only receive blood from others with the same type … which is about seven percent of the population."

"Interesting. And that alarm beeping was to remind you to give blood?"

"Yes." He picked up the phone and dialed his mother to make an appointment.

Sienna flopped back down on the couch and stared at the ceiling. "You learn something every day."

CHAPTER TWENTY-THREE

Balls

Bob Cutter flew back to Dallas a few hours after his meeting in Washington, DC.

He drove himself home from the airport in the four-wheel drive he'd left in the short-term lot. He wasn't going to pay some *foreign* cabbie to do a job that he could do himself.

He arrived at his ranch an hour later. He drove through the iron gates and up the long driveway that was lined with neatly painted wooden fences. Horses grazed in the paddocks behind each fence.

The driveway ended in an apron in front of the house. There were several vehicles parked there. Cutter didn't recognise the black Chevy Suburbans. They were big, imposing vehicles.

His eldest son, Richard, greeted him as he stepped out of the car.

"Who owns the two Suburbans?" said Cutter.

Richard looked anxiously past Cutter towards the main gate. "Not out here. Come inside and I'll tell you." He turned quickly and hurried back into the house.

Cutter frowned, but followed his son inside.

There were four men sitting in the kitchen. All of them were armed.

"Does somebody want to explain to me what's going on?" said Cutter.

Richard introduced the four men. "These guys are

here to protect you."

"To protect me? From what?"

"Your office has received a lot of death threats recently. Mostly directed at you. Someone even shot up our mailbox last night."

"So what?" said Cutter. "It's not the first time some commie bastard has done that."

Richard shook his head. "There's also the list."

"The list?"

"The App."

"Goddamit, Son. Not you too? I had enough of that crap in Washington."

"You need to take this seriously, Dad. The bounty on your head increased fivefold since you left. It took off right after you made that speech outside the Senate."

"What are you talking about? People loved that speech. The office told me donations increased by fifty thousand as a direct result."

"That's true. But so did the bets on your life."

"Seriously?"

Richard nodded.

Cutter laughed then he clapped his son on the back. "Shoot. Maybe we should get some posters made. Wanted - Dead or Alive."

"It's not a joke, Dad. And they only want you dead."

Cutter gestured to the armed men. "Who's paying for all this protection?"

The man who'd been introduced as Dan stood up. "Excuse me, Mr Cutter. But we're doing it for free. It's our way of saying thanks. For protecting our rights."

"You're NRBAA members?"

"Yes, sir."

"Done security before?"

"Yes, sir. We've done asset protection in Iraq."

Cutter nodded his head. "In that case, I guess it would be rude of me to say no. Many thanks, gentlemen." He held out his hand and they shook.

Two of the men went outside to take first shift.

Cutter turned and headed towards the stairs. "If you'll excuse me gentlemen, I've got a speech to prepare for tomorrow."

Simon was on the toilet when he heard the knock at the front door.

"Police. Open up, Simon."

Shit.

He hurriedly finished what he was doing and pulled up his jeans.

Sienna was waiting for him when he opened the toilet door. "Say nothing," she said. "And don't worry. Eli has a backup of your computer, remember?"

Simon nodded. He wiped his hands on his shirt and stooped to pick up Gizmo, who was barking loudly. Simon opened the front door.

Detective Peters stood in the doorway with a piece of paper. "Search warrant," she said.

Gizmo growled at her from the safety of Simon's arms.

Simon took the warrant. He glanced at it and passed it to Sienna. She studied it closely.

"It looks in order," she said. "But you should call Eli."

"You can do that in a minute," said Peters. "But first you need to let us in."

Simon opened the door wider.

A team of six police officers entered the apartment. They were wearing gloves and carrying an assortment of bags.

Gizmo snarled at the strangers. Detective Peters bared her teeth at the dog.

"Where's your partner?" said Sienna.

"Detective Kelly sends his apologies," said Peters. "But he's got more important business to attend to. He's having a little chat with your friend, Tom Roberts."

Simon's head shot up at the mention of Tom Roberts' name.

"I thought you'd find that interesting," said Peters.

Sienna placed a hand on Simon's shoulder. "Ignore her, Simon. She's full of shit."

Simon picked up his new phone. His old one had been erased and dumped on Eli's advice.

He called his lawyer.

"Are you with Tom Roberts at the moment?" said Simon.

"No. Why?" said Eli.

Simon explained about the visit from Detective Peters.

"Interesting," said Eli. "But not unexpected. Just do everything like we discussed."

Simon turned off his phone and was about to put it back in his pocket when Detective Peters grabbed it.

"That's covered by the search warrant," she said. She placed it in an evidence bag.

The police completed their search in just under an hour. They left with several bags of irrelevant paperwork and some brand new USB sticks that Simon had purchased for the occasion. He hoped the forensics experts would enjoy them. It had taken him several hours to download their contents.

The only thing Simon actually cared about was the loss of his computer. But it was only a temporary loss.

Eli arrived an hour later with a new machine. It was faster than his old one.

Simon re-installed the software on his computer in less time than it took for the police to conduct their search. Then he opened a beer.

Eli Rabinovich was waiting for Tom Roberts outside his apartment. "What did the police have to say to you, Tom?"

"What?" said Roberts.

"The police. What did they have to say?"

"What makes you think I was talking to the police?" Roberts' eyes darted up and to the right.

"Tom. Tom. Tom. You can't keep any secrets from me. You should know that by now."

Roberts folded his arms. "Um … they told me not to tell you."

Eli laughed. "They're not allowed to talk to you without your lawyer."

Roberts shook his head. "They said it was okay. There was a lawyer from the Ministry of Justice with them. She agreed."

Eli's gaze narrowed. "Really? Now that *is* interesting."

"She said that you might have a conflict of interest. Because of someone else you were representing."

"And let me guess," said Eli. "They wanted to offer you a deal? Your testimony against Simon Simpson for a reduced sentence?"

"Something like that. Supposedly I can help their case … by linking Simpson to Gelderman's murder."

It was Eli's turn to shake his head. "Please tell me you didn't fall for that one, Tom? Please tell me that you didn't accept their deal?"

"They gave me some time to think about it."

"How long did they give you, Tom? To make a decision that will affect the rest of your life?"

"They gave me forty-eight hours."

Eli sighed. "Well, for your sake, Tom, I hope you make the right decision. Because I guarantee you, things will work out better for you if you refuse their offer." He patted Roberts on the cheek. "I'll be in touch."

"You look stressed," said Sienna.

"I'm worried about Tom Roberts," said Simon.

"Is that all?"

"I'm also worried about the workload. The number of claims have increased dramatically and I don't have time to check them all. Plus, the claim notifications no longer come to my phone."

"Eli said it was risky to have that information stored on your phone. Or anywhere in Canada for that matter."

"I know. But it means the only way I can stay up to date is by logging on to the server in Russia."

Sienna moved closer and started massaging his neck and shoulders.

"That feels good," said Simon.

Sienna smiled. "I can do something else to help you if you like?"

"Thanks, but I'm not in the mood."

She laughed. "That's not what I meant. I meant that I can take on some of your workload if you want me to."

"Really?"

She stopped rubbing his shoulders. "Yes. You said you'd find something useful for me to do ... to justify my allowance."

"What did you have in mind?"

"Why don't you let me take care of confirming all the bets, and making the payments? That way you can just concentrate on making sure the software runs properly."

"That's a lot of work for you to take on."

Sienna grinned. "Don't worry. I can handle it. I'm not *just* a pretty face."

"Hm."

She resumed massaging his neck. "Another thing. Have you given any thought to an escape plan?"

"An escape plan?"

"Just as a precaution."

"Um … no. Why?"

"Well, if they charge you, they'll probably take your passport. Possibly mine as well."

"I hadn't thought of that," said Simon. "But what can we do?"

Sienna stopping massaging and moved so she was facing Simon. "I might know someone who can help."

"Really? How?"

"He can get us fake passports."

Simon arched his eyebrows. "You're full of surprises."

"So, what do you think?"

Simon paused then nodded. "Okay. Organise them. Just in case."

Sienna kissed him on the cheek and reached for her phone.

"One more thing," said Simon.

She paused with her finger on the keypad. "What?"

Simon looked down and shifted uncomfortably in his chair. He wiped his sweaty hands on his jeans.

"What is it, Simon?"

He cleared his throat, but it wasn't enough to stop the hoarseness in his voice.

"Um ... my mother wants to meet you."

Bob Cutter didn't care about being on the list. He had the right to bear arms, and by God he was going to.

There was an AR-15 rifle in the back of his four-wheel drive and a Desert Eagle .50 calibre in the driver's door.

And if that wasn't enough, there was an arsenal of weapons packed into the two Chevy Suburbans being driven by his bodyguards.

If anyone tried to claim the bounty on *his* head they'd be in for a surprise.

Cutter drove along the freeway. One of the Chevy Suburbans had taken up a position in front of him and the other immediately behind. Dan had given him a briefing on what they would do in the event of an attack.

In order to mitigate the risk of an ambush, Dan had insisted Cutter vary his route to work each day.

Today they were taking the new section of the freeway that had been open for a couple of weeks. It would cut ten minutes off the original trip.

He turned up the volume on the stereo that was part of the Internet-enabled entertainment system in his car. The voice of Bruce Springsteen, singing *Born in the USA,* reverberated throughout the car.

Cutter smiled. Bring it on, you bunch of left leaning fairies ... if you've got the balls.

Dwayne Rimmer had the balls.

Just.

He was fifteen years old.

Dwayne was sitting on his couch, fifty miles away. There was a half-eaten pizza in front of him and a laptop on his knee.

"Would you like a glass of Coke, Dwayne," said his mother from the kitchen.

"No, Mom. I'm good."

Dwayne enjoyed watching cooking shows and playing sudoku. And he knew a *lot* about computers.

He was also a student at the school made famous by William Childs.

In the aftermath of the shootings, Dwayne had reflected on how many of his friends might still be alive if William hadn't had access to an assault rifle.

While researching gun laws and associated lobby groups, Dwayne had learned about the NRBAA and Bob Cutter. He didn't agree with Cutter's views.

But he *did* agree with the thousands of people who'd bet money on Cutter's premature death. He'd even placed a bet himself.

It was pure chance that led to Dwayne's discovery about Cutter's car. He'd seen him being interviewed on television. A reporter had thrust her microphone through the driver's side window of the vehicle. A popular model four-wheel drive.

He remembered watching the webcast of a hacker's conference in Las Vegas. A couple of researchers had explained how to exploit a vulnerability in the vehicle's Internet-enabled entertainment system. Essentially, they proved it was possible to remotely take control of the four-wheel drive using a computer.

From that point on, it was relatively simple for someone with Dwayne's skills.

He hacked into the telecommunications provider to discover the IP address of the system in Cutter's car. Next he downloaded the specifications and source code for the system. Then he made the appropriate modifications and uploaded the software to Cutter's vehicle.

Dwayne's software modifications not only gave him the ability to control the vehicle, they also provided access to the GPS coordinates of Cutter's car.

The car's position was displayed on Dwayne's computer. It had just moved onto the new section of the freeway.

Time to go to work.

The first thing Cutter noticed was the change in music. The voice of Springsteen gave way to the orchestral strains of Wagner's *Ride of the Valkyries*. Not that Cutter was a Wagner fan. He only recognised it as the music from his favourite scene in *Apocalypse Now*.

The next thing Cutter noticed was Dwayne's voice.

"Hi, Bob."

"Who said that?"

"I'm you're new driver."

"Um … you mean that new driver-assist service the salesman talked me into buying?"

"I suppose you could call it driver-assist."

"What can I do for you?" said Cutter.

"You're the guy from that gun group, aren't you? The NRBAA?"

"Sure am."

"What's your favourite weapon, Bob?"

"Let's see … for personal protection it's hard to go past a Desert Eagle .50 caliber. Lots of power and made in the USA. A fine weapon. How about you, partner?"

"I'd have to say the Toshiba Ultrabook," said Dwayne. "Very light weight. Easy to carry. Available in gunmetal grey."

"Haven't heard of that one," said Cutter. "Sounds

foreign."

"It is, Bob. Comes from Japan. But I'll bet you it's more effective than your Desert Eagle."

Cutter snorted. "I doubt that."

Dwayne was watching the car's position on the map. It was approaching the end of the new freeway section. Beyond that, the next stage of the construction was already underway.

"How much are you willing to wager, son?" said Cutter. "My Desert Eagle against your Toshibaba Ultracrap?".

"I'm willing to bet it all, Bob. I'm willing to bet your life."

"What?" said Cutter. He was approaching the signs saying 'End of Freeway.' The Suburban in front of him took the exit. He flicked on his indicator and tried to turn the wheel. Nothing happened. "What the hell?"

He lifted his foot off the gas, but rather than slowing down, his car accelerated. The music volume increased.

Behind him, the other Suburban started honking its horn.

"Jesus," said Cutter. "What the hell's happening?"

"I've taken control of your car," said Dwayne. "With my Toshiba Ultrabook." Dwayne looked at the readouts on his computer. Cutter's car was already doing eighty five.

Dwayne watched via the front parking camera as the car ploughed through the barricades protecting the construction zone. Orange and white plastic crunched into the camera.

"Fuck," said Cutter. "Slow down." He could see the end of the blacktop two hundred yards ahead. After that, there was nothing. Nothing but air.

"I should also let you know that I've disabled the Airbag Control Unit," said Dwayne.

"Shit," said Cutter. He stamped his foot repeatedly on the brake. Nothing happened.

The car roared towards the chasm, its engine racing as the wheels left the road. Then it pitched forward and nose-dived gracefully, like a diver into an empty pool.

On Dwayne's computer, the image from the front parking camera went black.

A hundred yards behind Cutter's car, a perplexed Dillon Black exited the freeway. His mission aborted in the planning stage.

CHAPTER TWENTY-FOUR

Facts

Simon was sitting next to Eli Rabinovich in the interrogation room at police headquarters. They'd been waiting for fifteen minutes.

"Relax," said Eli. "It's just a ploy they use. Making you wait. Try and think about something you enjoy."

Simon wiped his hands on his shirt. "Okay, I'll try," he said.

He closed his eyes. An image of a spicy Thai chicken dish gradually formed. His stomach rumbled as he imagined its flavour.

His daydream was interrupted by three people entering the room. Simon recognised Detective Kelly and Detective Peters. He didn't recognise the third person. A tall man in a dark blue suit. He didn't look like a cop. More like a businessman or a lawyer.

"This is Special Agent Marks," said Detective Kelly. "From the FBI. He's going to sit in on the interview."

FBI. What the fuck?

"The FBI has no jurisdiction here," said Eli.

"We're aware of that," said Kelly. "But Simon's computer program has implications for some cases that Special Agent Marks is working on."

"Implications?" said Simon.

"For some murders," said Kelly. "Or perhaps assassinations is a better word." Kelly looked at Special Agent Marks. "They still have the death penalty down in the States, don't they?"

Marks nodded. "They certainly do."

Simon swallowed and looked at his lawyer.

Eli shook his head. "They're bluffing, Simon. Canada doesn't extradite in death penalty cases." He turned to Detective Kelly. "Now, if you've finished trying to scare my client, do you have anything else?"

"Relax, Mr Rabinovich. We're not trying to frighten your client." He looked at Detective Peters, who was leaning against the wall. He gave her a nod.

"That was some interesting information the techs found on your USB drives," she said.

A lopsided smile hoisted itself in the corner of Simon's mouth. "I thought they might find it useful," he said.

He'd downloaded hundreds of pages of documentation outlining the best methods for sanitising a computer's hard drive. This included deleting all files, overwriting the entire hard drive with zeros, and subjecting the hard drive to an intense magnetic field. Simon had used all these methods to sanitise his hard drive before re-installing the bare bones software for The App.

"The techs said they couldn't find anything on your hard drive, except for some code for The App. Why would you go to the trouble of completely erasing your hard drive, only to re-install some of the code?"

"I wasn't sure about your policy on pirated movies," said Simon. "I just wanted to make sure there weren't any still there … from my university days."

"Bullshit," said Peters. "You thought you were being clever. But the fact is we still have the code and the ownership papers linking you to The App."

"So what's your point?" said Eli. "Last time I checked

it wasn't illegal to write computer applications for cell phones. Or to own a company?"

"What's my point?" said Peters. "My point is that we can prove Simon created an app to kill people. He's part of a conspiracy."

Eli snorted. "Detective, I don't know what crime thrillers you've been reading. But I think you should stick to the facts."

Detective Peters pushed herself off the wall and walked over to stand in front of Eli. She leaned on the table causing it to creak. "I think we have all the facts that we need to put your client away." She turned to Simon. "For a very long time."

Eli shook his head. "Really? Perhaps we should go through them, shall we?"

He opened the folder in front of him. A neat list was written on a piece of A4 paper. Eli adjusted the folder so it was square with the table and his ballpoint pen.

"Fact 1. Simon owns a company which developed a cell phone application called The App.

"Fact 2. The App is a betting application that allows people to wager on anything they choose.

"Fact 3. The users of The App are responsible for defining the wager. Simon has no part whatsoever in specifying the wager. If someone chooses to bet on the name of a movie star's next adopted child, that is completely up to them. As is the case if some people choose to bet on how or when someone might die.

"Fact 4. Simon has no foreknowledge about any of the specific details of the wager. If someone bets that Angelina's next adopted child will be named Lucky, he has no knowledge of this before the adoption occurs. Similarly, if someone bets that Joe Bloggs will die on

January the first from a heart attack, Simon has no knowledge about this before Joe Bloggs dies. He only finds out after the event occurs, when someone claims a prize. Only then is he given the key to unlock the encrypted information in the database.

"Does that clear things up, Detective?" said Eli.

Peters glared at Eli and then at Simon. Muscles rippled on her face as she clenched her jaw.

Kelly leaned forward and touched Peters on the arm. He gave a small shake of his head before turning to face Eli.

"Our techs aren't stupid," he said. "They've been poring over Simon's code. If what you say is true, why did they find some code that prints out the details of a wager when it's first made? Surely if it's encrypted, the displayed text would just be gobbledygook?"

Simon had been waiting for that question. "That's only for testing purposes," he said. "The unencrypted print feature is disabled in the production system."

"What if someone re-enabled that feature?" said Kelly. "Wouldn't they be able to read the bets then?"

Simon shook his head. "It doesn't work that way. Even if someone *did* re-enable it — and I don't know why they'd bother — it *still* wouldn't work. The way things are set up, you'd need to know the user's ID *before they place the bet*. And you don't. It's only possible during testing, when a special user account is created. That account has a *known* user ID."

"So you're saying it's impossible?" said Kelly.

"In the production system, there's no chance of reading the details of a bet. I doubt even the NSA could crack the encryption."

"That sounds like a bunch of gobbledygook to me,"

said Peters.

"I don't expect you to understand it," said Simon. "But your techs will confirm what I'm saying."

Detective Kelly turned to Special Agent Marks. "Are you buying this?"

Marks shrugged. "I'll have our FBI techs analyse the code as well. They'll know if he's telling the truth."

Kelly nodded.

Eli closed his folder and placed his pen back in his suit pocket. "If there's nothing else, Detectives, we'll be on our way." He pushed his chair back and started to stand.

"Actually," said Kelly. "There is one more thing."

"What, Detective?"

"My colleague, Special Agent Marks, has some news to share with you. I think you'll find it interesting."

Marks inclined his head towards Kelly. "Thank you, Detective Kelly." He turned to face Simon. "The US government has formally requested that the platform vendors in the United States, who currently distribute your application, should cease doing so." He waited several seconds before continuing. "The platform vendors have agreed to this request. As of today, no one can download your application."

Simon turned to Eli and shrugged.

Eli nodded. "Thanks for keeping us informed about the status of your … um … investigation." He stood and placed his hand on Simon's shoulder. "Come on, Simon. We're leaving."

As they walked down the corridor towards the exit, Eli turned to Simon, chuckling. "I thought that went rather well."

"Hm, that didn't go like we'd hoped," said Detective

Kelly.

"He certainly threw us a few curve balls," said Special Agent Marks.

"He's an asshole," said Peters.

"Who?" said Kelly. "The lawyer or Simpson?"

"Both."

"Simpson didn't take the news about The App being blacklisted as badly as I'd expected," said Marks. "It's something that will seriously hurt his company. Yet he hardly batted an eye."

Kelly nodded. "I feel like we're playing a game of chess and we're two moves behind."

"I'll get our techs to pick apart his code," said Marks. "If there's anything incriminating, they'll find it."

"And we'll have another chat to Tom Roberts," said Kelly. "I think his testimony just became more important."

"I'm going to take the deal," said Tom Roberts.

"Are you sure you want to do that?" said Eli. He was clipping his nails while talking on the phone.

"I've made up my mind."

"Don't say I didn't warn you, Tom. The Crown Prosecutor isn't someone you should trust. She's not looking out for your best interests. Not like me." Eli held up his hand to inspect his work with the clippers. "When are you giving your deposition?"

"Next Monday. The prosecutor wants to get it done as soon as possible."

"I bet she does," said Eli. "In that case I won't take up any more of your time. It sounds like you've already made your decision. Goodbye, Tom."

They hung up and Eli picked up his nail file. He

smoothed off a troublesome burr. Satisfied, he picked up the phone and dialled the number of an old friend.

"I have a little job for you, Yuri. I'll meet you in an hour at the usual place."

CHAPTER TWENTY-FIVE

Invitation

Christine Hunter was contemplating how to tell her boss about the lack of progress, when her prepaid cell phone rang.

She threw herself across the bed and grabbed it from the bedside table.

"Hello. Simon. Is that you?"

"I'd like to complain about an order I made the other day," he said. "I asked for it to be mild, but it turned out to be extra spicy."

"Ahh. A little too hot?"

Simon made a low, throaty noise, somewhere between a cough and a laugh. "Not for me. But someone else had a few things to say ... once her voice returned, that is."

"Whoops," said Christine. She gave a small fist pump before composing herself. "But what are you really calling for? I assume it's not to complain about the food."

"Have you got time for a meeting with me and my lawyer?"

"Definitely. When and where?"

"My apartment. One hour."

"I'll see you then."

She hung up and raced to get changed. The call to her boss could wait.

Christine parked her car out the front of Simon's

apartment. A few journalists were still staking out the apartment from the grassy verge.

A couple of them waved to her. She waved back but kept walking.

"Hey, where are you going?" said one woman. Christine ignored her and knocked on the door.

"You're wasting your time," said another.

The front door opened. Simon's arm reached out and grabbed her hand. "Glad you could make it, Miss Hunter. Please come inside." He pulled her through the gap.

There was a chorus of unanswered questions from the journalists outside, followed by a stream of complaints. Their voices were blocked out by the closing door.

Simon led Christine into the living room and introduced his lawyer. She shook Eli's hand.

"And this is Sienna," said Simon. "You've spoken briefly on the phone."

Christine gave her a smile. Bitch.

Gizmo trotted up to Christine and stood on his hind legs. He leaned against her with his front paws. Christine squatted down and rubbed him behind the ears. "Who's this cute fellow?"

"That's Gizmo," said Simon. "He seems to like you."

"He can probably smell my Aunt Mabel's dog, Maisie."

Christine scratched Gizmo under his chin before standing again.

Eli stepped forward and took Christine's arm. He led her to one side. "Before we start, Miss Hunter, I'd just like to make it clear that everything Simon says here today is off the record. Unless we say, specifically, that you can report it."

"That's not usually how we operate," said Christine.

"Maybe not," said Eli. "But you need to understand the delicate situation Mr Simpson finds himself in. The police want to charge him with conspiracy to murder. We've even had the FBI threatening to extradite him so he can face the death penalty down in the US."

"Can I report that?" said Christine.

Eli nodded. "Yes, we're happy for you to report on the bullying tactics of the authorities."

"I'd really like to be able to report on everything that's said today."

"Sorry, Miss Hunter. Those are the conditions. I'm sure one of your colleagues outside would be more than willing to trade places."

"Hmm. I guess I can agree to those terms."

"Excellent. In that case, please have a seat."

She sat down at the dining room table. Simon sat directly across from her and Eli sat next to him. Sienna remained standing.

"So why did you ask me here?" said Christine.

"We wanted to give you the opportunity to have an informal interview with Simon. I understand you've gone to some extraordinary lengths to try and tell his side of the story."

Christine nodded. "Was that the only reason? You obviously want something from me."

Eli laughed. "I like you Miss Hunter. You don't beat around the bush."

She remained silent.

"And you're economical with words." He paused. "Of course, you're correct. We do want something else. We want people to hear about the tactics being used by the authorities."

"You've told me about the allegations and threats. What else have they done?"

Simon answered before Eli could respond. "The US government have pressured the platform vendors to stop distributing The App," he said.

Christine's eyebrows pinched together. "They what?"

Simon nodded. "The US politicians are running scared, and they've leaned on the vendors to make them pull The App from their online stores."

"Interesting. That effectively kills the growth of your app. And they haven't even charged you."

"You can report that," said Eli.

"But it won't work," said Simon.

"Why not?" said Christine.

"Because I've created a web-based version."

"A what?"

Simon grinned. He patiently explained what a web-based version of The App was. Then he demonstrated it for her on his phone.

"It looks just like the old one," said Christine.

"Yep," said Simon.

"But it doesn't need to be downloaded? You just navigate using a web browser?"

"Correct."

"Can I report that?"

"Definitely."

Christine scribbled notes quickly in her notebook, including the web address for the new version of The App.

"So why did you do it, Simon?"

"Do what?"

"Create a cell phone application that effectively lets people vote to have other people killed? Was it because you wanted to get back at Dick Gelderman? Because you lost your job?"

Eli interrupted before Simon could respond.

"Miss Hunter, I see that you're making the same erroneous assumptions that the police have made. The App is not a murder-for-hire application."

He went on to give her the same list of facts that he'd given to the police previously.

"You mean to tell me that you can use The App to bet on things like the weight of a newborn child?" she said.

"Exactly."

"How many people have done that?"

"That's not important," said Eli. "The important thing is that they *can* if they want to."

"Interesting," said Christine. "Okay, I'll ask the question another way."

"Sure," said Simon.

"How do you feel about the fact that people are using your application to bet on people's deaths?"

Simon shrugged. "I think it's significant that lots of people are *choosing* to use it in this manner. But they probably can't see any other way."

"Any other way…?" said Christine.

"To be heard."

"Ah. What is it that you think they're trying to say?"

"That they're angry. With governments and with the courts. They want them to change."

"Do you really believe there are *that* many angry people?"

"If there weren't, we wouldn't be having this conversation," said Simon.

"Because there wouldn't be enough money raised?" said Christine. "To make it worthwhile killing someone?"

"That's not what he meant," said Eli. "There's no evidence that any money is being raised to kill people. As far as Simon is concerned, people are just speculating about when someone might die."

"A lot of people," said Simon.

"Hmm," said Christine. "I guess I can understand why you're being circumspect with your answers. But can you answer this question?"

"What?" said Simon.

"How do you feel about the fact that Dick Gelderman has died?"

Simon paused, as he brought the tips of his fingers slowly together in front of his face. "I feel that there may actually be some justice in this world."

"Can you believe this?" said Detective Peters. They were watching Christine Hunter on the television as she described how US authorities had failed in their attempt to shut down The App. She also told viewers how to access the new web-based version.

Peters kicked the filing cabinet next to her desk. It rocked backwards and paused before thudding back into position. "Dammit. How did Simpson create this web thing so fast? Marks only told him about the shutdown yesterday."

"He must have anticipated the shutdown," said Kelly.

"That explains why he wasn't worried. He was laughing at us the whole time."

Kelly sighed. "I'd better go and call Marks. Ask him if he can shut down the website."

"No, we can't," said Marks.

"Seriously?" said Kelly.

"Not if it's hosted in Russia … which it is. We can't stop people accessing a website. This isn't China. And even if it was, there'd still be ways around it using proxy servers."

"Shit."

Marks paused. "I'm afraid that's not the only bad news."

"What else?" said Kelly.

"Simpson's computer. The FBI techs confirmed the encryption works just like he said."

"Hmm. If he doesn't know in advance about the murders, it will be difficult to nail him on premeditation and conspiracy."

"Sorry for the bad news," said Marks. "At least you still have Roberts."

Special Agent Marks checked his messages when he got off the phone. There was one from the field office in Washington, DC. He called them back.

"We think we've identified the vehicle," said Special Agent Dorner. "We went through the security tapes and cross-checked the licence plates of all vehicles entering the carpark."

"You got a mismatch on the vehicle type?" said Marks.

"On the model *year* of a Chevy van," said Dorner. "That's why it took so long. The plate had been stolen from a van at the airport."

"That's really good work," said Marks.

"Now we just need to narrow the search somehow."

"Agreed," said Marks. "I'm still waiting on the analysis of DNA collected from the Upton murder.

There was a lot of trace evidence at the motel. Hopefully it will reduce the size of the haystack."

Marks hung up. He thought about phoning Detective Kelly but decided against it.

It was getting late. And besides … the sniper was a US problem. The Canadians had more pressing concerns.

CHAPTER TWENTY-SIX

Thicker Than Water

Sienna twirled through the bedroom door and into the living room. "What do you think?" she said.

Simon looked up and lost control of his limbs.

The vacuum cleaner in his hand overshot its target and inhaled some curtain. The machine began to choke.

After several seconds, its screaming motor caught Simon's attention and he yanked the plug from the wall.

"What the hell are you wearing?" he said.

Sienna frowned. "Don't you like it?" She stopped twirling and the long floral skirt settled against her ankles. She self-consciously touched the high collar on her white lace blouse.

"You look like Anne of Green Gables," he said.

Sienna sighed. "I wanted to make a good impression on your mother. I didn't think she'd appreciate my *usual* wardrobe."

Simon shook his head. "I'm sure her *great-grandmother* would have been very impressed."

Sienna dropped her eyes to the skirt. "Too conservative?"

Simon nodded. "I think so. Mother will smell a rat. She's not stupid."

"Hmm." Sienna exhaled slowly and her shoulders drooped. "So, what should I wear?"

"How about ordinary jeans and a top that covers your breasts?"

"She won't think that's too casual?"

"Unlikely," said Simon. "Besides … that's all I'm wearing."

She nodded doubtfully. "Okay. If you think it will be all right."

She lifted her skirt and waltzed back into the bedroom. Simon rubbed his eyes.

Unbelievable. The things people did to impress their partner's mother.

He knelt down and ran the vacuum through the gap at the base of the couch. Stale cookie crumbs rattled along the pipe.

Simon made a quick visual inspection. At least his mother wouldn't find any crumbs *this* time.

Sienna emerged a few minutes later in a pair of faded hipster jeans and a midriff top. She raised her eyebrows at Simon. "Well?"

"That'll be fine," he said.

He put the vacuum away and checked his watch. Just in time.

A minute later, there was a knock at the door.

"She's very punctual," said Sienna.

Simon nodded as he hurried to answer it. "Coming, Mom."

He opened the door and his mother embraced him in a big hug. "How's my little boy?"

Simon's cheeks flushed.

"Don't be embarrassed by your mother, dear. Everybody has one." She looked over his shoulder. "Now where's this girl?"

She pushed past him into the living room. Sienna was standing with her back to the wall and her hands clasped together.

Simon slammed the door and dashed past his mother. He jumped between the two women.

"Mother, this is the young lady I mentioned on the phone. I'd like you to meet, Sienna."

His mother gave him a bemused look. "Well, it's hardly going to be a different girl, now is it, Simon?" She shook her head. "Unless, of course, you've started paying them."

Simon's cheeks bloomed again.

Sienna held out her hand. "Nice to meet you, Mrs Simpson."

Simon's mother ignored the outstretched hand. Her gaze slid down to Sienna's midriff then onto her jeans. "Have you been cleaning, dear?"

"Um … no," said Sienna. "Why?"

"The way you're dressed. I thought you must have been doing some manual work." She advanced past Sienna and ran a finger along the coffee table. It came up dusty. "My mistake."

Sienna glared at Simon behind his mother's back. She mouthed an obscenity in Russian.

Simon's mother turned and Sienna's expression morphed back into a smile.

"Simon's talked a lot about you, Mrs Simpson."

Simon's mother pressed her lips together. "Hm. He's only mentioned you once to me." She sat down on the couch and pressed her hand into the gap where Simon had just vacuumed. Her finger came away clean. A thin smile curled her lips. She patted Gizmo who was leaning against her legs.

Simon cleared his throat. "Sienna's originally from Russia, Mom."

"I thought I detected an accent. Perhaps that's why

she doesn't feel the cold."

Simon exchanged a confused look with Sienna.

"What makes you think I don't feel the cold?" said Sienna.

Mrs Simpson smiled. "Your *top*, dear. Or should I say *half a top*?"

Sienna took a step backwards and bumped into the wall.

"*I'm* sorry," said Simon's mother, holding up her hand. "*My* mistake. I can see now that you *are* cold."

"You can?" said Sienna.

"Yes, dear. Your nipples are sticking out." She shook her head. "But don't worry, it's nothing a bra won't fix."

Sienna's cheeks turned red. Whether it was from embarrassment or anger, Simon wasn't sure. But he didn't wait to find out.

"Mother, why don't you come into the kitchen and I'll make you a nice cup of tea. Sienna was just going to change out of her *exercise* clothes."

"I *was*?" said Sienna through gritted teeth.

"Yes," said Simon. "Into that lovely outfit you showed me earlier."

Sienna mouthed another obscenity. This time in English.

Simon fled into the kitchen.

An hour later, Simon escorted his mother to her car. Sienna said she'd remain inside — where it was warmer.

Simon opened the car door. "So, what do you think of her, Mom?"

His mother leaned forward and kissed him on the cheek. "She seems very nice, dear. For a prostitute."

She left her son speechless on the sidewalk.

"I'll book you in for a blood test," she said. "Just to be sure. Your girlfriend already has a regular appointment at our clinic."

"Shit," said Sienna. "I *thought* she looked familiar."

"Seriously?" said Simon.

She nodded. "Aleksei always made us get tested regularly. It was one of our selling points. *Disease free girls.*"

"Oh," said Simon, recalling how he'd liked that feature in their online ad.

Sienna sighed. "I guess she won't be inviting me over for dinner any time soon."

Simon reached out and took her hand.

"Look on the bright side," he said. "At least she liked your skirt."

CHAPTER TWENTY-SEVEN
Good Health

Yuri Aspidov was sitting in the Dubh Linn Gate pub, nursing his pint of Guinness. He'd been tending the same drink for the last hour.

Unlike his companion.

Tom Roberts was on his seventh pint.

"It's very generous of you to buy me drinks," said Tom. He raised his glass up to Yuri's. He missed his target and beer sloshed onto the floor. "Whoops."

"It's the least I can do for a fellow member of our fraternity," said Yuri. He raised his glass and took a sip. "To the Ski Patrol." Tom drained the rest of his pint.

Yuri wasn't actually in the Ski Patrol. But as a former special forces soldier in the Russian military, he did know how to ski and survive in the backcountry.

"Let me get you another one," said Yuri.

"Sure," said Tom.

Yuri went to the bar. He came back five minutes later with a pint and some shooters.

"To your continued good health," said Yuri. He handed Tom a vodka shot. He chose water for himself.

An hour later, the drinks were finished and most of the patrons had left. Tom swayed in front of Yuri.

"I should be going," said Tom. He burped loudly.

"Where are you staying?" said Yuri. Tom mumbled an address near the base of Blackcomb Mountain. It matched the one written on the paper in Yuri's pocket.

"Ha. That's near me," said Yuri. "We can walk together." He clapped his hand on Tom's shoulder and ushered him to the door.

They walked outside and headed towards Blackcomb. The temperature was below zero. Halos of white formed around street lamps that were cloaked in fog.

Yuri supported Tom as they shuffled through the snow. They followed a path which took them across a footbridge and over a stream. The freezing water flowed slowly beneath them, picking its way between ice-covered rocks.

"I need to piss," said Yuri. He stopped and propped Tom against the handrail facing the water.

"Good idea," said Tom.

Tom struggled with his fly for several seconds, but the combination of alcohol and gloves proved too much. He yanked hard on the left glove — then watched helplessly as it fell into the stream.

"Shit."

Tom unzipped his fly and took aim at a target beneath the bridge. He leaned over the railing to get a better view. "Bullseye," he said.

Tom didn't notice that Yuri wasn't peeing. Or that he'd picked up a rock.

The last thing Tom *ever* noticed was the crack on the back of his head.

His unconscious body slumped forward onto the railing, dangling over the edge.

Yuri stepped forward and grabbed Tom's legs. He lifted them and moved forward until a tipping point was reached. Then he let go.

Tom plummeted face down into the water.

"Bullseye," said Yuri.

He looked at his watch. Four minutes without oxygen was usually enough for brain damage. He waited five then walked away.

The phone next to Eli's bed rang. He answered it.

"It is done," said a male voice.

"Good," said Eli.

He hung up and imagined the expression on the Crown Prosecutor's face when she heard.

"He's what?" said the Crown Prosecutor. Her private school accent became more pronounced when she was angry.

Detective Kelly stood in front of the Judith Parker's desk. His lips were pressed tightly together.

"He's dead," said Kelly.

"When? How?"

"Last night, up in Whistler. Looks like he'd had too much to drink and stopped to take a leak. Fell into a stream and hit his head. He drowned."

"Are you pulling my leg?"

Kelly shook his head. "I wish I was." She had nice legs.

"Christ. There goes our link between Gelderman and Simpson." She paced towards the window, her high heels clicking on the wooden floorboards.

Long legs.

"Unless —" She turned suddenly, pointing at Kelly. He looked away guiltily. "Did Tom Roberts' name appear anywhere on that list?"

Kelly gave another shake of his head. "We already checked The App. His name wasn't there."

Parker swore. Her vocabulary surprised Kelly.

CHAPTER TWENTY-EIGHT

Senior's Moment

Graham Edwards was seventy one years old and totally bald. Fortunately, he'd been follicly challenged before entering hospital. So, nobody noticed the difference after his chemotherapy.

"Sorry, Mr Edwards," said the doctor. "I wish I had better news."

"Stage four?" said Edwards in a quiet voice.

The doctor nodded.

"Is there any treatment? I still have a few thousand dollars from selling my car."

The doctor hesitated. "You'll need more than a *hundred thousand* dollars, Mr Edwards. That's the price of the drug in the United States."

Edwards stared at his doctor. He felt tightness in his chest. "But that's more valuable than gold."

"About four thousand times more, actually."

"Jesus. Why is it so expensive?"

The doctor shook his head. "Don't get me started. Blame our health care system, the drug companies and their lobbyists. If you lived in Western Canada, you'd get the drug free."

"Seriously?"

"The Canadians use their buying power to negotiate a better deal."

"Don't we do that?"

The doctor snorted. "No. Our law makers are *funded*

by the drug companies. And *they* like the prices high."

Edwards sagged in his bed. "Maybe you should just euthanise me and let me die in peace."

The doctor gave him a wry smile. "Sorry, Mr Edwards. I can't do that either. Other lobby groups don't want you choosing your own fate."

Edwards shook his head. "What the hell has gone wrong with this country? Our politicians have made it too expensive for me to stay alive, but they won't let me die with dignity either. You call this freedom? I sure as hell don't."

Edwards lay there, staring at the ceiling.

His doctor apologised again before leaving to continue his rounds.

"Excuse me," said a patient from the next bed. Edwards turned his head. A gaunt man with no hair was propped up on his pillows, reading. "I wasn't eavesdropping," said the man, "but I couldn't help overhearing your conversation."

"Sorry," said Edwards. "Did we disturb you?"

"Not at all," said the man. "I'm sorry for your news." He introduced himself as Vincent. "I wanted to tell you about a man who was in here yesterday, handing out pamphlets. He was from GPA. Have you heard of them?"

Edwards shook his head.

"Grey Power Alliance. They want to harness the power of elderly people across the country — to help fix problems. Like those you were just talking about with your doctor."

Edwards scoffed. "How could a few old farts like us be of any use? Unless, of course, they capture and burn the methane we produce from eating this crappy hospital food."

Vincent smiled. "I was sceptical at first, too. But then I read their pamphlet."

"What did it say to change your mind?"

Vincent signalled for Edwards to wait while he retrieved the pamphlet from his bedside table. He opened it and peered over his glasses at him.

"Tell me Graham, what do you know about something called, The App?"

"Senator Criddle," shouted a journalist. "How do you feel about the campaign by the Grey Power Alliance to get elderly citizens to bet on your death?"

The senator turned to the woman who'd asked the question. "Cathy, it's just another campaign by a special interest group … and you know I've never been bothered by those."

He smiled mischievously while putting a finger to his lips. "But just between you and me, I doubt GPA members even *own* cell phones. It's unlikely they'll place many bets."

A few of the journalists laughed. Criddle searched their huddle for a friendly face. "Doesn't anyone have a question about why regulating drug prices is a *bad* idea?"

Before anybody could respond, a group of seniors unfurled a banner behind him. They began to chant. "Up The List. Up The List. Up The List."

The banner was about twelve feet long and four feet high. It was held aloft by two elderly men who struggled with the banner in the strong breeze.

At the top of the banner was the web address for The App. Underneath it was the text, "Vote One - Senator

Criddle." There was also an unflattering photo of Senator Criddle with a big red X through it.

The media scrum forgot about Senator Criddle and converged on the chanting seniors.

Criddle was left alone at the bottom of the steps with his aid.

"It doesn't matter," said Criddle. "I'm sure nobody watches television in the middle of the day."

The aid coughed. "Actually, sir … I think old people do."

Nancy Treacle was ninety-six years old. She'd lived in the *New Tricks* retirement village for eight years, ever since she'd fallen and broken her hip. Her eyesight was poor and she currently took eleven different medications per day. The doctors assured her they were all necessary … even the one that was used to kill rats.

"Is there anything I can do for you this week, Nanna," said her twenty-four-year-old great-granddaughter, Ashton. The young woman flicked a strand of blonde hair out of her eyes.

"Actually, dear, there is." Nancy reached out a wrinkled hand and placed it on Ashton's arm, covering the *trident* tattoo she'd always hated. "Do you have one of those cell phone contraptions, dear?"

Ashton laughed. "Of course, Nanna. Do you want to make a phone call?"

"Goodness no," said Nancy. "All my friends are dead. Who would I call?" She pursed her lips. "Actually, Ashton, I was hoping you might be able to help me place a bet."

Simon and Sienna had just started a game of chess

when Simon's phone beeped with a new message.

"I thought you'd disabled those," said Sienna.

"Don't worry. It's not one of *those* messages."

Sienna took her hand off the piece she was about to move. "What is it then?"

He looked at his phone. "A system message."

"A what?"

"A message that warns me when there's a potential problem with The App. This one is telling me that there's an unusually high load on the server."

He went and sat down at his computer. His hands flicked across the keyboard.

Sienna came and stood beside him. She peered over his shoulder.

"What is it? What's the problem?"

Simon opened a console window and logged on to the database.

"That *is* interesting," he said.

"What?" said Sienna. Her fingernails dug into his arm.

"There's been an enormous amount of activity on a single person. Their prize pool has jumped by half a millions dollars in the last six hours."

Sienna's eyes widened. "Half a million dollars? Is that even possible?"

Simon nodded. "It is if enough people don't like you. And a lot of people really don't like this guy."

"Who is he?"

Simon raised his eyebrows as he read the profile. "Some US politician who hates old people."

CHAPTER TWENTY-NINE

Records

Dillon had arrived back at his home in Seattle after another long drive.

He was tired and irritable.

In the last two weeks, he'd driven across the country to Washington, DC, then followed that up with a trip down to Texas.

And what did he have to show for it?

Half a kill in Washington, DC, and an aborted mission in Texas.

He was still confused by what he'd seen in the Lone Star State.

Dillon sighed. He needed a new mission. Something he could focus on.

He also needed the money.

Dillon started The App and waited for the list to load.

He looked at it. Then he looked at it again.

Surely that couldn't be right?

The leading prize pool was nearly half a million dollars.

"I have a favour to ask," said Detective Speed.

"Name it," said Kathy Anderson. "You know I'd do anything for my favourite crime-fighting detective."

Speed's first date with the headmaster's secretary had gone well. Well enough that they were now on their third.

The handcuffs had been used during their second encounter.

"That list of student's names you gave me. I need some help to reduce it."

"Reduce it? How?" Kathy's hand rested lightly on Speed's arm and she stroked it with her thumb.

He remained silent until the waiter had finished clearing their plates.

"In each of the photos with The Reverend Stiles, there's a different boy next to him. And in each case, Stiles has a hand on them. Like he's marking his territory."

"You think each boy might be a victim?"

Speed nodded. "Exactly. I'd like to speak to them."

"Hmm. Shouldn't be too hard. Twenty years worth of photos. Assuming the boys are all from the same age group, that's about twenty possibilities per year. Maybe four hundred boys in total." She chewed her lip. "I'll have to compare each boy against the individual student photos in the school records."

"Thanks," said Speed. "You're amazing."

"Give me a few days." She smiled at him. "In the meantime, what are you going to do for me?"

Speed grinned as he lifted a hand out of his lap. It was holding a set of handcuffs.

"Senator Nash, it's good to see you again," said Preston Shade. "I trust your campaign fund received our donations?"

"It has, thank you," said Senator Nash. "I'm *most* appreciative of your support." He grasped Shade's hand with a pair of sweating paws and shook it vigorously.

Shade wiped his hand. "Just be sure that it stays that

way, Senator." He picked up the newspaper and pointed to the main headline. "Terrible news about Senator Chisholm, wasn't it? Who'd have thought that he was having an affair with such a young girl? A girl from his daughter's school?"

Senator Nash's face dropped.

"Er … yes," he said.

Senator Criddle lived in Greenwich, Connecticut. Which meant Dillon had to drive his van across the country yet again.

But this trip would be worth it. For half a million dollars.

He drove at night and slept during the day. It took him four nights. He was exhausted by the time he crossed the Hudson.

Dillon found a Super 8 Motel in Stamford and crashed onto the bed.

"I've emailed you a spreadsheet," said Kathy Anderson. "It has the last known contact details of each boy."

"A spreadsheet?" said Detective Speed.

Kathy laughed. "Are you scared of a spreadsheet, *Wilbur*?"

He hated the fact that she knew his name. And he hated the fact that she *used* it even more.

"Can't you call me Speed like everyone else?"

She grinned. "Surely that's not something you'd want me to call you in the bedroom … Speedie?"

"Hmm. Perhaps we should get back to talking about the spreadsheet."

"Okay, *Wilbur*." She described how she'd combed the

school's records to identify the students. She'd also uncovered some troubling facts. "The rows in the spreadsheet with a grey background colour indicate the people who are dead. The rows with an orange foreground colour indicate people who took their own lives."

Speed clicked on the spreadsheet and opened it. Six of the twenty rows were shaded in grey. Of those, five had a foreground colour of orange.

"Jesus," said Speed. "That's a bit unusual."

"Yeah. Unless they were molested. In which case it's probably what you'd expect."

"You may be right."

"Um, there was one other thing I discovered," said Kathy. She hesitated.

"What?" said Speed.

"The surname of one of the boys, it's … the same as yours."

Senator Criddle's house was set back from the road behind a large stone wall. The main building sat in the middle of a six-acre block. It was surrounded by a big lawn that was in turn ringed by thick vegetation.

Dillon waited for the sky to darken, then he parked his van under some overhanging trees against the outside wall. He went through his checklist. After ticking each item, he slowly opened the rear door of the van. The air was cool against his painted face.

He shimmied onto the top of his van, and from there onto the wall. His night-vision goggles enabled him to see a criss-crossing network of laser sensors inside the grounds. The intersecting beams were at waist level, allowing squirrels and other animals to walk around without setting off the alarm.

Dillon silently thanked the system's designers.

He lowered himself to the ground and crawled towards the house.

An hour later he was in position on the edge of the foliage. From his hide, he had a good view of the house and lawn. There was also a tennis court.

Dillon shook his head. Tennis courts should come with a health warning: 'Caution, you may be shot.'

He reached into his pocket and pulled out a small plastic bag. Dillon had filled it with trace evidence from his motel after realising he couldn't use his van. He scattered the bag's contents around his position and checked his watch. Eleven o'clock.

Sleep when you can, soldier.

He closed his eyes.

Dillon wasn't worried about being discovered. His personalised ghillie suit made him virtually invisible. Someone would need to stand on top of him before they noticed anything suspicious. The fact he was wedged under a thick bush made that unlikely.

He drifted off to sleep thinking about ways to spend half a million dollars.

Dillon was awoken five hours later by a noise filtering through to his unconscious brain.

He remained motionless. Listening.

For thirty seconds there was nothing. And then there was a crack of a twig about fifty yards to his left.

He turned his head slowly and lowered his night-vision goggles. A bright figure crawled across an eerie green background. It settled behind a tree.

The figure was carrying a rifle.

Dillon's heart beat faster and his muscles tightened as

they prepared for fight or flight. But his military conditioning overrode his evolutionary instinct.

He willed himself to relax and formulate a plan.

Dillon measured the distance with a laser range finder and adjusted his bullet drop compensator. He carefully lifted his rifle and shifted position. Then he waited.

Dillon's plan was simple. When daylight arrived, he would determine what kind of threat the newcomer posed. If they were part of a security detail, he'd take them out before killing Senator Criddle. But if they were an assassin, he'd let them shoot the senator. Then he'd shoot the intruder in the stomach and use the distraction of their dying screams to help him get away.

Three hours later the first rays of light began to filter through the trees. He raised his night-vision goggles and peered through his rifle's scope.

Dillon could just make out the intruder, who was wearing a baseball cap pulled down low.

Adrenaline pulsed through his body as he recognised the cap.

He'd seen it before in Washington, DC. It was on the head of the repair man as he ran for the stairs.

We meet again.

Dillon stretched his trigger finger and settled down to wait.

An hour later, a noise from the back of the house drew Dillon's attention. A man in a suit appeared. There was a slight bulge under his left armpit. A handgun.

The man looked around. He checked both sides of the house before returning to the back door.

A minute later, Senator Criddle emerged in a pale-blue tracksuit and white trainers. He was talking on his cell phone in a booming voice.

"Of course I'm not worried," said Criddle. "I've got an expensive security system and a personal bodyguard. At the first sign of trouble I'll run to my panic room."

Dillon chuckled to himself. *The first sign of trouble will be your head exploding, Senator.*

He was wrong. The first sign of trouble was a red cherry blossoming on Criddle's chest.

Dillon heard the crack of the other shooter's weapon.

He quickly aimed his own weapon at the other sniper and was just in time to see their second shot.

Dillon's finger tightened on the trigger. He was about to apply the final pressure when he saw it.

Hair.

Long. Blonde. Hair.

Dillon's training and instincts kicked in.

We do not shoot women and children.

He froze. His brain refusing to issue the command that would override the prime directive.

Unaware of his dilemma, the young woman calmly flicked a wisp of hair out of her eyes and adjusted her aim. Then she shot the bodyguard in the thigh.

She replaced her baseball cap on her head and pushed herself off the ground. The sleeve of her shirt momentarily rode up her arm to reveal smooth white skin.

Through his scope, Dillon noted how the woman's milky complexion contrasted sharply with the dark shape of her tattoo. The trident was visible only for a second before her sleeve slipped down.

The woman picked up her rifle and began moving towards him.

Shit.

He needed to leave.

Dillon leapt up, causing the woman to gasp. He ignored her and sprinted towards his van.

He reached the wall and vaulted over it. Then he jumped in the driver's seat and took off. He sped towards the interstate. As Dillon drove, he used a towel and some baby wipes to remove the paint from his face.

Dillon was twenty-five miles away when he remembered the bet.

Shit. In the excitement he'd forgotten to update the time and date.

He pulled over to the side of the road and picked up his phone. He selected *The App* on his home screen.

He drummed his fingers on the steering wheel while the Internet connection was established.

Thirty seconds later, the list appeared. Dillon scrolled to the top.

He relaxed when he saw Senator Criddle's name.

And then he swore.

The senator's name had a padlock symbol next to it.

Betting had closed.

CHAPTER THIRTY

Revolution

Christine was half-way through the stack of pancakes her Aunt Joan had cooked when she saw the bulletin on CBC News.

"It seems our American neighbours may soon have access to affordable medications … a benefit Canadians have enjoyed for many years. This comes after a group of US politicians decided to switch camps and support a bill that enables the FDA to cap prices on many life-saving drugs. Seasoned political observers are putting this change of heart down to self-preservation, after a campaign by elderly citizens arguably led to the assassination of Republican senator, Morton Criddle."

Joan made a huffing sound. "About time *someone* made them see sense."

Christine looked up. "You really believe that, Aunty Joan?"

"Of course I do, dear."

"What about the way the change was achieved? Using intimidation and assassinations?"

Joan pointed her fork at Christine. "I'll tell you this much. This cell phone thing never would have taken off if our political and legal systems worked. But they don't, and instead we've got politicians, lobbyists and paedophiles – all running around, doing as they please. People are sick of it."

Joan stabbed a strawberry with her fork before

continuing. "Tell me this? What are ordinary folks supposed to do when the system stops working? Nobody listens to them. What *can* they do? Sometimes the *only* option available is … revolution."

Christine stopped halfway through pouring her maple syrup. "You think The App has started a revolution?"

"What else would you call it? History's filled with examples of ordinary people overthrowing a system that doesn't work. But the nice thing about *this* uprising is that it's being done with cell phones instead of guns."

"Um … they haven't been killing people with their cell phones, Aunty Joan."

"Maybe not. But look on the bright side, dear. At least with *this* revolution, the only people being killed are the ones who deserve it."

She bit into her ripe strawberry.

"Mr Shade will see you now," said the young woman from behind her desk. She pressed a button and the door next to her clicked as it unlocked.

Senator Nash stood and wiped his sweaty palms on his trousers. He walked to the door then paused, his hand hovering over the doorknob. He took a deep breath then turned it.

Nash froze when he'd taken two steps into the office.

Preston Shade stood just inside the door. He was holding a live mouse by its tail. He swung the mouse gently, backwards and forwards in front of his eyes. Like a hypnotist.

"What do you see, Senator?"

"Er … a mouse."

"Very astute, but that's not all there is to see." He thrust the creature towards Nash, who recoiled. It swung dangerously near his nose. Nash could see its little whiskers and nostrils as they sniffed the air.

"It's also a victim," said Shade. "It just doesn't know it yet."

Nash exhaled slowly. "I see."

Shade licked his lips. "Yes, Senator. This innocent little mouse had the misfortune to be born into a world that is full of predators."

He turned and walked to a glass tank beside his desk. Nash noticed it for the first time.

Inside the tank was a snake.

"Don't be shy, Senator. Come over here and meet Fate."

Nash forced himself to walk towards the snake. "Your snake's name is Fate?"

Shade nodded. He pressed a button and the enclosure was bathed in red light.

"Fate prefers to be warm when she eats."

Shade gently lowered the white mouse into the tank then crouched down with his face next to the glass. The mouse furiously sniffed its surroundings.

The snake flicked the air with its tongue. Then its head twitched and turned toward the mouse.

"It's only a matter of time," said Shade.

Sure enough, Fate struck swiftly, seizing the mouse as it cowered in the corner of the tank. The snake wrapped its body around the mouse and squeezed. Each time the mouse exhaled, the snake squeezed tighter. Until the mouse stopped breathing.

Shade stood, smiling. He walked around to his chair and sat down.

"Now, Senator, to what do I owe the pleasure of your visit? And please don't tell me you've come to return my money."

"Um … no. Well … not exactly."

Shade stopped smiling. "Excuse me?"

"Um … it's just that there's been a lot of anger from the public directed towards me. And it's not only me. It's other politicians too. Like those opposing gun control, drug price regulation and stronger health warnings on tobacco products."

"By 'anger from the public', I assume you're taking about those assassinations?" said Shade.

Nash nodded. "Senators Quaid and Criddle have both been murdered. Admittedly, Quaid was careless and didn't take precautions. But Criddle was extremely careful. I was actually talking to him on the phone when he was shot. It was horrible. I had to listen to him die."

"You could have hung up," said Shade.

"What?"

"You didn't have to listen. You could have hung up the phone."

"He was dying."

"There's no room for sentimentality in this business, Senator."

"I can see that, now."

"Good," said Shade. "You'd do well to remember that advice." He paused before continuing. "Now if you don't want to return my money, what is it you want?"

Nash leaned forward in his seat and placed his hands on Shade's desk. "Protect me, Preston. Please. Me and my family."

"Protect you?"

Nash nodded. "I'm happy to take your money and support whatever legislation you want me to. But I don't want to die."

Shade stood and walked around his desk. Slowly. Deliberately. Until he was standing behind Nash's chair. The hairs on Nash's neck stood as Shade's talon like fingers descended on his shoulders.

"I think we can manage that," said Shade. "After all, it's only prudent that we protect our investment."

Nash bowed his head. "Thank you, Preston. I'm in your debt."

Shade nodded. "Yes, you are." He held Nash a moment longer to emphasise the point, then released his grip.

Nash stood and turned toward the door. He caught a glimpse of Fate as he did so. The snake appeared to be smiling at him as she swallowed the last of the mouse's tail.

After talking to her aunt, Christine went upstairs to do some research on her computer. But every few minutes, her thoughts returned to what her aunt had said.

Revolution.

Was that really what this was?

She was interrupted by her phone ringing. It was her boss in Moncton.

"Guess what I just heard?" he said.

"What?"

"A old friend from *Time Magazine* called me. He was hoping you'd introduce him to Simon Simpson."

"I'm listening," said Christine. Her tone said otherwise.

"Don't worry. I didn't commit you to anything. But he *did* reveal that they're adding Simpson and The App to their shortlist."

"Shortlist for what?"

"*Time Magazine's* Person of the Year."

"What? I thought that didn't come out 'til December?"

"It doesn't. But The App has been so influential in the first few months that they're already adding him to the list."

"Shit."

"Yes. And you know what I expect from you now?"

"A televised interview. And a reaction from Simon to being included on the shortlist."

"That's my girl."

He hung up, leaving Christine stunned.

Time Magazine's Person of the Year.

Winston Churchill. Adolf Hitler. Mark Zuckerberg.

And Simon Simpson?

Maybe Aunty Joan was right.

She picked up her phone and called Simon.

Senator Nash hadn't left his house since he'd gotten home from his meeting with Preston Shade. He was too scared to go outside.

He jumped when his phone rang, but it was only his rent-a-cop calling from the gatehouse.

"Senator Nash. I have a group of people here who wish to see you. A Mr Shade sent them. Some sort of security experts? They said you'd know who they were."

"Send them in," said Nash.

That was quick. Shade didn't mess around.

Nash peered through the window as six black Chevy Suburbans roared up his driveway. They parked nose to tail in front of his house.

Four men jumped out of each car. They were dressed identically in black T-shirts and camouflage pants. They began to unload bags and boxes of equipment.

Nash opened the door to greet them and took a step onto his porch. The leader of the group saw the front door open and raced up the stairs. He shepherded Nash inside.

"Stay inside, Senator. Until we know it's safe. You'll need to give us some time to set up a perimeter."

"Oh. Of course."

"My name is Jack Fyfe and I'm the leader of your security detail. We'll get set up, then I'll give you a security briefing."

"Thank you."

"You can sleep soundly now, Senator. Nobody can get past us. We're the best in the business."

That didn't surprise him. Preston Shade didn't settle for second best.

Nash picked up his phone and called the gatehouse.

His security guard answered. "Yes, Senator?"

"You're fired."

CHAPTER THIRTY-ONE

Makeup

"Is that necessary?" said Simon. He was sitting on a chair in his living room and a woman he'd just met was trying to apply makeup to his face.

Christine Hunter stopped talking to her two cameramen.

"Trust me," she said. "You may feel silly wearing it, but you'll look sillier without it. Nobody likes a shiny face." She bent down and picked up Gizmo. "Do they, sweetie?" She rubbed him behind his ears.

Simon grimaced as the makeup artist dabbed at his nose with a brush. She made a tut-tutting sound.

Translucent powder. Setting spray. He hadn't realised a television interview was this complicated. He was beginning to wish that he'd refused Christine's request.

Eli Rabinovich spoke quietly in his ear. "Remember, I'll be standing just over there. If I think there's a question you shouldn't answer, I'll let you know."

"How?" said Simon.

"I'll pull my finger across my throat, like this." He made a cutting motion with his finger across his Adam's Apple.

Simon raised his eyebrows. "Isn't that a bit dramatic?"

Eli shook his head. "You need to choose your words carefully. The Crown Prosecutor will scrutinise everything you say."

The makeup artist interrupted them to apply more

powder to Simon's cheeks. Simon coughed as she sprayed him with a concoction that supposedly kept the rest of his makeup from sliding off.

"Remind me why we agreed to do a televised interview?" said Simon.

"Because it gives us the chance to shape the narrative," said Eli.

"The narrative?"

"The story. So that people believe your invention's a good thing."

The artist stepped back to admire her work. "All done, Mr Wriggle and Squirm."

Simon stared at the powdered stranger in the mirror and shook his head.

The cameramen and lighting assistants left their huddle and moved into position. Christine sat down facing Simon.

"Very nice," she said. "You'll look good for all your fans."

"Fans?" he said. "You're joking right?"

Christine grinned.

"The arrogance of this guy," said Judith Parker. "He's thumbing his nose at me and the Canadian justice system on national television."

Detective Kelly nodded at the Crown Prosecutor. He'd been summoned along with Detective Peters to the prosecutor's office. The three of them were watching a recording of Simon Simpson's interview.

The camera angle switched to Christine Hunter's face. "How do you feel about the way people have chosen to use your cell phone application?" she said. "Betting on a person's death, which arguably increases the chances of them being killed?"

The camera switched back to Simon. "Just to be clear, Christine. I've never personally condoned the taking of another person's life. I think there are better ways that reasonable people can resolve their differences. By talking and treating each other with respect. That being said, I can understand why so many people are frustrated. They're not being treated with respect by our political leaders, or by others who exploit them for personal gain. I *understand* why they're angry and why some of them believe this is the only way to change things."

The camera zoomed out and Christine checked her notes. "As I mentioned in the introduction," she said, "*Time Magazine* has added you to their shortlist for Person of The Year. How does it feel to rank as one of the most influential people in the world?"

The camera zoomed in for a close up on Simon's face. Pink circles bloomed on his cheeks. "Um ... to be honest, I find that story hard to believe. I'm just a software engineer who was lucky enough to create a betting app that people find easy to use. I'm not the one who deserves the credit." He turned to look straight into the camera. "*You're* the ones who acted. It was *you* reminded our political leaders that they serve *us*. And *you're* the ones who should be recognised by *Time Magazine,* not me."

Judith Parker pressed the pause button on the television. "Do you see what he's doing?"

Detective Peters nodded. "He's sucking up to the public. He thinks if they like him enough then no one will want to touch him."

"Exactly," said Parker.

"Can't you prosecute him on a lesser charge?" said Kelly. "Like being an accessory?"

"Possibly," said Parker. "But it would make us look weak. And there's still no guarantee of a conviction. The existing laws were never designed for technology like The App. Simpson's software is clever and Rabinovich could probably sell a jury on reasonable doubt." The Crown Prosecutor shook her head. "If a prosecutor wins a case like this, it can make their career. But if they lose it, they may as well go and work pro bono for legal aid."

The two detectives exchanged a glance.

"So, you're going to let him walk?" said Kelly.

"No," said Parker. "This arrogant prick isn't going to ruin my career."

"What are you going to do?"

"I'm going to get the Federal Government to change the law."

Eli patted Simon on the back. "You're a natural," he said. "The public will actually believe that stuff about *them* deserving the credit. Hell … you were so convincing, even *I* believed you."

"Um … thanks," said Simon. "It's easy to be convincing when you mean it."

Eli laughed then winked at Simon. "Of course it is." He looked at his watch. "I've got to go."

He waved at Christine Hunter on his way out the door. "Miss Hunter. Thanks for the opportunity. You look lovely as always."

After he'd left, Christine walked over to where Simon was having his makeup removed.

"Did you hear about Tom Roberts?" she said.

Simon's head twisted towards her, causing the

makeup artist to poke him in the eye.

"Ouch." He rubbed his watering eyeball. "No. Why?"

Christine paused. "You really don't know?"

Simon looked at her with his good eye and shook his head. "The last I heard was that he'd been arrested. Why? What's he done?"

Christine leaned forward and touched Simon's shoulder. "He died."

Jack Fyfe spoke into his microphone. "Alert in Orange Sector. Possible intruder." He was inside Senator Nash's house watching the bank of security monitors that were set up on the pool table. An orange square was flashing on one of the screens. "Oscar One, proceed to the perimeter fence to investigate. Oscar Two, provide cover."

Fyfe checked the monitors for indicators in adjacent sectors.

"Blue and Green Sectors, be alert for possible intruders."

There was silence for about a minute before the radio crackled. "This is Oscar One. The perimeter has been breached. I repeat, the perimeter has been breached. They've used wire cutters to cut through the razor wire."

Fyfe keyed his microphone. "Alpha Team. Secure the package. We have an intruder."

Upstairs, the two men assigned for close protection of the senator burst into his bedroom. One of them covered the door while the other ran to the senator's bed and threw back the covers.

"What the hell -"

"Quiet, Senator. Come with us. We have a situation."

The senator opened his mouth but before he could ask what the 'situation' was, he was yanked out of bed. The two Alpha Team members hustled him through the door and down the stairs. They didn't stop until they'd reached the basement. One of the team swung open the door to the senator's panic room. The other bodyguard hustled the senator inside and closed the door behind them. There was a clunking sound as he turned the internal handle, sealing them inside.

The guard who remained outside activated his radio. "The package is secure. Repeat, the package is secure."

"Acknowledged," said Fyfe. He was watching the monitors when a blue square suddenly appeared on the screen. "Blue Sector, I'm showing movement in the north-west corner of your sector. Sierra One, do you have eyes on the north-west corner of Blue Sector?"

The sniper on the northern side of the building responded. "Affirmative, Tango Lima." He raised his infra-red binoculars and scanned the area one hundred yards from the house. A bright figure could be seen crawling along the ground. It was carrying a rifle.

"This is Sierra One confirming. I have eyes on a single target. Target is armed and moving south. Range approximately one hundred yards."

"Roger that. Sierra One, you have over-watch responsibilities."

"Acknowledged." The sniper lifted his rifle and adjusted his thermal sight for the new range and angle.

The radio crackled to life again. "Bravo and Golf Teams. Move in and apprehend. The target is armed. Repeat, the target is armed."

From the roof, the sniper could see four bright images slowly converging on the target. "Bravo Two, this is

Sierra One. Target is thirty yards north of your position. Heading directly towards you."

"Roger."

Sierra One watched as Bravo Two hurled a flare in the direction of the target. He could hear Bravo Two yelling. "Stay where you are. We have you surrounded. Kneel with your hands behind your head. Leave your weapon on the ground."

The prowler froze for several seconds before apparently making a decision.

Through his scope, Sierra One could see the target reach into a pocket and remove a round object.

"Grenade," said Sierra One. He moved the cross-hairs of his scope onto the intruder. As the man stood and pulled the pin, Sierra One pulled the trigger.

The bullet struck the would-be assassin in the chest and both he and the grenade fell to the ground. The body of the man covered the grenade. Several seconds later there was an explosion.

"Target is down. Repeat, target is down."

"Good job," said Fyfe. "Bravo team, secure what's left of the target."

"Roger," said Bravo Two.

Bravo Two carefully approached the bloody remains and was surprised to find the man's head completely intact. It was wearing a balaclava. He knelt down, careful to avoid the chunks of bloody flesh.

"Shit," said Bravo Two as he lifted the balaclava. "This guy looks old enough to be my grandpa."

CHAPTER THIRTY-TWO

Cabin Fever

"I'm bored," said Sienna.

"Would you like a game of chess?" said Simon. "I could give you a few tips."

Sienna's facial muscles tightened, compressing her eyes into narrow trenches. Simon took a step back.

"Winning two games in a row doesn't make you an expert," she said.

"You're right, of course," said Simon. "But it *is* better than losing two in a row."

He ducked the cushion aimed at his head and tried to stop laughing.

Gizmo's wrinkled brow rose from inside his basket. He tilted his head, and looked quizzically at Simon.

"Okay," said Simon. "Truce." He held up his hands. "Is there anything you'd like to do?"

"I'd like to go *outside*. I'm starting to get cabin fever."

Simon took a tentative step towards her. He kept one eye on the cushion next to her hand. "Where would you like to go?"

"Shopping."

"Of course you do."

"I want you to buy me some nice things."

The grin slid from Simon's face.

"Isn't that what your allowance is for?"

Sienna shook her head. "It's not the same. *This* way gives you a chance to demonstrate your affection."

"Hmm. I thought that's what I did in the bedroom." Simon twitched as Sienna's hand moved towards the cushion. "No. You're right. It's not the same."

"Does that mean we can go?" she said.

"I think so. The journalists have all disappeared. Ever since Christine's interview aired —"

"Christine? You mean Ms 'Slutty Dress' Hunter?"

"Um … I quite liked what she was wearing."

"You were meant to."

"What's that supposed to mean?"

"She's after more than just your story."

Simon snorted. "A beautiful media personality throwing herself at me? That'll be the day."

Sienna folded her arms. "I didn't mean she'd want to have sex with you. I'm sure that slut already has several boyfriends."

"Oh. You think she has a boyfriend?"

Sienna rolled her eyes. "She's after your money, Simon."

"My money?"

Sienna nodded. "With people like that, you can never be too careful."

"I'll bear that in mind."

"You'll thank me later." She touched his cheek. "So, can we go shopping?"

"Um … sure."

"Excellent," said Sienna. "We'll go first thing tomorrow."

"Tomorrow? Why don't we go now?"

Sienna flicked her hair back over her shoulders. "It's already lunch time, Simon. You're not getting off *that* easy. A proper shopping trip takes all day."

Simon slumped into a chair.

"And besides," said Sienna. "I'll need this afternoon to compile my list."

Judith Parker had flown to Ottawa to meet with the Attorney General of Canada, Owen MacDonald. He was also the Minister for Justice in the governing Conservative Party.

"Thank you for seeing me," said Parker.

"A pleasure," said MacDonald. "A lot of people are taking an interest in your current case."

"I'm sure *many* politicians are concerned about the outcome."

MacDonald held up his hands defensively. "It's not just politicians. Some of my most important constituents are outraged. They're demanding we stop this … this dangerous invention."

"I thought all constituents were equal, Minister?"

MacDonald's face tightened. "Don't play dumb, Ms Parker."

Parker lowered her head slightly. "Of course, Minister. I imagine the lobbyists are getting nervous."

"Yes. And we're *all* hoping that you'll make this problem go away."

"That's why I'm here, Minister."

She explained her problem with the existing legislation and how it would be difficult to get a conviction.

MacDonald toyed with the miniature Canadian flag on his desk while she spoke. When she'd finished, he sat forward and pointed it at her. "So you want us to pass some specific laws that target The App?"

"Yes, Minister."

MacDonald nodded. "I shouldn't have too much

trouble convincing my colleagues. It's in their interest, after all."

"One more thing, Minister."

He peered over his glasses at her. "What?"

"You might want to keep the proposed legislation quiet."

"Quiet? Why?"

"If word leaks out to your *less important* constituents, you might find your name on the list."

"What about this one?" said Sienna. She was with Simon in Tiffany's on Burrard Street. Sienna was holding a string of diamonds against her throat.

"It looks magnificent," said the store's manager.

"Not *you*", said Sienna. "*Simon?*"

Simon was jolted out of his stupor. He was sitting on a stool holding several shopping bags from Holt Renfrew and Club Monaco, having endured a morning unlike any other.

His only moment of respite had come when he'd sat on an oasis-like 'man couch', strategically provided in one of the stores. A young woman in a short dress had served him coffee. But the reprieve had been all too brief and he'd been summoned by Sienna for his opinion. The glassy eyed man next to him had wished him well.

Now Simon had been summoned again. He hauled his eyes up from the floor to look at the necklace. The main diamond was huge.

"Um, it looks a bit big."

"Big? That's the whole point of diamonds."

"Oh. I thought it was more about the quality."

Sienna turned to the store's manager. "We'll take it," she said.

"An excellent choice," said the man.

Simon handed over his credit card.

While the necklace was being wrapped, Sienna sidled up next to him. "You're in luck," she said.

"Why?" He didn't feel lucky as he signed the credit card slip.

"I've booked a three-hour beauty-treatment and massage at a spa."

Simon dropped his credit card on the ground.

"You what?"

"Don't worry. You don't have to come with me. Just look after the bags until I'm finished."

She handed him the packaged necklace, which he juggled into one of the bags he was holding.

"I'll meet you at the car at five o'clock," she said. "Don't be late." And then she was gone, out through the door.

Simon groaned. What was he going to do for three hours?

Three hours on his own. He looked aimlessly around the store. Simon's attention was drawn to his own picture on the security monitor. As he stared at it, he was ambushed by an idea.

His stomach churned.

The more he thought about it, the better his idea seemed.

Simon placed his bags in a pile on the floor and pulled out his phone. He hesitated before selecting the name.

It was answered on the third ring.

"Christine. It's Simon. Would you like to grab a drink at the pub?"

Christine Hunter took a sip of her beer and gestured

to the pile of shopping bags. "I have to give your girlfriend credit, Simon. She has good taste in clothes."

"Having a girlfriend is more expensive than I thought," he said.

"I can imagine."

Simon took a sip from his drink.

"You might want to keep an eye on your wallet around her," said Christine.

Simon laughed. "She said the same thing about you."

Christine sprayed beer on the table. "What?"

"She thought you might be after my money."

"I think she's projecting."

"She said you wouldn't be interested in me for any other reason … and that you probably had several boyfriends."

Christine looked down into her drink and took a long sip. "She'd be wrong on both counts."

It was Simon's turn to spill beer. He mopped it up with a napkin.

"Um … you don't have a boyfriend back in Moncton?"

She shook her head. "Not for a year."

"Interesting," said Simon.

"Interesting?" She cocked an eyebrow.

"Surprising," said Simon quickly. He gulped down the rest of his beer and signalled to the waitress.

After she'd left, Christine reached across the table and touched his arm.

"You're an interesting guy, Simon. Intelligent. Perhaps a little naive when it comes to women."

Simon raised his eyes and noticed the half-moon curve of her lips. He reached for his empty glass.

"Sienna's complicated," he said. "She's had some

difficult experiences that have shaped her view of the world."

Christine bit her lower lip and removed her hand. "I've thought a lot about what you've been doing," she said.

"Really?"

She nodded. "And I want you to know I support you. As a journalist, I've seen a lot of things to make me cynical about the system. Backroom deals. Greed."

"Don't forget injustice," added Simon.

"That too. And when I mention this stuff to my more experienced colleagues, they say it's always been like that."

She paused while the waitress placed their drinks on the table.

Christine raised her glass and clinked it against Simon's before continuing. "But then *you* came along with The App. And everything changed. Even my colleagues agree."

"I didn't set out to change the world," said Simon.

"But you have."

"Sometimes I wonder what I've unleashed."

"You need to be careful," said Christine.

"Eli seems pretty confident about my legal position."

"I'm not just talking about the police. You've upset some powerful people. It's hard to imagine they won't respond."

"I'll try and stay out of trouble."

She touched his arm again. "If there's anything I can do to help, let me know."

He placed his hand on top of hers and squeezed it gently. "Thanks. That means a lot."

He looked down at their overlaid hands and noticed

his watch.

"Christ. Is that the time?"

CHAPTER THIRTY-THREE

Revelations

Detective Speed worked his way through the twenty names that Kathy had provided.

Six were eliminated straight away because they were already deceased. Of the remaining fourteen, five were living overseas or in other cities on the dates that Stiles and Hinkley were killed. Another three were in prison; two for sexual assault and one for killing someone in a bar fight.

Of the original twenty, only six people still lived around Fredericton. Speed had interviewed five of them, but they all had alibis for the killings.

Which left him with one person to interview.

His father.

Speed drove up the driveway to his father's house under an overcast sky. His Dad came down the steps to greet him.

"Two visits inside a month, son. To what do I owe the pleasure?"

"It's kind of official business, Dad."

His father laughed and raised his hands. "Don't shoot, son. I didn't do it."

"Perhaps we should go inside, Dad."

The smile gradually disappeared from his father's face. "Okay. Sounds serious."

He led the way up the stairs and into the empty house.

"Can I get you a drink, son?"

"Not while I'm on duty."

"Hope you don't mind if I still have one." Speed's father opened the fridge and grabbed a beer. Then he sat down across the kitchen table from his son.

"What's on your mind?"

"The Reverend Stiles."

The beer stopped half way to his father's mouth. His eyes narrowed before taking on a distant stare.

Speed remained silent.

Eventually his father exhaled. "That's a name I've tried to forget."

"Why?"

His father put his beer back down and slowly rubbed his eyes. "If you're here asking about that man, then I assume you already know."

Speed leaned forward and touched his father's arm. "Why didn't you tell me you were abused?"

His father pulled his arm away. "It's not the sort of thing you discuss."

Speed nodded. He took a deep breath. "Were you abused the entire time you were at that school?"

His father looked down and shook his head. "No. It seemed like an eternity when it was happening. But it was only one year." A tear slid down his father's cheek.

Speed's eyes became moist when he saw it. His father never shed tears. Even when his mother had died.

He reached out and took his Dad's hand.

"Stiles used to give us a choice," said his father. "A lashing with his belt ... or sex education."

Speed squeezed his father's hand. "Is that why you killed him?"

His father looked up slowly, as if he hadn't heard.

"What?"

"Don't worry, I understand. I probably would have killed him too."

Speed's father recoiled back in his chair, yanking his hand away. "What the hell are you talking about?"

"I can understand you killing Stiles," said Speed. "But why did you kill Stephen Hinkley?"

"Hinkley? That other paedophile priest? Have you gone mad?"

"I know you were in Moncton the night Hinkley was killed."

"What?"

"You called me the next day, and told me that you'd stayed in a motel."

"So that makes me a killer? That's what passes for evidence these days is it? I stayed in a motel in the same town, so I must have killed him."

"What were you doing there, Dad."

"None of your goddamn business."

"You've always stayed with me before when you came to Moncton. But not this time. Why?"

"I'm not telling you. I *can't* tell you."

"Dad, if you get a good lawyer, he can use the fact that you were abused to help."

"I'd like you to leave now."

"What?"

"Do you have any evidence to charge me?"

"You bought a new car right after Hinkley's murder. Where did you get the money?"

"None of your fucking business."

Speed's hands were balled into fists. "Don't you understand? I can't help you if you don't tell me the truth. I'm not here to arrest you. I'm here to offer you advice."

"I told you to leave, *Detective*. And don't come back until you're ready to apologise."

Speed stood slowly. He felt as if he'd aged a hundred years since coming inside. He wiped away tears with his sleeve.

As he walked past his father, he hesitated, extending his hand towards him.

His father turned away.

Speed lowered his arm and trudged down the stairs into the rain.

CHAPTER THIRTY-FOUR

Modern Warfare

Amit Chopra was a second generation American. Though to many in his native country he'd always be considered a foreigner. A fact painfully reinforced during his school years.

But Amit overcame the taunting and was accepted into a prestigious technical college. His parents were incredibly proud.

Amit's father and mother had saved hard for his college education fund. They'd invested the money on advice from a man at their bank. Unfortunately, he'd advised them to invest in sub-prime mortgages and they'd lost it all.

When they phoned the man for help, he'd refused to take their calls. Finally, they tried pleading with him in the bank's car park. But he slammed the door of his Porsche and sped away.

Amit applied for a scholarship to attend college, but narrowly missed out. There was only one option after that to pay the bills.

Amit's mother cleaned offices and public toilets for minimum wage, while his father drove cabs at night and limousines during the day. Amit had a part-time job at a restaurant.

He felt guilty that his parents had to work so hard. It wasn't fair. After all they'd been through to come to America.

He hated the men who'd stolen their hard earned savings.

Amit knew other students who were Trust Fund Babies. Their parents had gotten rich on the backs of people who worked hard like his parents. For *those* students, life was a breeze. They attended class, went to parties and looked down on people like him.

Amit was sick of politicians who peddled the myth that if you worked hard, you reaped the rewards. The reality was different.

If you were rich, you made more money. If you were poor, you survived. Barely.

Amit desperately wanted to improve his lot and to repay his parents for their hard work.

So when a friend told him about *The App*, he studied the list of targets.

He found a senator near the top who was being paid to protect the banks. The banks that had robbed his family.

Amit's area of study was Mechatronics. He was particularly interested in autonomous drone collectives and swarm algorithms. Put simply, he was able to make flying drones act towards a single purpose, like foraging bees. The scouts would search and report, and then the hive would act.

Amit's scouts had been programmed to identify Senator Nash using on-board facial recognition software.

"What's that noise?" said Senator Nash.

He was sitting in the sun, in his enormous backyard, watching his daughters playing tennis.

Two minders sat several yards away, scanning the trees. Alpha Team.

"Sounds a bit like bees," said one of the minders.

The buzzing sounds got louder.

"Lots of bees," said the other minder, looking from side to side. "They seem to be all around."

"Tango Lima, this is Alpha One. We're hearing something that sounds like swarming bees. Does anyone have a visual?"

"Roger that, Alpha One," said Jack Fyfe. "Hold for visual confirmation. Sierra One, are you seeing anything from the roof?"

The sniper on the roof of the house raised his binoculars and scanned the trees.

"I can hear something," he said. "But I can't see them." He panned west towards the trees behind the tennis court. "No … wait. I see something. It's not bees … it's … an aerial drone."

"A drone?" said Fyfe.

"Roger that," said Sierra One.

"Alpha Team, secure the package," said Fyfe. "Possible drone attack."

The two minders leapt to their feet and lifted the senator out of his chair by his arms.

"What the —" said Nash.

"We have another situation," said Alpha One.

The two teenage girls on the tennis court noticed the commotion and stopped playing.

Senator Nash made it half way to the safety of his house before two more drones rose from the trees and moved to cut him off. The drones jinked violently in different directions, making them difficult to shoot.

His minders stopped abruptly and propelled Nash back the other way. Towards his daughters.

"Run," screamed their father.

They didn't move.

Another two drones approached from either side, channeling him towards the tennis court.

Each time his minders tried to change direction, several drones ducked and weaved to cut them off. Nash counted at least twelve drones in total.

As they reached the tennis court, the rest of Nash's protection detail responded. They raced from the house and surrounding trees with their weapons raised. Shots were fired, but none of them hit their targets. The drones were too small, too agile.

Several more drones joined the jitterbugging collective until they surrounded Nash in an ever decreasing hemisphere. He spun around, searching for help. The rest of his guards weren't going to make it before the swarm contracted to a single point.

Nash could make out the tiny payload that each drone carried. He didn't know what it was, but he assumed it wasn't good.

It was actually a high explosive that Amit's friend, Jennifer, had developed. She was a chemistry major.

Jennifer had also missed out on a scholarship.

Nash turned to his minders, who were trying in vain to lock onto a target with their weapons.

"Protect my daughters," he said.

"What?"

"That's an order. Protect my daughters."

The two minders looked at each other then reacted in unison. They raced the five yards to Nash's teenage girls and picked them up, carrying them away. When they reached twenty yards they threw themselves on top of the girls.

They felt the explosion behind them as the sixteen

drones converged on Nash simultaneously and detonated.

Amit watched the scene from his laptop. It was being streamed live over the Internet from another drone circling high above the tennis court.

He was relieved when the two girls stood.

Nash hadn't known it, but the drones were programmed *not* to detonate until the girls were out of range.

Amit typed in a command, telling the observer drone to return, then he turned off his computer.

He picked up the phone and called his parents.

"You can stop working two jobs now, Mom. I've managed to get a scholarship."

CHAPTER THIRTY-FIVE

Tips

Christine Hunter opened the email. It was marked urgent. The message had been sent from an anonymous government email address using the pseudonym, John Smith.

She opened the attachment. It was a draft bill that was being prepared for the Federal Government.

As she read the title, the hairs on her arms bristled.

An Act to amend the Criminal Code (criminalising the software betting program, The App).

She picked up the phone and made two calls. The first was to Simon. The second was to her boss.

"Bitch," said Judith Parker.

Detective Kelly remained silent. He was getting used to the Crown Prosecutor's range of expletives.

Up on the television screen, Christine Hunter was outlining the details of the draft bill to criminalise The App.

"Reliable sources have confirmed the bill is being pushed through quietly by Attorney General, Owen MacDonald. However, these sources also claim that the *original* request for the legislation came from *outside* his office.

"I'm told that, Crown Counsel, Judith Parker, recently flew from Vancouver to Ottawa for a meeting with the Attorney General, and that *this* meeting was the catalyst for the legislation."

Kelly winced at Judith Parker's next remarks. The Crown Prosecutor had surprised him again.

Speed was sitting on Kathy Anderson's couch. He'd gone straight to her house after the argument with his father.

She came downstairs after putting her daughter, Ellie, to bed.

"How is she?" said Speed.

"Fine. Though it's hard to convince her to sleep. She's *always* on her computer."

Kathy sat next to Speed and gently rubbed his neck.

"I don't know what to do," said Speed. "I *want* to believe my father, but he won't tell me where he was when Hinkley was killed."

"He may have a good reason for not telling you," said Kathy. "Everyone has their secrets."

"But if he doesn't tell me everything, I can't help him. I'll have to hand the case over to someone who has no personal involvement."

Kathy started to knead Speed's neck and shoulders. He gave a small sigh.

"There might be another way," she said.

"Another way? How?"

"Catch whoever killed Hinkley. If your father is telling the truth, then the real culprit is still out there."

Speed made a tsk sound. "Don't you think that's what I've been trying to do?"

Kathy dug her fingers in sharply, causing Speed to gasp.

"With respect, *Wilbur*, you've been eliminating suspects on your list of twenty names. That's not the same thing as trying to catch the killer."

"I'm not following you," said Speed. "Eliminating suspects is *how* we do that."

"I'm just saying that you could take a different approach."

He turned around to face her. "Such as?"

"You could set a trap."

Attorney General, Owen MacDonald, took the phone from his secretary who pointed at the screen displaying The App. "There's your name, Minister."

"Thank you," said MacDonald dryly. "I *can* recognise my own name."

He looked at the dollar figure next to it. A little under six thousand. And it had only been two hours since that CBC story went to air.

He shook his head.

There was a brief moment of *schadenfreude* when he noticed Judith Parker's name there too.

He handed the phone back to his secretary. "Call a press conference," he said. "Immediately. Tell them it's urgent."

Christine Hunter was watching the live press conference from Ottawa in her aunt's kitchen.

The Attorney General was telling the packed room that he'd decided the bill to criminalise The App was unwarranted. He emphasised that it wouldn't proceed as long as *he* was Attorney General, and he urged the journalists in the room to make that clear to the public.

Christine snorted.

Self-interest had triumphed again.

Her thoughts were interrupted by a phone call. It was

Detective Speed.

"I'm calling to ask a favour," he said. "I figure you owe me one."

He told her of his strange request.

Christine listened and made notes. Then she hung up and phoned her boss.

CHAPTER THIRTY-SIX

Deception

Preston Shade sat in his private board room in New York. Behind him, piranhas swam restlessly in their tank.

His eyes shifted around the table, pausing to acknowledge each of the holographic projections in front of him.

Shade cleared his throat. "Our usual methods of persuading politicians are no longer effective. And despite taking great precautions to protect our investments, these measures have had limited success. We all know what happened to Senator Nash. In addition, our hopes that our Canadian friends would rectify the problem with legislative changes have also been in vain."

Shade paused to stare at the only Canadian in their group.

"Don't blame me," said the silver haired man with a long nose. He spoke with a slight French accent. "Once the public found out about the draft bill, there was nothing we could do. That damned computer program saw to that."

Shade nodded. "It seems to me, that all of our problems stem from the same source."

There was a general murmur of agreement from the holograms around the table.

"I've given this matter a great deal of thought," said

Shade. "And I may have a solution."

The men and woman fell silent. Their holographic projections leaned forward in their chairs.

"I propose that we initiate a takeover of Mr Simpson's company."

"A *hostile* takeover?" said the French Canadian.

Shade smiled. "If necessary."

Detective Speed sat in the armchair of the large house owned by the Church. They'd agreed to let him use it as part of his ruse.

When Speed had phoned Christine Hunter, he'd asked her to help him by planting a story in the news. After discussions with her boss she'd agreed.

The story announced that an accused paedophile priest was being temporarily housed in Church accommodation. No address was given, but it was suggested that it was the same property where Stephen Hinkley had stayed. The story said he'd be there for three days, before being moved to another province.

The first two days had passed uneventfully. Speed had donned his grey wig each morning then pottered around the house. He'd spent a lot of time watching afternoon television.

By lunch on the third day, Speed was convinced their plan to lure the killer wouldn't work. But out of desperation to help his father he continued the charade.

Evening arrived on the final night. Speed dimmed the downstairs lights before slowly making his way up to the main bedroom. He radioed his uniformed backup across the road. "Keep your fingers crossed, boys."

"Give Pamela a kiss for me," came the reply.

"Whatever," said Speed. "You're just jealous."

Pamela was his stunt double.

He rolled the blow-up doll onto its side and adjusted the blanket. Then he turned off the light and sat in a lounge chair in the corner of the room.

His breathing gradually deepened and he fell asleep.

He was woken several hours later by the tinkling of breaking glass. Initially he didn't realise what had roused him. Then he heard the creaking of a floorboard on the stairs.

Speed's adrenal gland kicked into action. He reached for the pistol next to his hand.

There was a noise outside the door. The handle turned and the door creaked open, casting a thin light onto the floor. A tall figure squeezed through the gap and crept inside. It moved to the head of the bed and stopped. There was a glint of reflected light as the shadow raised its arm. An ice pick trembled in mid-air before the arm swung down.

There was a loud popping sound as the metal lanced through Pamela's head

"What the hell?" said a man's voice.

Speed pressed a button and several spotlights blared into life, capturing the figure in their intersecting beams.

"Freeze. Armed Police."

The man turned.

"*You*," said Speed.

The headmaster of St. Anthony's boarding school for boys stood there. A surprised look on his face.

"*You*," said the headmaster.

"Put down the ice pick. We have the house surrounded."

As if to confirm this, loud voices could be heard coming from downstairs as other police entered the house.

The headmaster dropped the ice pick on the floor.

"You tricked me," he said.

"You lied to me," said Speed.

"I never did," said the headmaster.

"When I asked whether you disliked The Reverend Stiles, you said you'd never met him."

The headmaster shook his head. "I said he left before I started *teaching* at the school. I didn't lie. He *did* leave before I started teaching. But he was there when I was a *pupil*."

"But you weren't in any of those twenty photos."

"No. I was the boy he chose at the start of his twenty first year. He abused me for several months until I bit him."

"Bit him?"

"Down there." He gestured to his groin.

Speed lowered his gun a fraction.

"You bit his penis?"

"His injuries were quite severe. For some reason he found it hard to justify a student's teeth marks being there, and he was given early retirement."

"And that's why there was no photo for his twenty first year?"

"Exactly. Otherwise I would have been the boy standing next to him."

"I can understand you wanting to hurt Stiles. But what about Hinkley?"

"Predators like those two mustn't be allowed to hurt any more boys. There's only one way to be sure."

The door opened and several uniformed police officers entered the room.

"Get him out of here," said Speed.

Speed had phoned his father the next day and told him that he wanted to apologise in person. They'd arranged to meet in Fredericton.

When Speed arrived at his father's house the next evening, there was another car already in the driveway. He didn't recognise it.

His father opened the door and came out onto the porch. He closed the door behind him.

Speed started to speak, but his father held up his hand.

"Son, before you say anything, I have a confession."

An icy chill crept down the back of Speed's neck.

"A confession?"

His father nodded. "Something I should have told you a long time ago."

Speed took a deep breath, preparing for the worst. His father opened the front door.

"Son, I'd like you to meet your sister."

A woman stepped into view. She was a few years older than Speed. The woman held out her hand.

"Hello, Wilbur. I'm Robyn."

Speed stared at her. His head moved backwards and forwards between the woman and his father.

"My si... sister?"

His father nodded. "Your older sister. She was given up for adoption before you were born."

"Adoption? You had another child?"

"Your mother gave birth to Robyn when she was only sixteen. We weren't ready to be parents. At the time we thought it was for the best, but that turned out not to be the case. Your mother never forgave herself. Neither of us did."

"But —"

"If I could change the past, I would."

Speed turned to Robyn and took her outstretched hand. "Hello, Robyn. I'm … Wilbur."

She smiled at him and then they embraced. Cautiously at first. Afraid of making a mistake.

Eventually they released each other.

"How did you find one another?" said Speed. "I thought adoption records were sealed."

"Robyn tracked me down," said his dad. "The agency sent me a letter asking if I wanted to meet."

"And that's why you were in Moncton on the night Hinkley was killed?"

"Exactly. I was meeting my daughter for the first time in forty years."

Speed wiped his eyes. "I'm sorry, Dad. For thinking you might be capable of murder."

His dad touched his arm. "It's okay. I realised how it must have looked after you left. When I wouldn't answer your questions."

Speed embraced his dad and held him for several seconds.

"I understand you not telling me why you were in Moncton that night. But what about the new car?"

His dad looked sheepish.

"I won some money gambling."

Speed stiffened. "Gambling?"

His dad noticed the reaction. "Don't worry. I wasn't using The App. I won it in a poker game down at the Legion."

"Sounds like a high stakes game," said Speed. There was a hint of disapproval in his voice.

"Yeah. It's a good thing I didn't lose, or I'd have been

coming to live with you."

His father didn't wait for a response. He linked his arm through his daughter's and led her towards the door. "Don't worry, Robyn. He doesn't *normally* accuse his family of committing crimes."

CHAPTER THIRTY-SEVEN

Negotiations

"Eli insisted that I talk to you," said Simon. "He said it was in my best interests."

Preston Shade leaned forward on the dining chair with his hands spread either side of him on the table.

Simon was reminded of a toad he'd once seen in Australia.

"Mr Rabinovich is a wise man," said Shade. "Quick to spot an opportunity."

"I've noticed," said Simon.

"He had some complimentary things to say about you, as well." Shade shifted his gaze to Sienna and his mouth stretched into a thin smile. "He had *very* nice things to say about you too, Ms Volkov."

Simon's head snapped around to face Sienna. "Volkov? Does that mean you were —"

"His wife," said Sienna. Her face was devoid of expression.

"Sorry for your loss, Ms Volkov," said Shade. "Terrible news about your husband's death."

"Don't be sorry. I don't consider it a loss."

Shade nodded. "Eli said you were a survivor."

Simon shook his head. "Why didn't you tell me?"

"It wasn't relevant," said Sienna.

"Not relevant?"

"Let's discuss this later." She turned to Shade. "For now, why don't we hear what Mr Shade has to offer."

Her eyes narrowed. "I presume that's why you're here, after all."

Shade inclined his head. "Of course, madam."

Simon stared at Sienna for several more seconds before turning back to Shade.

"All right, Mr Shade. Why have you come all the way from New York to Vancouver? You don't look like the type who enjoys skiing."

Shade laughed. "You're quite right, Mr Simpson. I prefer my sport in the boardrooms and corridors of power." He leaned back in his chair and reached into his suit pocket. He pulled out a rosary and began moving its beads between his fingers. "I'm not sure why you created your computer application, Mr Simpson. May I call you Simon?"

"Just tell me why you're here."

Shade's lips tightened. "Very well. A business transaction then. It's not important *why* you created The App. But the fact is, you did. And it has caused significant difficulties for many people."

"You mean for the people who died?"

"For them too. But I was referring to the people I represent."

"And who exactly *do* you represent, Mr Shade."

"They prefer to remain anonymous. Let's just say they're the people who make things happen in the world."

"You mean the puppeteers who pull the strings?"

Shade's lips stretched across his face. "Exactly. The *real* people who drive economic growth. The people who grease the axle on which the planet spins."

"You actually believe that?"

Shade shrugged. "It doesn't matter. What matters is

that they're the ones who control things. Which countries have wars. The price of oil. Who has enough to eat."

"Most people think it's the politicians who determine that," said Sienna.

Shade snorted. "Most people are naive. The politicians do what they're told. Or at least, they used to."

"Used to?" said Simon. "Until I created The App, you mean?"

"Yes," said Shade. He leaned forward. "Until you created The App."

"And now your puppet masters aren't happy?"

"No, they're not. With your little computer program, you've highlighted something politicians care about more than money." His brow furrowed. "And as a result, it's harder to control them."

"You mean I've cut their strings?" said Simon.

"*Some* of their strings," said Shade. "There *are* others. But money has always been the simplest string to pull."

"So, why are you here, Mr Shade?"

"To make you a proposal, of course."

"A proposal?" said Sienna. She leaned forward.

Shade smiled. "A generous proposal."

"Interesting," said Simon. "How do you define *generous*?"

"We'd like to buy your company?" said Shade.

"Excuse me?" said Simon.

"What are you offering?" said Sienna.

Shade looked at Sienna then back at Simon. He rubbed his rosary beads.

"Buying your company isn't our first choice. We've tried other means to keep our politicians in check. Regrettably, those methods had mixed results. But then it occurred to us that *your* method is more effective. And cheaper."

"*My* method?" said Simon.

"Yes. They do *your* bidding for a fraction of what it costs us to bribe them."

"It's not *my* bidding," said Simon. "It's the bidding of the people."

"Ha," said Shade. "That's just semantics. You're still controlling them. And we'd like to do that too."

"By using The App?"

He nodded.

"How much?" said Sienna.

Shade licked his lips. "Straight to point, Ms Volkov. Very well. We're prepared to offer you twenty million dollars. US."

"Not enough," said Sienna.

Shade looked at Simon who shook his head.

"The App is very profitable," said Sienna. "You have no idea how many people are placing bets."

Shade frowned. "Oh, I think we do." He chewed his lip. "Hmm … very well. I had to *try* low-balling you. Part of the game. But I can see you appreciate your company's true value."

Sienna folded her arms. "How much?"

"I'm authorised to offer you one hundred million dollars."

Sienna smiled. "That's more like it."

"I'll have to think about it," said Simon.

"What?" said Shade.

Sienna turned to face Simon, a hand covering her mouth.

"I'll have to think about your offer," said Simon.

"I assure you, Mr Simpson, this offer is very generous.

It takes into account future earnings. And there's no risk to you. The authorities will become *our* problem."

"Even so, I'll need to think about your offer."

Shade arched his eyebrows and stared at Simon for a good ten seconds.

Then he stood. "I'll give you a day, Mr Simpson. The people I represent are not known for their patience. I'll return tomorrow."

He picked up his briefcase and walked to the door. "Don't get up. I'll show myself out."

When the door had closed, Sienna turned to Simon.

"Do you think he'll increase his offer?"

Simon shrugged. "Maybe. But it doesn't matter."

Sienna chewed on her fingernail. "Why not?"

"Because I'm not selling."

"Not selling?" she said. "But you'll be rich. One hundred million dollars." She touched his arm. "We'll never have to work again."

Simon pulled away. "Don't you get it? It's not about the money."

"It's always about the money."

"Can you imagine what will happen if Shade gets control of The App?"

She moved closer and placed a finger on Simon's lips. "He'll give us more money than we can ever possibly spend."

Simon snorted. "Somehow I think you'd give it a good go."

A smile creased Sienna's lips. She chuckled. "Yes. I suppose you're right." She gently traced her finger down his chin and onto his chest. "But you'll be there to make sure I don't get carried away."

Simon placed his hands on her shoulders and gently

pushed her away.

"Shade and his kind would have complete control. They'd manipulate the database so only their enemies became targets. Good people would die, rather than those who deserve to."

"Good and evil is sometimes just a matter of perspective."

Simon sighed. "When I initially built this thing, I'll admit it was for revenge. But since then … it's become so much more. It's given people a voice. And they've used it to make the world better."

Sienna put her hands on her hips. "I'm afraid I don't share your optimism for the world. In my experience, it's better to eat too much than become someone else's meal. And Shade is offering you a feast."

"Sienna, I understand you've had a different experience in your life … and that *may* explain the way you feel. But you're wrong." He turned and opened the front door. "I'm taking Gizmo for a walk. I need to clear my head." He called to Gizmo and attached his lead. They left her alone.

Sienna stared at the door as it swung shut behind him. The loud bang releasing her from her trance.

She shook her head. "You're the one making a mistake," she said.

She picked up the phone and called Eli.

He'd know what to do.

When Simon returned, he was met by Sienna as he entered the apartment. Gizmo made a beeline for his water bowl.

"I'm sorry," said Sienna. "I didn't mean to get angry. It's *your* company and *your* decision. I was out of line."

Simon reached for her and pulled her towards him. "Thanks for understanding. It means a lot."

Sienna squeezed his hand. "It's just that I've been so stressed lately," she said. "With everything that's happened."

"I know," said Simon.

Sienna whispered in his ear. "You know what we need?"

"What? And please don't say another shopping trip."

"A holiday."

Simon nodded thoughtfully. "That's actually not a bad idea."

"Somewhere remote," she said. "Away from the city."

"How about a ski trip to Whistler? There's still some good spring skiing. We can hire a chalet with a hot tub on the slopes?"

Sienna frowned and sucked on her bottom lip — a trait Simon had observed during their chess games. It meant she was thinking.

"I'm only an intermediate level skier."

"There's some boutique clothes shops up at Whistler."

Sienna's frown disappeared. "Hm ... in that case, I think skiing is an excellent idea."

Simon was surprised when he opened the front door the next day. Eli was standing slightly behind Preston Shade. His lips were pressed firmly together.

"I wasn't expecting *you* as well, Eli," said Simon.

"I thought you might need my advice," said Eli.

"Um. All right. Come in then." Simon stepped back from the door and waved them inside. There were two large men behind them who could have been clones. They wore dark suits and sunglasses.

Gizmo bared his teeth at them and made a growling sound.

Shade turned to the nearest clone. "Wait outside, Jonus."

The two bodybuilders stepped back and Simon closed the door. He raised his eyebrows at Sienna who just shrugged.

"Before we start," said Eli. "I'd like to emphasise some of the benefits of Mr Shade's offer."

"You know what he's offering?" said Simon.

"We've had some discussions."

"Interesting."

"Um … apart from the obvious benefits of such a large amount of cash, I think you need to understand the potential *legal* benefits."

"Legal benefits?"

"The only reason the authorities are pursuing you so vigorously is because of pressure from behind the scenes. But with you out of the game, all that will disappear."

"Won't their attention just be redirected to Mr Shade and his associates?" said Simon.

"Only in part," said Eli. "Once Mr Shade possesses both carrot *and* stick, he can nip most investigations in the bud."

"And for those he can't?"

Eli paused. He exchanged a look with Preston Shade.

"Mr Rabinovich will be paid a retainer, to help with any legal arguments," said Shade. "I understand he has an intimate knowledge of the inner workings of your application. Something he's used to good effect so far."

"A retainer?" said Simon.

Eli took a sudden interest in his own feet.

"A very generous one," said Shade.

Simon nodded. "I see." He walked over to where Sienna was sitting and stood behind her. He placed his hands on her shoulders. "I'm sorry to disappoint you, Mr Shade. But I can't accept your offer." He frowned at Eli. "As generous as it is."

Sienna's shoulders tightened beneath Simon's hands.

"There's no such thing as *can't*, Mr Simpson," said Shade. "Not as far as my backers are concerned. I think the word you're looking for is *won't*."

"That's just *semantics*, Mr Shade. It still means *no*."

"The group I represent aren't used to hearing that word."

"What can I say?"

"You're making a mistake."

"It wouldn't be the first one."

"I don't suppose it would help if I increased our offer?"

Simon shook his head.

"I didn't think so," said Shade.

Shade emerged from Simon's apartment with Eli walking briskly behind him.

"Mr Shade. Wait up." Eli reached his hand out to touch Shade's shoulder.

One of Shade's bodyguards moved to intercept him. Shade raised his palm, stopping the minder in his tracks. "It's okay, Jonus."

Eli stepped closer and lowered his voice. "I have a proposition you might find interesting."

"Really?" said Shade.

Eli nodded. He checked over his shoulder. "But we should probably talk about it in your limousine."

The edges of Shade's lips curled. "I knew there was a reason I liked you, Mr Rabinovich."

"Please, call me Eli."

"Let's organise that ski trip," said Simon. "I need to get away after meeting that man."

"All right," said Sienna. "Just let me get changed into something more comfortable." She disappeared into the bedroom.

She returned a few minutes later in a pair of black silk pyjamas.

Simon gave a low whistle.

Sienna sat next to him and put a hand on his leg. "It's one of the things you bought me."

"Good to see that shopping trip produced some benefits." He ran his hand over the silk.

Sienna smiled and pointed at the computer. "Didn't you want to book our trip?" She removed his hand and placed it on the keyboard.

He reluctantly brought up the web page for Whistler's central reservations. There were plenty of options.

"How about this one?" said Simon. "It's ski-in/ski-out *and* it has a hot tub."

"Hmm. It looks okay." She tapped another item in the list. "But this one's better."

Simon read its description.

Close to shops.

He suppressed a groan.

"It *still* has a hot tub," she said.

He pulled out his credit card and made the reservation.

"What about Gizmo?" said Sienna. "He can't stay here for five days."

"I'll ask my neighbour, Mrs Martinelli, to take him. She's lonely these days and loves Gizmo. And he loves her lasagne."

Gizmo looked up and wagged his tail.

"Okay," said Sienna. She rose from her chair and faced Simon. "And now I think you need to relax. Why don't you help me with my pyjamas?"

CHAPTER THIRTY-EIGHT

Targets

"Finally," said Dillon.

A target that didn't involve driving for days across the country.

True, it *was* in Canada. But Vancouver was only two hours from Seattle by car.

Dillon had had enough of long trips.

He picked up the phone and dialled an old buddy from the Corps.

"Hey, John. I'm coming to Canada on business. Is it okay if I crash at your place for a few days?"

"Sure, man. *Semper Fi.*" They chatted about the old days in Afghanistan for a few minutes before saying goodbye.

Dillon rechecked The App. He whistled at the ten million dollar prize pool.

The target must have *really* pissed someone off.

He wouldn't want to be Simon Simpson.

"Who was that on the phone?" said Simon.

Sienna jumped. She hadn't heard Simon approach.

"Um … it was just Eli. He wanted to know where we were staying. In case he needs to contact us."

"Hmm. I'm not sure I trust him anymore. He seems to be more concerned with his own interests."

"I *did* warn you he wasn't very ethical. But at least he's predictable. He can always be relied on when it comes to his greed."

"That's what worries me," said Simon.

"He knows you need to be kept out of jail, or he won't get paid. And you *know* he wants to get paid."

"I guess," said Simon. "But I still don't trust him."

"Stop worrying and come and help me pack."

The break in the case came as Special Agent Marks was about to sit down to his T-bone steak. An enthusiastic lab technician phoned him with the news.

"Are you sitting down?" said the tech.

"Almost," said Marks. He looked at the juicy beef on his plate.

"We've analysed the trace evidence from Senator Criddle's death in Connecticut. The pattern of evidence was similar to your Jerry Upton scene in LA."

"Similar? How?" said Marks.

"There were a lot of different hairs and fibers left at the scene … as if someone had deliberately dumped evidence to confuse us."

"Interesting. Did you get any matches between the two scenes?"

"No."

"That's too bad," said Marks. He dipped his finger in the mushroom sauce and stuck it in his mouth.

"Not with the Jerry Upton scene. But we *did* get a DNA match with the trace that we collected from the Los Angeles motel."

Marks removed his finger from his mouth. "You mean the one where Randy Lee met the hooker?"

"That's the one. Do you know how many DNA samples we found in that motel room? *Hundreds*. We had a field day with the blue light."

"What was the match?"

"Um … we got a match with a sample from Senator Criddle's front yard. A solitary match, which —"

"Makes it highly likely that it's our perp," said Marks.

"It gets better. We've got an ID. You're going to love this."

Marks had forgotten all about his steak. "Tell me."

"The guy we matched is former military. Did you know that all military personnel have their DNA taken —"

"Tell me his name."

"Not *only* is he military. He's a former Marine *sniper*. And the best bit is that he owns a Chevy van."

"Goddammit. What's his fucking name?"

"Dillon Black."

Marks arrived in Seattle four hours later. He was met by the commander of the Hostage Rescue Team. Marks recognised him from the botched takedown of Randy Lee.

"Can you try and leave my suspect alive this time?" said Marks.

The HRT commander huffed. "We can probably manage that … for a couple of pizzas."

Dillon's phone beeped. It was a message from The App. He'd received it because he'd registered for notifications about Simon Simpson.

The target's profile information had changed. A new location.

According to the update, Simon was staying at a chalet in Whistler for the next five days.

Dillon went down to the basement and picked out two

sets of skis. Downhill and cross-country. Then he went upstairs to pack.

The Hostage Rescue Team was in position. They'd surrounded Dillon's pink, two-storey house in Puyallup, south of Seattle.

Several snipers were deployed in adjacent buildings, and neighbouring residents had been discreetly moved away.

The assault teams climbed the stairs at the front and back of the building and waited for the signal.

"Breach."

The doors burst open. Flash bangs were hurled inside and the operators charged into the darkened house.

There were loud explosions and a cloud of white smoke. The teams methodically cleared the basement and ground floor. Then they moved up the stairs.

The first operator to reach the top was nicknamed Arnie. He was built like *The Terminator* and almost as lethal. He was closely followed by his hairy companion, Chewie.

They stopped on the landing at the top of the staircase. A banging noise was coming from behind a closed door. According to the house plans it was the master bedroom.

They signalled each other with their hands and cautiously approached the door.

Arnie held up his fingers.

Three.

Two.

One.

He kicked open the door and moved in to cover the left side of the room. Chewie followed, covering the right.

Something metallic rattled in the back corner. It was followed by a rustling noise.

"Fuck you," shrieked a voice from the darkness.

Arnie swivelled and aimed his gun at the voice. He fired. There was a crash and thud. The shrieking stopped.

He slowly approached the lifeless form on the floor, his weapon raised. A third operator, Hank, turned on the lights.

"Fuck," said Arnie. "Not again."

Lying on the floor amongst the blood and feathers was Dillon's parrot. It was very dead.

"We're never going to hear the end of this," said Chewie.

Hank shook his head. "You know what this means?"

"Yup," said Arnie. "No pizza."

CHAPTER THIRTY-NINE

Borderline

"Fuck," said Marks.

"It was only a parrot," said the HRT commander. "Even with waterboarding, it couldn't have told you much."

Marks ignored him.

Instead, he turned on his phone and started The App. Who would Black's next target be?

He scrolled to the top of the list.

"Shit."

Marks opened the contact list on his phone and stabbed at Detective Kelly's name. Kelly answered on the seventh ring.

"This better be good," he said. "The Canucks are a goal up with only three minutes to play."

Marks apologised and explained what he'd found.

Kelly forgot about the score. "I'll alert them at the border," he said.

At the precise moment that Dillon's parrot left the world, its owner was driving over the Canadian border at the Peace Arch crossing.

"Passport," said the Canadian official.

Dillon handed his American passport through the van's window.

He smiled. But not too much. He'd seen those television shows about border security and was aware of the types of behaviour that raised suspicions.

He was keen to avoid closer inspection. Partly because he was in a hurry, but mainly because of the weapons hidden inside his van. His rifle was in pieces beneath the floor, and he had a pistol in a compartment under the dashboard.

"What is the purpose of your visit to Canada?"

"I'm visiting a friend in Vancouver. We're going skiing for a few days."

"What does your friend do?"

"He's a fireman."

"Where does he live?"

"In Vancouver." Dillon gave him the address. He waited while the official typed something into his computer.

"Your friend's name?"

"John Williams".

"Are you skiing in Vancouver? It's very late in the season for the local mountains."

"No. We're heading up to Whistler. My friend's organising the accommodation."

The official nodded and peered through the van's window at the skis lying in the back.

He made a note on his computer then handed Dillon his passport.

"Welcome to Canada, Mr Black. *Bienvenue.*"

"You were right," said Detective Kelly. "He came across the border."

"Did you get him," said Special Agent Marks.

"No. We missed him by an hour."

"Goddammit. This guy keeps getting lucky."

"Yeah … well maybe his luck just ran out. He gave the

border guard an address where he's staying. And we're going to pay him a visit."

"Finally," said Marks. "It seems like I've been chasing this asshole forever."

"I've put in the call to our Emergency Response Team."

"Shit," said Marks. "I hope they're not as trigger happy as the HRT?"

"Don't worry," said Kelly. "They promised not to shoot anything with feathers."

Dillon loved Canadians. They were like polite Americans who spoke French.

He phoned his buddy, John Williams.

"*Bienvenue*," said Dillon.

"Fuck off, Dillon," said John. "Don't you start with that French crap too."

Dillon laughed. "I think it's kind of cool."

"Do you realise that almost every document or sign in Canada has to be printed twice? Once in English and once in French."

"Seriously?"

"Except the French words have to be bigger in Quebec."

Dillon laughed again. "You're kidding, right?" He paused. "Aren't you?"

"I wish," said John. "Are you in Canada yet?"

"Just crossed the border, but there's been a change of plans. My business meeting has moved up to Whistler, so I won't need to stay with you."

"Whistler, eh? Some kind of swanky conference in a luxury resort?"

"If only. I'm on a budget … at least until I pull off this

deal. Can you recommend a cheap place near here?" He read out the address of Simon's chalet.

"Just a minute." Dillon heard the clicking of a keyboard in the background. After a couple of minutes, John returned. He gave Dillon a list of three possible places.

"Thanks," said Dillon. "I'll drop in to see you on the way back. If the deal turns out as I expect, dinner and drinks are on me."

"I'll hold you to that," said John.

They hung up. Dillon checked for traffic, then eased his van off the shoulder and onto Highway 99.

Next stop, Whistler.

Simon and Sienna had driven to Whistler in the morning. The roads were clear until about ten kilometres from the resort, where late season snow had left a thin white blanket on the ground.

After picking up the keys, they drove to their chalet and unpacked.

"We still have enough time for an afternoon ski," said Simon. "Which would you prefer? Downhill or cross-country?"

He willed her to say downhill.

"Cross-country's easier," she said. "And more private."

"Okay," he said. "I can live with that."

They had lunch then got changed into their ski clothes. Simon was ready first. He went outside to secure the skis to the car's roof.

He was too engrossed in what he was doing to notice the van parked across the street.

Dillon Black had just turned off his engine when Simon stepped out of the chalet carrying some skis.

"Damn," said Dillon. Another thirty minutes and he would have retrieved his rifle from its hiding place.

Dillon started to reach for his pistol before hesitating. Should he take a risk? Or wait and observe?

A professional would wait.

He was glad he did.

Sienna walked out of the chalet. "Where are we going?" she asked.

Her voice carried through Dillon's open window.

"Lost Lake," said Simon. "I thought we'd ski the beginner's trail around it."

"An easy trail sounds good to me."

Dillon googled the trail map for Lost Lake. He noted an advanced trail that intersected the beginners loop on the far side of the lake. Simon would have to ski past the trails' junction. A plan began to form.

By the time they'd arrived in the Lost Lake carpark, Dillon knew exactly what to do.

The Vancouver Emergency Response Team had surrounded the address they'd been given in the suburb of Marpole. It was a single story house at the end of a cul-de-sac.

"Go," said the team's commander.

The team member next to him checked his equipment. Then he picked up the phone.

It rang twice before being answered.

"Hello," said a male voice.

"Is that John Williams?"

"Who's asking?"

"I'm from the Emergency Response Team. We have

your house surrounded. Please come out with your hands up."

Five minutes later, Williams was in handcuffs, sitting on his front lawn. One of the police officers offered him a cigarette.

"Nice job," said Detective Kelly.

"We prefer our suspects alive," said the ERT commander.

Detective Peters approached Williams. "What can you tell us about Dillon Black?"

He told them everything he knew.

"I'm a bit confused though," he said. "What's Dillon done?"

"I guess you could say that he's been doing what he was trained to do," said Peters.

The ERT commander motioned to Kelly, and twirled his finger in the air. "Do you two fancy a chopper ride up to Whistler?

Kelly nodded. "I'll have the local police meet us there with some cars."

On the way to the airport he phoned Marks.

"Whistler?" said Special Agent Marks. "Wait a minute." He recalled something he'd seen earlier when he'd discovered the bet on Simon Simpson.

He opened The App.

"That's where Simpson is supposed to be staying for a few days."

He read Kelly the address of Simpson's chalet.

Kelly copied it down on a piece of paper and handed it to the ERT commander. "Can you get the helicopters to drop us near there?"

"I'll talk to the pilots."

CHAPTER FORTY

Cross-country

Simon and Sienna walked from the carpark to the entrance of the cross-country trails. There was hardly anyone else around.

"You were right about it being more private," said Simon.

They stopped at the main ticket booth then fitted their skis. Behind them, a serious looking man in his early thirties purchased a ticket.

Simon smiled at the man. "Nice day for a ski, eh?"

The man nodded back. "The location is perfect," he said. "Glad I made the drive."

Simon recognised the man's accent as American. "Welcome to Canada. Hope you enjoy your stay."

"I'm sure I will," said the man. He turned away to adjust his skis. Then he skated off to the advanced trail.

"He looks like he knows what he's doing," said Sienna.

Behind them a woman with blonde hair was also buying a ticket. She had a rifle strapped to her back.

Sienna nudged Simon and pointed at the gun. The woman noticed and laughed. "Don't worry, it's not loaded. I'm training for the biathlon. It's more realistic this way."

Simon nodded and touched Sienna on the shoulder. "Let's go," he said. He led her to the beginner's trail.

The woman with the blonde hair adjusted her jacket,

momentarily exposing her trident tattoo to the winter sun. Then she headed to the beginner's trail.

Dillon pushed himself along the Upper Panorama trail. He wanted to be at the junction well ahead of Simon.

In his knapsack was his pistol. A Glock 17. He hadn't had time to retrieve his rifle.

But Dillon wasn't concerned. A handgun would do the job. There'd be no mistakes this time.

Seven minutes later, Dillon stopped just before the junction. He placed his knapsack on the ground and was about to remove the gun when he heard helicopters.

He looked up. Two *CH-146* helicopters flew low in formation about a kilometre away. Black clad figures could be seen sitting inside, reminding him of his time in Afghanistan.

He laughed. Someone was in for a nasty surprise.

He removed the pistol from his bag and waited.

From the air, the white expanse of Lost Lake stood in stark contrast to the dark green fir trees surrounding it. Several ant-like skiers moved slowly around the frozen water in a clockwise direction.

"I'd love to be down there," said Detective Peters.

"Skiing?" said Detective Kelly.

Peters shook her head. "Skating."

They were interrupted by the ERT commander. "Two minutes," he said.

The helicopters banked and headed towards a line of police cars in a clearing.

"We're getting close to them, now," said Kelly. "I can feel it."

Sienna was skiing slowly next to Simon. She looked back over her shoulder at the blonde woman for the third time.

"For someone who's training for a biathlon, she's not very fast. She's only just keeping pace with us."

Simon turned. The woman with the blonde hair was about two hundred metres away.

"You're right. I don't think she'll be representing Canada any time soon."

"She sounded American," said Sienna.

Simon nodded. "A lot of Americans out skiing today."

They resumed skiing towards the place where several white trails intersected.

"Which way do we go?" said Sienna.

"To the right. The other two trails are more advanced."

They reached the junction at the same time as another skier. It was the American man from the ticket booth.

"Hello, again," said Simon. Then he noticed the pistol in the man's hand. "I don't think you're allowed handguns here."

Dillon raised the weapon and pointed it at Simon. Simon froze.

"Simon Simpson?" said Dillon.

"How do you know my name?"

"Someone doesn't like you, Simon."

"What do you mean?"

"The App says you're worth ten million dollars."

"What the —" said Simon.

"Ten million dollars?" said Sienna.

"I s'pose I should thank you," said Dillon. "For being worth so much."

Sienna moved crab-like away from Simon, leaving him alone on the trail. She pushed one hand into her jacket pocket.

"Any last words?" said Dillon.

Simon turned his head towards Sienna. "Don't hurt my girlfriend."

He never heard Dillon's response. There was a loud bang, and a red cherry blossomed in the centre of Dillon's chest.

"Jesus," said Simon.

Sienna screamed and released the pistol in her pocket. "It wasn't me."

She was telling the truth.

The helicopters touched down in a swirl of white. The Emergency Response Team members jumped out.

A police sergeant came forward to greet them.

"We've rounded up some transportation for you. Mr Simpson's chalet is two minutes from here by car."

Detective Peters and Detective Kelly climbed into the first vehicle with the ERT commander. The cars took off in a convoy.

"We've set up road blocks," said the sergeant. "And we've told the neighbours to stay indoors."

"Let's try calling Simpson first," said the ERT commander. "See if he's okay."

"There's no landline in the chalet," said the sergeant.

"Try this," said Kelly. He handed his cell phone with Simon's number to the ERT commander. "We've spoken to Mr Simpson a few times."

The commander selected Simon's number.

The phone rang.

After a minute, he terminated the call.

"He's not answering."

The police sergeant interrupted them. "There've been reports of shots fired out at Lost Lake. The cross-country ski course."

"Shit," said Peters. "We just flew over that."

"We'll get there quicker if we drive," said the sergeant. He gave instructions over the radio and the convoy turned around.

"It was me," said a female voice.

Simon and Sienna turned towards its source. The blonde woman was skating quickly towards them on her cross-country skis.

She moved gracefully despite the rifle she was holding in front of her chest.

Ashton Treacle slid to a stop next to Dillon, then squatted to feel his pulse. Satisfied, she stood.

"You must be Simon Simpson," she said.

Simon nodded.

"So much for your rifle not being loaded," said Sienna. She slowly moved her hand into her own pocket.

Ashton gestured with her rifle and shook her head. "Hands where I can see them please."

Sienna removed her hand and raised her arms above her head.

Ashton turned to Simon. "Did you know someone has placed a ten million dollar bounty on your head?"

Simon nodded towards the dead man on the ground. "He just told me."

The woman grimaced. "I've seen him a lot, lately. The two of us keep showing up for the same assignments."

Sienna stared at the blood spreading on the man's chest. "I guess there won't be any more clashes," she said.

Ashton ignored her and addressed Simon. "The question now, is what to do about you?"

"Ten million dollars is a lot of money," said Simon.

"It is," said Ashton. "And until recently, I would have been happy to claim the prize. But then I realised what you're doing."

"Which is?"

"Transforming society," said Ashton. "For the better." She explained what had happened with her great-grandmother in hospital, and how they'd used The App to force down the price of medications in the US. Millions of people were better off as a result. "So when I saw your name at the top of the list, I thought you might need some help." She jerked her head towards Dillon's body. "Seems I was right."

"Thanks," said Simon. "I appreciate it." He looked at Sienna then back to the woman holding the gun. "So what happens now?"

"You should probably remove your name from the list."

"Um … there's a few problems with that. Firstly, I'm not dead. And secondly, if I remove my name before I'm dead … I soon will be. People know I'm on the list now and they won't tolerate that kind of double standard." He paused. "I also want the transformation to continue. But in order for that to happen, The App *must* remain credible."

"I see your point," said Ashton. "In that case, you need to disappear."

Simon tensed. "Disappear?"

"If you stay in the open, assassins will keep coming until the prize is claimed. They have ten million reasons."

Sienna nodded in the background.

"I'm not sure anywhere would be safe," said Simon.

Sienna took a step forward and slowly lowered her hands. "I might have an idea."

"What?" said Simon.

"We can hire a boat and sail around the islands. At least until we work out a long term plan. No one will know where we've gone and it will give us time to think."

"Do you know how to pilot a boat?"

Sienna nodded. "I had a rich father in my former life, remember?"

Ashton glanced at her watch. "I need to leave you now. Someone may have reported the shot. Your girlfriend's plan sounds like a good one." She adjusted her goggles and paused. "Keep up the good work." Then she skied back towards the car park.

Simon's phone started to ring. It was Detective Kelly's number. He ignored it.

"I think we might have some company soon, Sienna."

The convoy of police cars drove down the highway towards Lost Lake. They ignored the blonde woman in a Subaru Outback heading the other way.

As they pulled into the carpark, Detective Peters pointed at Dillon's van.

"That looks like the van Marks told us about."

Kelly nodded then pointed at a woman running towards them. "Isn't that Simpson's hooker girlfriend, Sienna?"

Sienna was waving at them frantically with her hands in the air. "Help," she said. "There's been a shooting."

She led them back along the trail. Her progress was much quicker without the cross-country skis. She'd dumped them next to Simon and run back to the carpark to wait for the police. She'd just had enough time to hide her pistol before the police pulled into the carpark.

"They're just around the next bend," she said.

The Emergency Response Team fanned out in front of them with their weapons drawn. As they rounded the bend, two figures could be seen lying on the ground.

They approached the figures and Simon slowly raised his hands. "Don't shoot," he said. "It was the other guy who tried to kill me."

They moved in and secured Simon with flex-cuffs.

Detective Kelly compared Dillon's face to a picture he'd been sent. He took a photo on his phone and pressed send. "This should make Special Agent Marks very happy."

Detective Peters grinned at Simon.

"I didn't think you'd be so happy to see me alive," said Simon.

"I'm not," said Peters. "But now we've got you on murder, which is the next best thing."

Simon laughed. "Sorry to spoil the party, Detective."

He told her about the other shooter. Though he didn't mention she was a woman.

Simon and Sienna were driven back to Vancouver under the watchful eye of Detective Peters. She scowled at them the entire way.

When they arrived at the station, Sienna used her phone call to contact Eli.

He was surprised by her news.

"I'll have you out of there soon," he said. "Both of

you."

Sienna was led back to where Simon was being held.

"What did he say?" said Simon.

"Not to worry. He'll take care of everything."

CHAPTER FORTY-ONE
Bon Voyage

The autopsy on Dillon Black's body had been performed as soon as it reached Vancouver, and the fatal bullet retrieved. The relevant data had been sent immediately to the local lab and to the FBI for analysis.

Special Agent Marks doodled on his pad as he read the FBI's ballistics report. He paused when he reached the conclusion.

Dillon Black was shot by the same weapon that had killed two US Senators.

Marks phoned Detective Peters.

"Simpson didn't kill Dillon Black," he said. He held the phone away from his ear for the reply.

"Don't look so disappointed, Detective Peters," said Eli. "Justice has prevailed and an innocent man goes free."

Peters clenched her fist and took a step towards Eli. She was prevented from hurting him by Detective Kelly's hand on her shoulder.

Eli winked at her then turned to Simon and Sienna. "See, I told you I'd get you out."

"We never doubted you," said Sienna. She squeezed Simon's hand.

Simon remained silent.

They left the police station. Eli walked them to their car, which the police had transported back from

Whistler.

"Sienna tells me you're planning on lying low for a while," he said. "Sounds like a good idea. Just make sure that I know where to find you."

Simon gave a non-committal shrug then drove off.

Eli went back to his office and phoned Preston Shade.

Simon's knuckles whitened as he tightened his grip on the steering wheel. "We're *not* telling Eli where we're going this time."

"Okay," said Sienna. "It's your call."

They drove through back alleys and darkened roads until they reached Simon's apartment. The street outside was deserted.

"I can't see anyone lurking around," said Simon. "But that doesn't mean there isn't someone waiting inside."

"Wait here and pop the trunk," said Sienna. She jumped out of the car. When the trunk opened, she dug inside the rim of the spare tire for the pistol she'd hidden earlier in the day. She opened the driver's door.

"Jesus," said Simon. "Did you bring that thing with us?"

"Are you complaining?"

"Er ... I guess not."

"Good. Then follow me."

She led him quickly to the front door then waited while he fumbled with the keys. Eventually he managed to unlock the door. They entered the apartment.

"Stay here," whispered Sienna. "I'll check the rest of the rooms."

He watched with a mixture of fascination and terror as Sienna went from room to room with the gun held in front of her. Eventually she returned.

"All clear," she said.

Simon sighed. "We need to hire that boat. I can't stay here."

He turned on his computer. While he was waiting for it to boot up he checked The App on his phone.

His jaw clenched. He'd hoped it wasn't true, but it was.

Preston Shade evidently didn't take *no* for an answer.

Sienna sat beside him and rested her hand on his knee. "We'll be safe on a boat. Just you and me."

He opened a web browser on his computer and searched for boats in Vancouver. He was surprised by how many there were.

"How long should we hire it for?" said Simon.

"Start with a month."

"Does it matter what kind of boat?"

"Get one with a motor. Easier for us to handle." She pointed at a picture of a sleek cruiser. "How about this one?"

Simon opened the link for a *Marquis SC 40*.

"Nice," he said. "It looks brand new. But I wonder why it's so cheap?"

Sienna gave a wry smile. "I imagine there's a lot of luxury boats being leased because of the GFC."

Simon nodded, appreciating the irony.

"Have you noticed that boats are almost always painted white?" he said.

They made their booking online. The boat would be available at lunchtime the following day. The marina was just down the road, on Granville Island.

"Excellent," said Sienna. "Tomorrow we'll be on the water and you can stop worrying."

"We still have to get there first."

She patted his cheek. "I'll protect you, my little computer genius. But first I'm going to have a shower. A day of skiing, shooting and police interrogations. You sure know how to show a girl a good time."

She picked up her phone and headed to the bathroom.

Simon needed a shower too. But he could wait.

He opened the website for CBC News and clicked on a video clip of Christine Hunter. She was interviewing people on the streets of Vancouver about The App. Most were saying positive things.

Simon paused the video on a close up of Christine's face. He was twirling his pencil and gazing at her picture when his phone beeped.

A system message from The App.

As he read it, his fingers tightened around the pencil. The thin wood bent under the pressure. Eventually the pencil snapped, splintering into shards.

One of the fragments pierced his finger. Simon put the injured finger in his mouth. He sat like that for several minutes. Tasting blood. Thinking.

Then he made two phone calls. The first was to his mother.

The second call was to Christine Hunter.

When Sienna came out of the shower, she noticed his change of mood.

"Are you okay?" she said.

He held up his bandaged digit. "I cut my finger."

Simon got up early the next morning. He began to prepare what they'd need. Sienna joined him an hour later.

"I have to run some errands," said Simon. "And I'm going to leave Gizmo with my Mom. He can't stay with

Mrs Martinelli indefinitely."

"Do you *need* me to come?"

"No. You finish packing. Grab as much food as you can find, and bring those passports you got us."

She raised her eyebrows. "Are we going somewhere?"

"Just making sure we have options." He paused. "There's one more thing."

"What?"

"Can I borrow your pistol?"

"Seriously?"

"Just while I'm running my errands. It's me they're after. Not you. And I'd feel better if I had some protection."

Sienna chewed her lip. "Do you even know how to use it?"

"I watched an online video while you were in the shower last night."

"Hmm. Okay, but let me show you again in case the video was wrong."

She showed him the basics then he tucked the gun into the waistband of his jeans.

"See you in a couple of hours," said Simon. "We'll need to put that double kayak on the car when I get back."

"The kayak?"

"Yes. Just because we're hiding out, it doesn't mean we can't have some fun."

Sienna gave him a strange look.

"Have you ever paddled around the islands?" he said.

"No. I was kept locked up most of the time."

"Oh. Of course. Well … you'll love it. The scenery is beautiful."

She nodded doubtfully. "Okay."

Simon turned to Gizmo. "Hey, Giz? Do you want to go for a ride in the car?"

Gizmo jumped off the floor and ran to Simon. He leaned against him with his front paws. His tail smacked loudly against the wall.

"I'll take that as a *yes,*" said Simon. He attached Gizmo's lead. Then he waved goodbye and walked out the front door.

The first stop Simon made was at Christine's aunt's house. Christine met him on the front steps.

"I'm sorry," she said. "About you being a target. And about the other thing." She took his hand.

"Are you sure you want to go through with this?" said Simon. "I'll understand if you don't."

Christine squeezed his hand tight. "I've been giving it a lot of thought. You. The App. The revolution." She smiled. "Count me in. One hundred percent."

Simon grinned. "Thank you."

Christine turned and started to tug him up the stairs. "Come in and meet my aunts. They're dying to meet you. Aunty Joan even baked you a cake."

"Gizmo is in the car," he said.

"Even better. Bring him in and I'll introduce him to Maisie."

An hour later, Simon had left Christine and was driving to see his mother at the clinic. His stomach hurt from the four slices of cake that he'd been forced to eat. Gizmo's stomach was bulging too.

Simon parked out the back of the clinic in the loading zone and phoned his mother. Two minutes later, the door opened and his mother came out to give him a hug.

She held him for thirty seconds without saying anything. When she pulled away there were tears in her eyes.

"My little boy. All grown up. And in trouble."

"I'll be okay, Mom."

She wiped her cheeks with the back of her hand. "Everything is here," she said. "Just like you asked." She pointed to the two coolers on the loading dock.

"Thanks Mom."

He handed her Gizmo's lead. "Take good care of him."

Simon knelt down and squeezed his dog. "And you behave yourself, Giz." Gizmo licked Simon's face.

Simon stood and loaded the coolers in the back of the car. Then he kissed his Mom and drove away.

"What's in the coolers," said Sienna.

"Just some more food," said Simon. "Mom couldn't let me go without giving me something. You know what she's like."

"A fusspot?" said Sienna.

"Yeah. But I never said that if she asks."

They finished packing the car then secured the double kayak to the roof.

"I'm still not convinced about this thing," said Sienna.

"Trust me, you'll be glad we brought it."

They got into the car and Simon felt something pressing into his lower back. "Oh. Almost forgot." He reached for the gun and handed it to Sienna. "Thanks."

She checked it and put it back in her handbag.

Simon started the car and they drove to Granville Island.

The formalities with the boat had taken an hour. Sienna had inspected the boat and was confident she could drive it.

Simon slipped a five hundred dollar tip to the owner. "If anyone asks, we were never here. My girlfriend's ex is a stalker. A boat is the only place she feels safe."

"Of course," said the owner. "My lips are sealed. I hope you have a pleasant trip."

They thanked him and waved goodbye as he jumped onto the jetty.

"Shall we get underway?" said Simon.

"You mean, 'Shall we get underway, *Captain*?'"

Simon arched his eyebrows. "It's going to be like that is it?"

Sienna nodded. "And the first thing you can do is secure that damned kayak. Lash it down tight."

"Aye, aye, *Captain*."

Twenty minutes later, everything was stowed and Sienna turned the key. The twin Volvo engines gave a low growl.

"They're quieter than I thought," said Simon. He reached for a joystick on the console. "What's this?"

Sienna smacked his hand. "Don't touch the controls without my permission."

"But it's a joystick for a computer."

"It's not," snapped Sienna. "It's for maneuvering the boat in tight spaces."

"Oh."

"Now go and cast off the ropes … and don't fall in."

He did as he was told. Sienna used the joystick to slowly move the boat out of its pen. They stuck to the speed limit in False Creek and gradually picked up speed in English Bay.

Simon sat down to enjoy the view. On the right was Lighthouse Park, with a backdrop of snow-covered mountains. If he closed his eyes, he could almost forget why he was here.

"Are you sure you want to head to the Broken Islands?" said Sienna.

"Yes," said Simon. "It's very remote. And the kayaking is sensational."

"You *do* realise that it's over three hundred kilometres? We're not going to make it tonight."

"That's fine," said Simon. "We can spend the night at Salt Spring Island." He pointed at the chart. "We can moor in Long Harbour."

Sienna examined the chart. "It looks very populated."

"It'll be okay for one night. No one knows we'll be there." He pointed at another location on the chart. "Just make sure that we stay north of this line."

"The US border?"

"Yes. The US authorities would love to get their hands on me. And I'm not keen on them sticking a needle in my arm."

Sienna guided the boat between the various islands for the next two hours. They were covered in Douglas Firs and edged with pebbly sand. Driftwood logs, rubbed smooth from their journey, lay strewn across the shore.

Simon pointed to some killer whales on the port side.

They eventually reached Long Harbour in the late afternoon and found a berth in the marina.

"Are we going ashore?" said Sienna.

"Probably better we stay aboard. How about some dinner and a game of chess?"

"Dinner sounds good. I'm not so sure about the

chess."

"Are you chicken?"

Sienna ignored the barb. "I'd prefer lamb," she said.

He laughed and went to heat up some frozen meals. Sienna disappeared into the bedroom to get changed.

Simon's silenced phone vibrated in his pocket. Another system message.

After dinner they went to bed. Simon immediately fell asleep.

Sienna lay there, listening to the water lapping against the hull.

CHAPTER FORTY-TWO
Endgame

The following morning, Simon woke feeling refreshed.

Sienna woke with bags under her eyes.

"Couldn't sleep?" said Simon.

Sienna shook her head. "Must have been the motion of the boat."

After breakfast, they topped off the fuel tanks at the jetty then headed out of the harbour.

"We should get there by mid-afternoon," said Sienna.

They took it in turns to steer. The boat hugged the coast of Vancouver Island as they navigated the Juan de Fuca Strait. As the craft rounded the southern tip of the massive island, the urban sprawl of Victoria gave way to the sparsely populated south-west coast. Miles of deserted coastline, where rocks met waves in the shadows of dark green trees.

They motored past East Sooke Park and saw a bear running along the beach with a fish in its mouth. It was being chased by another bear.

Simon grimaced. "Survival of the fittest."

"It's a brutal world," said Sienna.

They sped towards their final destination.

They reached the Broken Islands in the late afternoon.

The dark blue of the Pacific was speckled with islands that were different shapes and sizes. As if some giant had smashed a larger island into hundreds of pieces.

Simon pointed to the chart. "Head for the far side,

near Forbes Island."

Twenty minutes later, they moored in a protected cove on the eastern side of the island. There was nobody for as far as the eye could see.

"Give me a hand with the kayak," said Simon.

"We're not going kayaking now, are we?" said Sienna.

"No. But I want to be ready first thing in the morning."

Sienna rolled her eyes. She reluctantly helped him untie the kayak and lower it into the water. Simon secured it to the back of the boat. Then he went inside.

He returned a moment later with a bottle of champagne.

"What's that for?" said Sienna.

"Just a little something to help us relax. And to celebrate getting away."

He poured a glass for each of them then raised his in a toast.

"To our future together," said Simon.

"To the future," said Sienna.

They clunked plastic glasses. She waited until he took a sip before drinking hers. Then they sat on the back of the boat, drinking champagne and watching the sun go down in the cold night air.

The white stars gradually appeared against the black sky.

"I need to pee," said Simon. He went downstairs into the cabin.

When he returned, Sienna had moved into his seat. She was holding her pistol.

"No need for that," said Simon. "You can have my seat. All you had to do was ask."

Sienna shook her head. "You never take things

seriously." Her brow was creased and she chewed her bottom lip. "Why couldn't you have accepted Shade's offer? Then none of this would have been necessary."

Simon took a step towards her. "What do you mean?"

She raised the pistol. It shook unsteadily. "Stay where you are."

He held up his hands. "Jesus, Sienna. What's wrong with you?" said Simon.

Sienna gripped the pistol in both hands to stop it shaking. "If you'd done the smart thing, we could have happily lived out the rest of our lives. But now, we're always going to be looking over our shoulders. Running from place to place." She nodded her head towards the island. "I don't want to live on a deserted island for the rest of my life, kayaking every damned day."

"You haven't even tried kayaking," said Simon.

"There you go again. You can't even be serious when someone is pointing a gun at you."

"Is that why you placed the bet?"

"What bet?"

"The one where you said I'd be shot this evening on a boat in the Broken Islands."

Sienna's eyes widened. "You knew?"

Simon nodded.

"But how? The bets are anonymous and encrypted. And you don't even receive notifications anymore."

"It's your fault really."

"*My* fault?"

"When you claimed the bet on Aleksei."

"You knew about that as well?"

"I recognised the user ID."

Sienna shook her head. "That *damned* ID. You told me it was anonymous."

Simon shrugged. "After you killed Aleksei, I made some modifications to The App."

"Modifications?"

"Something the police noticed, but I was able to convince them the code was only used during testing."

"Those unencrypted bets they asked about?"

"Yes," said Simon. "I knew your user ID. So I added it to the relevant database table and monitored your bets."

"But how did you know about my final wager? I only made it last night."

"System messages," said Simon. "I still get those, remember? The test messages are routed differently to the regular betting notifications."

Sienna used one hand to wipe a tear from her eyes. The pistol began to wobble again.

"Damn you. If you'd just taken Shade's deal, we could have been rich beyond our wildest dreams."

"It was never about the money, Sienna."

"It's always about the money."

Simon took another step closer to Sienna.

She steadied the pistol with her other hand. "Don't come any closer."

"You're not going to shoot me," said Simon.

He took another step and held out his hand.

"Give me the gun, Sienna."

"I'm warning you, Simon," she said. Tears were running down her face.

He took another step.

Sienna's body trembled as she aimed at Simon's legs and squeezed the trigger.

Click.

Silence.

"You might need this," he said.

Sienna stared in disbelief at Simon's hand.

He was holding the firing pin in his outstretched palm. His fingers closed around it.

Christine Hunter was being driven to Vancouver International Airport by her two aunts when the news bulletin came on the radio.

"The creator of The App, Simon Simpson, has died in mysterious circumstances off the coast of Vancouver Island. The luxury boat he'd recently hired with his girlfriend was found abandoned and drifting on Tuesday morning, near the Broken Islands. Although Simpson's body has yet to be found, forensics experts located more than ten pints of his dried blood at the scene. Coroner, Dr James Thomson, said no one could survive that amount of blood loss.

"There was no trace of Simpson's girlfriend, Sienna Volkov, and police haven't ruled out foul play"

Mabel shook her head in the back seat. "You can't trust those Russians," she said.

Christine nodded. "I know what you mean."

The car slowed as it pulled into the drop-off area at the airport. Christine was about to open the door when her phone rang. There was a slight delay before a male voice spoke.

"Is this Mai Thai? I'd like to place an order for some food. And can you make it spicy, please?"

Christine laughed. "It's the only way to eat Thai."

"I couldn't agree more," said Simon.

"My aunts are dropping me at the airport now."

"Okay. I'll meet you when you land," said Simon.

She hung up.

"Who was that, dear?" said her Aunt Joan.

"Just my new boss."

"I wouldn't have thought many places sell Thai food in Russia. It's all cabbage, potatoes and boiled meat. You should watch you don't starve."

"Yes, Aunty Joan. I'm sure I'll be fine."

Her Aunt Mabel leaned forward from the back seat. "Make sure you stay away from the seafood, dear. You never know *where* it's been."

Simon's mother waited until the other nurse had left the office then she logged on to the computer.

At the prompt she typed in her son's name.

After several seconds a list of Simon's frozen blood donations scrolled across the screen. A cumulative total was displayed at the bottom. Eleven pints.

She selected the third option on the 'Update' menu. 'Blood discarded.' In the 'Reason' field, she typed 'Deceased.'

Mrs Simpson smiled. Simon had always complained when she took his blood. He'd said it was a waste of time. But Mother knew best.

He could thank her when she and Gizmo visited him in Moscow.

Simon logged on to his new computer. He opened the admin console and clicked on his own name in the betting list.

He shook his head when he saw the two valid claims.

Then he typed some commands to confirm his death and transmit the funds.

Somewhere in the world, Sienna's phone was beeping. He hoped she'd spend her five million wisely.

Simon knew she wasn't perfect. She'd almost killed

him. But she *had* aimed at his legs.

The mistakes she'd made weren't entirely her fault. Sienna had been forged in a harsh furnace. The world of a sex slave. No one could blame her for wanting a better life.

In a dog eat dog world, she'd learned to be ruthless.

By showing mercy, Simon had hoped to guide Sienna to a different path.

She'd jumped at the deal he'd offered. Five million to walk away and start a new life. All she had to do in return was keep his secret.

They'd staged the scene with the blood that Simon had brought on-board in the food coolers. It had clotted into a sticky pool on the deck.

Then they'd cut the anchor rope on the boat and paddled ashore in the double kayak. Despite the headwind, Sienna had done her share of the paddling without complaint.

Christine had been on the coast of Vancouver Island to pick them up. She'd caught the ferry from the mainland and driven across the island to Ucluelet.

Christine had nodded to Simon when she saw Sienna, affirming his decision to forgive her.

They'd caught the ferry back to the mainland and Sienna had asked to be dropped at the train station.

She'd kissed him on the cheek and whispered in his ear. Then she'd walked away.

"What did she say?" said Christine. "Sorry for trying to kill you?"

Simon smiled. "She said she will miss our games of chess."

Christine had arched an eyebrow. "Sounds interesting."

"It is," said Simon. "I'll have to teach you."

Christine had dropped him at the airport where they kissed goodbye. Then he'd flown to Moscow on his false passport. He'd been there for two days.

Simon's phone beeped. His five million dollars had been received.

He went to the fridge and opened a beer.

Then he returned to his computer and placed a bet.

Five million on Preston Shade.

DON'T LET THE STORY STOP HERE

If you'd like to read a bonus epilogue for *The App*, navigate to the following hidden web-page:

www.paulruthven.com/
books-theapp-epilogue.html

You can also follow Paul Ruthven on Facebook at

www.facebook.com/paulruthvenauthor

for the latest news and updates.

Find out more about the author at

www.paulruthven.com